Alec wanted to kiss her

In all his adventures over the years, Alec had never been so tempted to lose himself in a woman, to press his mouth against the pulse point at her throat and count the beats.

Sara tensed. He was going to make a move, and she wasn't going to stop him. All the warning signals flashing behind her eyes were drowned out by the drumbeat of her blood. It had been so long since a man had regarded her with such raw desire. Too long.

With his finger, he hooked the high-ribbed neck of her sweater, gently tugging it away from her throat. He kissed her throat tentatively, stamping it with a trail of small nips. Pleased by her groan, he captured her mouth and kissed her deeply, thoroughly.

When he felt her soften helplessly, he dared to slip his hand up beneath her sweater, to stroke the smooth skin of her belly. When she responded, he climbed higher, cupping her breasts, losing himself completely in Sara.

And then reality intruded. What was he doing, making love to a possible criminal?

Leandra Logan thoroughly enjoyed writing this Christmas romance. Stepping back in time to celebrate an old-fashioned Christmas appeals to her. Naturally, she was forced to settle for the joys of researching life in the thirties, rather than being actually able to time-travel back. Her mother, Dee, was a tremendous help, though Dee was quick to assure Leandra's readers that she was a mere child at the time!

Leandra wishes her readers a very Merry Christmas and hopes that they will find comfort and peace throughout the upcoming year.

Books by Leandra Logan

HARLEQUIN TEMPTATION
472—JOYRIDE
491—HER FAVORITE HUSBAND
519—HAPPY BIRTHDAY, BABY
535—BARGAIN BASEMENT BABY
564—ANGEL BABY
611—HEAVEN-SENT HUSBAND
650—HOLD THAT GROOM!

Don't miss any of our special offers. Write to us at the following address for information on our newest releases.

Harlequin Reader Service
U.S.: 3010 Walden Ave., P.O. Box 1325, Buffalo, NY 14269
Canadian: P.O. Box 609, Fort Erie, Ont. L2A 5X3

Leandra Logan
MY JINGLE BELL BABY

Harlequin Books

TORONTO • NEW YORK • LONDON
AMSTERDAM • PARIS • SYDNEY • HAMBURG
STOCKHOLM • ATHENS • TOKYO • MILAN
MADRID • WARSAW • BUDAPEST • AUCKLAND

To my mother, Dee, and my husband, Gene.
Thanks for the information and inspiration.

ISBN 0-373-25763-5

MY JINGLE BELL BABY

Copyright © 1997 by Mary Schultz.

This edition published by arrangement with Harlequin Books S.A.

® and TM are trademarks of the publisher. Trademarks indicated with ® are registered in the United States Patent and Trademark Office, the Canadian Trade Marks Office and in other countries.

Printed in U.S.A.

1

"WAKE UP, ALEC WAGNER! Wake up!"

Alec burrowed deeper into his warm, cushy bed, trying hard to ignore the pinch of his new dime-store pajamas and the familiar motherly voice that had talked him into the pajamas in the first place. *She* could talk him into anything it seemed. He was halfway into his two-week stint at this rural bed-and-breakfast, *her* paying guest, yet he'd become her pawn, putty in her hands!

Surely he had to be in the midst of a vivid dream. Even Mrs. Beatrice Nesbitt had her limits, always respecting his privacy once he closed the bedroom door for the night. A bedroom door he routinely secured. He was absolutely certain he'd locked it as usual, and almost as sure he'd slid the bolt.

"There's trouble, Alec. Serious trouble."

Mrs. Nesbitt's voice sharp with insistence, sounded all too real. The steel bed frame creaked as Alec flopped over on his broad back, ever-so-reluctantly cracking open one eye.

The proprietress of the Cozy Rest Inn was on hand, all right, up close and in person.

Alec surveyed her hovering figure in the rosy glow of the bedside lamp. She was certainly taking this nocturnal invasion over the top. Rather than her customary pink chenille robe with buttons down the front and the funny little shoes she called mules, she was sporting oversized olive-green combat clothing straight out of an old war movie: woolen slacks, a huge bomber jacket zipped up tight and a fur-trimmed hat with ear flaps.

It was a sight that best belonged in a dream!

"Do you hear me, Alec?" She leaned over, gripped his solid shoulder with a plump, gloved hand, and gave him an impressive shake.

Struggling like crazy to climb out of the foggy depths of slumber, Alec cleared his throat and inched up on the bank of downy pillows propped against the headboard. During his twelve years with the FBI as a field agent, he'd learned to sleep just one level below alertness, ready to respond to as little as a feather under the chin.

But seven days in this frozen western Wisconsin wonderland had completely disrupted his body clock. He'd been sleeping as deeply as a boy, and liking it. Liking it so much, in fact, that he wanted to drift right back off into that special land of nothingness where his troubles couldn't follow.

But the worry deepening the lines in Beatrice Nesbitt's round, cheery face couldn't be dismissed. With a groan he raised himself up higher on his forearms. "What's the matter? Your old furnace go out?"

"A car's slipped into the ditch," she briskly reported. "Right out front, at the foot of the drive!"

Alec raised his eyes to the plaster ceiling. The end of the drive was a good half mile away. And it might as well have been a half million in the season's swirling wintry gale. He'd watched nature's fury whip across the rolling farmland for hours on end from the window seat in Mrs. Nesbitt's front parlor this week. It was something Chicagoans born and bred like himself didn't see in the concrete jungle. A danger to be respected.

"Something *must* be done, Alec."

So true, he conceded, rubbing a hand over his whiskered jawline. And the way she said his name, with such affectionate intimacy, was a foolproof way to garner his full cooperation. But even he couldn't work miracles. They had no practical transportation at hand to effect a rescue. He'd arrived by taxi and knew that neither Mrs. Nesbitt nor the inn's other occupants owned any sort of vehicle. In the time he'd spent here, not a one had even shown a desire to leave the premises.

"How do you propose we reach the road?" he said. "What with the drifts so deep, visibility poor..." He paused as a thought occurred to him. "Which brings up the question, how did you see the accident from such a distance in the first place? Are you sure it happened at all?"

She raised her fleshy chin, and folded her arms against her bulky coat. "I'm up and about at all hours, especially this close to Christmas. Looked out the window just in time to see the headlights wobble and dive." Her glare of indignation left no room for argument.

"Taking everything into account, it would be safest for everyone to call the authorities," he declared. "A plow-and-rescue squad must be standing by—if not in your Elm City, then surely in Madison."

She clucked in dismay. "You certainly didn't wait for a squad in Iran, when you rescued that young mother and daughter from the jaws of danger."

"Blazing sun and a little blowing sand were a piece of cake compared to conquering this frozen tundra—" He clamped his mouth shut. That Iranian mission was classified information! He didn't recall spilling it, yet he must have. Probably while lubricated with some of the inn's fine brandy during one of their evening fireside chats. With no TV or radio to entertain them, the guests did rely on storytelling for entertainment.

In any case, he was insulted that she would try to bait him into action with visions of damsels in distress. He was an equal-opportunity rescuer; he'd saved his share of both shapely ladies and portly bankers with equal skill and fortitude.

His judgment call in either case would be to alert emergency services. State troopers could be on the scene pronto.

"Mrs. Nesbitt," he begged, "can't you see that you're wasting precious time bickering with me? Pick up the telephone."

"It's you who complains that the telephone's always a fuzzy jumble, Alec."

He shook his head in bewilderment. "But it seems to work for you, for some wild reason. Have you tried 911?"

"Don't you try and dodge me with a fancy FBI code," she scoffed, her hat's earflaps slapping the sides of her bobbing head. "Do you realize people in these parts even stood firm against Bonnie and Clyde back in '33?"

Alec hit the heel of his palm against his forehead. That argument seemed a little outdated. By his calculations, Mrs. Nesbitt had been a baby at that time! "You simply don't understand about 911. Now—"

"Country folk simply rise to the call!" she bellowed. "I have a perfectly dandy sleigh in the barn. And a fine Belgian draft that can easily trot through knee-high drifts."

His dark brows lifted in surprise. "You *are* prepared."

"Naturally! Would I be in here without a plan, boy? Dressed in my husband Jim's duds if I didn't mean business? Now get out of bed. This very instant!" With a flick of a gloved hand she whipped the covers off his mattress. It seemed physically impossible, but Alec found himself soaring through the air, entangled in his flying bedclothes. He ultimately landed on the stone-cold polished pine floor, missing the buffer of the brown braided rug by inches.

She stood over him, hands set on her hips. "You'd have known about the sleigh if you'd been using your investigative skills around the place, instead of planting yourself in my parlor window seat like a potted petunia." She moved to the highboy against the wall, yanked open the bottom drawer and produced some bright red long johns. "Put these on, Alec. Quickly, now."

Alec began pulling the one-piece suit on right over his pajamas. Mrs. Nesbitt turned away with a ladylike discretion, but he was darn sure she had X-ray vision, along with her magician-like dexterity and soothsayer's crystal ball.

He rose first to his knees, then his feet, tugging at the roomy red garment. Judging by his woolies and her bomber jacket, Alec figured that Mrs. Nesbitt's husband, presently on the road selling shoes, was a tall and brawny man, even larger than Alec's impressive six-foot frame.

Alec stalked over to the highboy to retrieve the jeans he'd draped over it several hours ago, fuming behind gritted teeth. He wasn't accustomed to being ordered about this way. It would be different if he'd been convinced by her story. But he hadn't. He didn't know what she'd seen out the window, but in this blizzard it couldn't have been a car's headlights half a mile away! Still, what choice did he have but to cooperate? She was determined to make him take some action.

He eased his tight-fitting jeans over the long johns with difficulty, venting his frustration by grumbling about his disrupted retirement.

Mrs. Nesbitt turned and gave him a concerned look. "A young man of thirty-five can't retire from livin' altogether," she admonished gently. "From being a member of the God-fearing human race."

Alec's large mouth thinned in the shadows. Couldn't he? Gee, it certainly was the plan. As he struggled to button the waist of his jeans over the bulky underwear, he felt a stab of pain in the gristle above his heart, a reminder of how his life had taken this sad detour into uselessness. He'd taken a slug in the collarbone region during a drug raid six months back. If he hadn't been wearing a bulletproof vest, he'd be stone-cold dead right now.

Instead he'd become one of the living dead, stripped of his prestigious and exciting field position, parked at a desk in a windowless room at the Bureau's downtown Chicago office. It had been sheer torture plotting the strategies for his old team, then being left behind during the execution stage. He'd put up with it during his convalescence in the hope that he'd eventually pass muster again, be out on the line again. But the brass hadn't judged his doctor's report with the necessary open-mindedness.

Ultimately, it had been the desk job or nothing.

Alec had chosen nothing, bluffing his way out with a story about seeking new adventures. What he really had to show for his career was a heart full of defeat, a modest pension and a gift certificate for Christmas here at the Cozy Rest Inn. Even now, as he sat on the edge of the mattress to lace up his leather utility boots, he was burning at the memory of his departure. He knew his team had sent him here deliberately, hoping he'd be bored out of his skull, ready to dash back in the New Year and beg for that desk job.

He'd show them! Half a loaf was *not* better than none. Without the field as his playground, he was nothing but an aimless zero, satisfied with loafing around in the boondocks.

With new determination to be the best layabout ever hatched from the inn, he marched up to yank open the door. To his surprise, it was locked and bolted! He turned to find Mrs. Nesbitt at his side, unperturbed by his gasp, waving him off so she could handle the sticky catches.

Alec raked a hand through his tousled brown hair. "What's with the security? Afraid I'd escape?"

Her bosom jiggled beneath her coat. "Oh, you can't run away from me, Alec Wagner."

Alec bit his lip. Hard. She wasn't going to explain herself—again! A trick she'd been playing a lot over the little curiosities around here.

Mrs. Nesbitt led the way down the steep open staircase to the first level, which was already ablaze with lights. Every nook and cranny of the place was decorated in honor of the festive season, the varnished wood molding along the walls and doorways plastered with mistletoe and holly. Alec tramped across the foyer to the octagonal window beside the heavy mahogany door for a look at the current weather conditions. Pushing aside the lace curtain, he stared out through the center of a red straw wreath. Things seemed the same as he'd left them two hours earlier at eleven; a mad swirl of flakes spun wildly in the moonlight.

How could this fiesty innkeeper keep insisting that she could see action on the road, with visibility down to twenty feet or so?

"I know what you're thinking," she chortled. "That I'm out of my mind. A silly old lady on a wild-goose chase."

"Oh, Mrs. Nesbitt. You're not so old." He smiled thinly, crossing the foyer to where she was rummaging through a closet conveniently built into the side of the staircase. As observant as he was, Alec hadn't noticed a door in the dark paneling.

Within moments she produced another green jacket and bomber hat, which she handed over with anxious hazel eyes. Alec took hold of the outerwear, meeting her gaze squarely for a long, electric moment.

"You do trust me on this, don't you, Alec?"

"I trust that you have amazing faith in yourself," he said mildly. As her soft gray brows furrowed in hurt, he added, "I'm more than willing to check things out, put your mind at ease."

"That's a very crafty way of saying that you're humoring me."

"Is that so bad?" he asked dryly. "I'd like nothing better than for you to humor me. Like letting me have an extra strip of bacon at breakfast, and ignoring the mess I leave in my room."

She thought about it for a full thirty seconds. "Too high a price to pay."

He gave her shoulders a squeeze. "All right. Whip me into shape. But this is no night for you to be outdoors. I'll handle this alone."

"Know anything about horses?"

"Not much. But enough," he assured her.

She sighed hard. "No, it will take the two of us to bring the girls back to safety. Can't put the wee one to any unnecessary distress." She shook her head as she closed the door of the closet. "I'd never forgive myself, Alec."

Girls? Wee one? The last of Alec's patience dissipated into thin air. "You don't need to play on my gallantry, I tell you. I'm up. I'm here—at your service. Whether it's Christie Brinkley or Rodney Dangerfield out there!"

Beatrice Nesbitt's eyes shifted in confusion behind her small spectacles. "Do you believe these are friends from the FBI, Alec? Are you expecting them?"

Alec sighed in resignation. With so little contact with the outside world, the hopelessly old-fashioned sixty-five-year-old probably didn't recognize the names, or get his point. "Never mind, Mrs. Nesbitt."

The innkeeper took him at his word and trotted off down the hallway like a sturdy little steam engine.

Alec trailed close behind, and upon reaching the large country kitchen, was unable to resist trying the heavy black rotary phone sitting on the counter just inside the swinging door. It would be nice to summon somebody—even the Elm City sheriff—on the off chance that there was an emergency. As usual, the line was humming with static.

Unable to conceal his ire over the phone, he slammed the receiver back down on its hook. Not once during the past week had he been able to raise a dial tone. Sometimes he heard distant voices on the wire, which Mrs. Nesbitt attributed to the fact that the inn was on a party line. He had caught all of the Cozy Rest's inhabitants—Beatrice, her sister Camille and their permanent boarders, eighty-year-old Lyle Bisbee and the middle-aged Martha Doanes—in the midst of animated chats. But surely they were putting him on, only pretending to have a connection, then hanging up when they spotted him. He understood; entertainment was scarce in these small towns. What fun it must be for the Cozy Rest gang to torment uptight guests like him who stumbled into their mundane existence.

Some pampered getaway this was. Claims of modern conveniences in a quaint but bustling atmosphere advertised in the inn's brochure were a bald-faced lie!

The guys and gals back at the Bureau had to be splitting their sides over this campaign. Send grumpy Alec to a rest home and watch him beg for a reinstatement. Some thanks for his mentoring them so well in the dirty tricks department.

There was a small service porch off the kitchen. It was a chilly box of a room on the side of the house, the entrance designed to accommodate farm workers coming inside. There was a long, narrow bench against one wall, boots lining the concrete floor beneath it. The opposite wall boasted a series of jacket pegs and a tall cabinet stocked with jars of home-canned fruits and vegetables.

Mrs. Nesbitt was rummaging through a cedar chest near the door leading outside. She turned, offering him a pair of large chopper style gloves. "Mustn't lollygag, Alec."

Alec inhaled sharply, a protest dying on his lips. "No, ma'am. Sure you won't stay behind?"

"Arguin' is lollygaggin'." She opened the white door a smidgen but Alec stopped her with a hand on her sleeve. "At least let me go first, shovel a path to the barn."

"But your shoulder's bound to ache, Alec. Let me lead."

Alec stiffened in embarrassment and frustration. It was bad enough his superiors at the Bureau had attempted to coddle him, but a little old lady trying to blaze his way was the ultimate affront. "I'm good and tired of people underestimating me!"

She patted his cheek with her glove. "All right, dear, all right. I meant no offense. It's just that I'm well accustomed to the layout of my property, have the health of a draft horse myself."

"I'm fine enough," he said on a quieter note. Embarrassed

by his show of emotion, he quickly peeled back his glove for a look at his watch. Amazingly, only ten minutes had passed since Mrs. Nesbitt's invasion of his room. He'd done more feeling and fretting in that space of time than he'd done in a month.

A snow fence of slatted wood flanked the fifty-foot path leading to the barn, efficiently keeping drifting caused by northwest winds to a minimum. Trudging ahead in his giant boots and using his shovel sparingly to save his shoulder, Alec opened a trail for his companion.

The land was a vast blanket of white as far as the eye could see. The moon was incredibly bright against the velvet blackness of the sky, casting a glittery silver light on the earth. It was a heavenly picture, but so very, very cold. The bracing air stung his face and crystalized his breath.

Concerned for his spunky companion, Alec turned to check on her. With a scarf covering the lower half of Mrs. Nesbitt's face, it was impossible to gage her condition. But she was right on his heels, so he figured she had to be faring well.

"Barn's not locked, Alec," Mrs. Nesbitt half shouted, passing by him to throw open the great door's latch.

Too bad, Alec thought. After the smooth way she'd entered his room, he'd have liked to see her spin her magic on it. With a shrug Alec followed her into the hollow stillness of the barn, coughing as the earthy smells of hay and horseflesh assailed his nostrils. Moonlight poured through the windows and door, giving the space shape and shadow. With confident steps, Mrs. Nesbitt strode over to a workbench and with the swipe of a match, brought two brass lanterns to life. He met her halfway to take one of the glass-domed lights, blinking as his eyes adjusted to the brightness.

Swinging the lantern one way, then the other, Alec took in his surroundings. This was certainly a functioning farm, a small old-fashioned one, but operational on its own basic level. To the left was a pen full of bales of hay and burlap sacks of grain. Stalls to the right held two neighing horses.

Mrs. Nesbitt headed for the stalls, and Alec went in search of the sleigh, finding it and a plow near the rear doors on the opposite wall. Along the way he discovered a chicken pen. Peering inside, he found a good fifty chickens roosting on dowels behind wire mesh, sound asleep.

"Come meet Sugar and Spice," Mrs. Nesbitt invited. Alec admired the handsome Belgian drafts, chestnut in color, with curly manes and tails. He knew enough about horses to appreciate the quality of the animals.

He helped Mrs. Nesbitt guide Sugar out of the stall, backing the horse between the two wooden shafts of the sleigh and hook up its leather traces. A bellyband lined with bells gave a merry jingle so fitting to the season. The sleek black-laquered wood sleigh with thin, curled-up runners was ancient, but in remarkably good condition.

Santa Claus himself couldn't ask for fancier transportation.

Alec assisted Mrs. Nesbitt into the sleigh and she immediately took firm hold of the reins. When Alec was settled in beside her, she gently flicked the leather straps and they zipped out of the barn.

The large, powerful draft galloped through the snow-drifts, easily pulling its load. The sleigh's smooth wooden runners skimmed over the crystalized snow with speedy efficiency.

The long winding drive was filled in by the blizzard, but easy enough to discern from the tall pines bordering it. Remembering how lovely the inn had appeared from his taxi that first night, Alec shifted round for a another look.

The exterior of the three-story turn-of-the century Victorian house was indeed spectacular. The gray-painted lady was strung with golf-ball-sized Christmas bulbs that added a merry sparkle to its ornate lines, accentuating the turned posts supporting the front porch and every shuttered window up to the turret-shaped attic room on the top level.

The barn, with its dormers, cresting cupola, and rooftop weather vane, all in period, was charming, but definitely a poor relation without the bulbs.

How grand it all looked from a distance, the twinkling rainbow of lights against a black-and-white canvas of bare rolling land.

To some degree Alec could understand why genteel Mrs. Nesbitt and her boarders were so satisfied in their surroundings. There was certainly comfort and a sense of security in the sturdiness of everything from the old stained furniture to the hand-loomed rugs. The house itself had been crafted with pride with longevity in mind, back before disposable was a buzzword, a way of life for most.

Alec himself had been weaned on disposable everything. How many Chicago apartments had he flitted in and out of during his lifetime, first in his mother's lackluster care, then on his own, never staying long enough to hang a picture, or get to know his neighbors? How many women had he shied away from, the second they cooked him a decent meal or mended his shirts?

He'd done a lot of thinking this past week at the Cozy Rest, dwelling among those who thought constancy was an anchor rather than a shackle. Unfortunately, his study of the two contrasting life-styles hadn't brought him any enlightenment. Instead it had left him hanging in midair, feeling that he was a nowhere man. Without his work he was dislodged, disoriented. Alone.

The wind and snowflakes bit his bare face like a stinging, angry slap, crusting his whiskers with spray-gun force. Alec ducked his head for relief.

When he looked up again, the sight up ahead took his breath away. A car had indeed slipped into the ditch on the edge of the property between the drive and the split-rail fencing, a nice new Lincoln Town Car. Tipped at an angle, its headlight beams were aimed haphazardly into the darkness.

As Mrs. Nesbitt reined in Sugar, Alec instructed her to stay put and leapt off the sleigh into the deep cushion of snow. He waded through the knee-high drifts, half-scrambling, half-sliding into the slippery trench. All the while he was piecing together the circumstances. Fortunately, the sedan hadn't rolled. He theorized that the driver, sensing a loss of control, had slowed way down, and the car had glided into its awkward position.

The passenger door was wedged into the ground, so he climbed up on the driver's side and yanked open the door. Dangling on the frame for moment, he stared mutely into the front seat.

There was a baby bundled up in a hooded pink snowsuit strapped into a car seat at the opposite end, with a woman's purse lodged beside her.

Evidence of two girls, large and small, just as Mrs. Nesbitt had predicted.

No doubt about it, the innkeeper belonged in a government think tank, serving her country.

"Couldn't resist coming closer, Alec." Mrs. Nesbitt's sturdy hands clamped his shoulders; her voice, gusty with confidence, filtered through the fur flap of his hat. "Don't you dare fuss about it, either."

He stayed quiet, making room for her as she inched alongside him to look into the car. She could not only tackle a think tank, he decided, but probably jump behind the wheel of an armored one as well!

Together they surveyed the situation. The driver apparently had been in good enough shape to climb out. The snoozing baby she had left behind certainly looked no worse for wear.

But why hadn't they spotted the woman along the driveway? The inn was the only house in sight. Alec and Mrs. Nesbitt stared at each for a long tense moment.

"Does seems strange," Alec muttered.

The child opened her eyes the moment Alec spoke. Taking one look at the pair of olive-drab-clad commandos peering down at her, she let out a piercing cry.

Alec hastily unzipped his jacket, eased his torso into the upturned car, and with soothing sounds carefully freed the baby from the molded plastic car seat. Using his coat to shield the child from the bracing wind, he cradled her against the softness of his red long johns, studying her face for any obvious signs of injury. "She seems fine."

Mrs. Nesbitt clucked in agreement, grazing the baby's cheek with her glove. "A hundred-proof cry of indignation I'd say. And how nicely you handle her, Alec," she said approvingly. "As if you were born to it."

He was. Being big brother to two petulant sisters had given him plenty of experience. But he wasn't comfortable talking about his formative years, even two decades later, so he left her observation unanswered.

Together they gingerly scaled the ditch, Alec with the baby and Mrs. Nesbitt with the car seat. Alec moved swiftly to get the pair settled in the sleigh, then returned for a look around the vehicle.

That was when he discovered the woman, lying behind the tilted Lincoln, an arm raised up to her cheek as though to shield her face from the elements. "She's down here!" he shouted, causing a new outbreak of cries from the baby. "And the little fool's in tennis shoes!"

2

THE BABY'S VOICE pierced the harsh cold night and penetrated the dazed benumbed mind of Sara Jameson. *Precious Rosie! Where is she?*

Judging by the distant echo of the child's voice, it seemed that she'd been removed from the car. Someone had really found them! For a while she'd wondered if the jingle she'd heard in the distance was a cruel trick of her imagination. The bells had been so lively, so melodic...so unreal.

Sara tried to respond, but found she was too frigid to move. To her relief her arm was lifted from her face. She forced her eyes open just as a dark masculine form reached for her and hauled her onto his knee. Warm fingers delved into the collar of her cloth coat and pressed her pulse point. The man posed short, terse questions as he probed her with a physician's touch.

Expressing satisfaction over her croaked responses and ability to focus, he jammed his hand back in his glove, then hoisted her over his shoulder and began to stomp around the sedan to the shallowest point of the trench.

Sara felt incredibly fortunate to have been saved by this strong, capable stranger. But her gratitude quickly soured during her bumpy trip to safety. Bouncing against his back, Sara could hear him grumbling about her light coat and shoes, skimpy earmuffs, her dim-witted attempt to push the car to safety like Wonderwoman!

Who was this rude Hercules, making pained sounds of his own with every step? Was he some nutty motorist who happened to be passing on the two-lane road?

Perhaps her luck would hold, perhaps this was someone from the house. The last thing Sara remembered seeing before the accident was the stately old Victorian home, trimmed in strings of colorful lights, rising out of vast empty plains. A welcoming bulb-trimmed sign near the drive had identified it as the Cozy Rest Inn.

The temptation to stop at this unexpected port in the snowstorm had been powerful. But she'd reminded herself she'd made a promise to stick to the itinerary. It was Saturday, December 20th, which meant she was due in Madison, with reservations made at the Super 8 Motel.

But traveling with a baby had proven a lot more complicated than she'd expected. Rosie required lots of rest stops and detours. And detours made the chance of a wipeout greater.

Oh, there were so many things she could tell this guy. Starting with her unfamiliarity with icy conditions, her desperation to follow through.

But there were so many more things she couldn't. Keeping her mouth shut was more important than flexing her ego. With her spitfire temper she'd have to remember that.

Finally, with a grunt and a stomp, her hero stopped. A horse whinnied and the bells she thought she'd imagined jingled merrily. Sara hadn't the strength to move her head, but she managed to open her eyes and from her upside-down vantage point found herself staring at the shiny runners of a sleigh. A polished black side moved into her line of vision as her rescuer, with a gentleness in clear contradiction to his harsh tone, lifted her from his shoulders and set her down on a bed of blankets, then climbed up beside her. Rosie was nearby, cooing and sniffling. Sara so desperately wanted to sit up, but she was paralyzed, chilled to the bone.

"Rosie?" she croaked pitifully.

A merry face topped with a furry green hat appeared overhead in the light of a lantern. "Rosie's her name? She's fine, just fine. I promise you that. Raised a son myself and I know what you're feeling. He's a man now, of course—"

"Mrs. Nesbitt—please!" The masculine interruption came from Sara's rescuer, who sounded frazzled. Comforted that the matron had the upper hand, Sara closed her eyes, settled into the warmth of her covers and listened to their exchange.

"As you say, Alec. So, how is she?"

"Seems in decent shape, considering."

"Here, now. Put this flask of brandy to use." There was a rustle and a sniff. "Not to your mouth, fool, to hers!"

"A rescuer must first serve himself in order to efficiently aid the others," he staunchly claimed.

"My bags," Sara pleaded softly. "All my bags. Need..."

"I'll take care of it, Frosty."

The gruff promise was carried on a waft of brandy breath. *Frosty?* This guy she had to see. Sara struggled, managing to open her eyes. Moonlight was spilling over her hero as he knelt beside her, cupping her head, plying her with alcohol. She sipped gratefully and gazed up dazedly, wanting to pin a face to the gruff and insulting but gentle person who was her savior. A fur-trimmed hat covered his forehead, and encrusted snow whitened his brows, moustache and chin stubble.

If it hadn't been for the crimson suit underneath his open jacket, she might not have believed it. But it was Christmas and she'd distinctly heard sleigh bells.

This grumpy guzzler had to be none other than Santa Claus himself!

"No, Mrs. Nesbitt, I don't think it's a very good idea."

Back in the coziness of his bedroom at the inn, Alec paced around under the watchful eye of the innkeeper. She'd changed into her pink chenille robe and mules, undone the gray braids she usually kept up in a neat coronet, and was quickly reassembling the bedcovers she'd torn apart. Though intent on her work, she never let him out of her sight, not even while tucking in the corners. He was getting smarter, though. He'd left the door wide open this time. If there was more "trouble," he was determined to awaken the whole house for reinforcements.

"You've been a rock, Alec," she praised, straightening up, massaging the base of her spine. "A mighty oak. But the crisis isn't over yet."

It was tough to maintain any sort of dignity in red long johns, but Alec was trying, keeping his chin high, his arms folded across his chest. This was the absolute limit. He'd braved the perilous outdoors, brought damsels large and small back safe and sound—luggage included. He was even grudgingly glad that Mrs. Nesbitt was so proud of him. But to take little Frosty into his bed without her permission seemed like a suicide mission. She might not awaken to appreciate him as much as she would have an electric blanket.

But Mrs. Nesbitt had scoffed over the electric blanket alternative as she snapped his crisp white sheet in the air, as angry as if he'd suggested the electric chair for their foolish visitor. Alec had interpreted this response to mean she had no electric blankets, considered them to be as unnecessary as other power-driven conveniences like dishwashers and microwaves.

It was a whole different kind of electricity that kept bringing Alec's eyes back to the feminine figure huddled under two down-filled quilts on the chaise longue in the corner of the room. Mrs. Nesbitt had instructed him to carry her in here first thing because his room had the most efficient heater, then sent him down to the kitchen to have hot cocoa while she stripped off Frosty's icy layers of clothing and got her into a ruffled flannel gown.

He'd eventually returned to ask for directions to another room. But Mrs. Nesbitt wouldn't hear of it. She insisted that his mission was only half-over. They still needed his body. For heat.

Alec had been called into beddy-bye service in any number of ways over the years, but this was a first. *Body heat. Hell.*

Didn't Mrs. Nesbitt realize that Frosty was just too damn intriguing for her own good? Her glossy mane of auburn hair spilled over the chaise longue's tapestry upholstery like the inn's fine brandy, and her features were as delicate as a porcelain figurine's. And the few words she'd spoken—anxious questions about the beautiful child, assurances that there was no special someone to contact on her behalf—all had threatened to pull his long-buried heart back up to daylight.

His body quaked at the very idea, as though under attack from a sudden virus.

Taking a deep fortifying breath, he attempted to calm himself with practicalities. She was so very young, certainly not a day over twenty-five, putting her a full decade behind him. As for the good sense and experience that he found so attractive in his women, forget it. She had been on the road in tennis shoes, for Pete's sake!

So why was he tingling right down to his stockinged feet? Young and foolhardy she might be, but these factors only managed to heighten her mystique.

All things considered, it seemed she was too damn intriguing for *his* own good!

Mrs. Nesbitt watched his measurement of their new guest, her cheeks bunched in a knowing smile. "Surely you're the model of self-control, Alec."

Alec's huge chest heaved. "You have a very annoying habit of trying to bring out the very best in me, Mrs. Nesbitt."

"And what a fine thing it is, Alec," she said blissfully, "to do your very best each and every day." She gestured to the chaise. "Let's move her to the bed now, so I can go tend to the wee one."

Alec obligingly scooped up his personal guest. Struggling to keep the pain shooting through his shoulder from registering in his expression, he quickly deposited her on the open bed. "Let's trade," he suggested with sudden inspiration. "I'll take the wee one and you take the...wow-wow-wee one."

"And give up my chance to dote on a beautiful baby with the face of an angel?" Mrs. Nesbitt protested. "It's not every day that such an opportunity comes my way."

"Nor mine, Mrs. Nesbitt," he swiftly returned. "I...happen to like babies very much." Alec reared slightly, his own admission catching him by surprise. It was the truth, but he wasn't accustomed to sharing such personal information without sending it through a series of mental filters.

Mrs. Nesbitt stared up at him with twinkling hazel eyes. "You'll have every chance to enjoy the child *tomorrow*. Now if you'll excuse me, I'll be turning in."

He clenched his fists at his sides as she whisked off. "How dare you?" he demanded.

She paused with her hand on the brass doorknob, her face puckered in bewilderment. "How dare I what?"

"How dare you...trust me?" he sputtered incredulously. "With this woman? In my bed!"

"I know you well enough, Alec. Perhaps even better than you know yourself right now, with all your trials clouding your good sense. What better guarantee could there be, than when given the choice of mother or child, you choose the child, *beg* for her in fact?" A soft chuckle jiggled her bosom. "Like it or not, you're undoubtedly a fail-safe fellow. Not a security risk." On that note she closed the door with a gentle thump.

"Safe?" he squawked. "I'm considered dangerous the world over. Banned from several countries and one tropical resort! You hear? Dangerous and liking it!"

Alec stood in the center of the oval braided rug, a long, lean figure in red, primed for further argument. She'd be back. She always wanted the last word, insisted on having the last word.

But the old paneled door remained closed. Didn't she give a rip about his lethal credentials?

But why should she, he reasoned with a sigh, when he'd been humoring her all week long because she personified all the nurturing qualities his own mother had sadly lacked.

He sagged a little, raking his hands through his tousled hair. What a sad beginning to a grand retirement, his body reduced to a human heater. Part of him nagged on about his uselessness, his hard fall from his high-level ranking at the Bureau. But a stronger voice suggested that saving silly little Frosty and her baby was a gallant deed, and that by climbing into bed now he was only following the mission through.

Several floors below in the dank cellar, the furnace switched on with a noisy clank, which in turn brought the coiled heater under the window to crackling life. His thunderous pleas to Mrs. Nesbitt hadn't disturbed Frosty, but the mechanical sounds did. She stretched and twisted in the roomy bed like a tiny kitten in a large box, making a soft husky sound that made him ache with hunger.

Duty called. Straightening his long johns, trying to ignore the pinch of his cheap pajamas underneath, he crossed the rug. His carriage was so stiff he tripped over her overnight bag. Catching himself in midfall, he muttered a quiet oath as pain shot through his big toe. Liking order, Alec took the time to right the boxy green leather case on the floor beside two larger ones. He noted for the first time that they were all genuine Gucci, and had gold initialing beneath the handle.

K.H. So Frosty went by K.H. What did it stand for? Karen Hall? Kris Heath? Katrina Halvorson?

His brain was humming with possibilities as he switched off the bedside lamp and climbed under the pile of quilts. The puzzle was bound to help pass the time. Until he could drop off, and find merciful release from the carnal urges stirring him.

Before he could decide just how he was going to hold his guest to keep her warm, she snuggled up against his back, all soft and cuddly, smelling deliciously of peach shampoo. Desire curled up his spine like a flame from a Zippo lighter.

To think Mrs. Nesbitt had proclaimed this setup secure! But she was right, of course. As always. Alec had a wealth of willpower.

But the new tamer image of himself taking shape in this anachronism called the Cozy Rest Inn, would be downright insulting to any self-respecting, globe-trotting bachelor: Alec Wagner, who doted on an old woman, could be trusted in bed with a young one and who liked babies. If his colleagues hadn't already driven him out of the Bureau, they would have just cause to laugh him out.

SARA JAMESON OPENED her eyes the following morning to a wall of red. Holiday-crimson woollies on a broad expanse of back.

By golly, she was in bed with last night's old St. Nick.

Cuddled up to his backside was a better description. Molded to his long, lean form. However she described her position, it was all too intimate, too embarrassing. How had this happened? Even more urgent in her mind, *what* had happened? Disengaging herself from her new friend, Sara gingerly sat up. Ever so cautiously she sneaked a peek between the sheets. Thank goodness, she was dressed; rather primly too, in a ruffled flannel nightgown.

She scanned the room for her clothes, finding them neatly draped over a chaise. Unfortunately, she couldn't recall taking them off herself. With a hammering heart she pulled at the neck of her gown, and to her relief, found that both bra and panties were in place. A fairly reliable sign that she hadn't fallen into a hanky-panky trap for lost female travelers.

Gut instinct assured her that she was safe for another more basic reason. *This man didn't want a thing to do with her.* That had been clear last night.

Gradual awakening brought this negative memory and

others flooding back. The rescue from the driven snow. The matron comforting Rosie. The brandy. The warmth of this man's embrace. The chilliness of his complaints.

Her reluctant savior. A Scrooge in Santa's clothing.

With a hasty, uneventful getaway in mind, Sara slipped one leg off the mattress. A large hand suddenly clamped onto her arm, holding her firmly in place. Sara's head spun in panic to find her Scrooge wide awake and sitting up beside her.

"I want my baby!" she cried, attempting to pull herself free.

"She's safe and sound," he asserted quietly. "I swear."

"How 'bout my stuff?"

"Your suitcases are piled against the footboard and your groceries are down in the kitchen."

Sara stopped struggling and sized up her bedmate. The woman had called him Alec, she remembered. The name, basic and no-nonsense, fit him well. He was incredibly handsome without the snow crusting his face, and exceptionally strong, judging from the grip he had on her arm. His manner was disturbingly direct; he was staring her down squarely, with the deepest blue eyes imaginable.

Delicious trouble, Sara thought, the kind of Christmas gift many a single girl hoped to find under her tree.

The last thing she needed right now, however, was more trouble.

"So you got lost, huh?"

Mental giant, she thought with a frown. "Yes, I got lost. Stopped for groceries and got all turned around."

He returned her disparaging look. "Damn fool stunt, running around in tennis shoes."

"The freeways are plowed, for your information. I got confused after leaving a supermarket. It could happen to anybody!"

"All the more reason to dress for the worst."

"I'll remember that." Sara sniffed, her voice nervously

high. "I'd really like to see Rosie now, if you don't mind." To her surprise, he kept his grip firm. "You have no right to hold me—"

"You should be thanking me for holding you! You were one cold icicle last night."

"I mean," she said, "that you have no right to detain me now, this way."

He abruptly released her. Unprepared, her feet hit the braided rug in a skid.

"You really shouldn't be up yet," he insisted as she flapped her arms, struggling for balance.

"I'm fine now. Really!" With huffy disbelief she watched him adjust his pillows on the spindle headboard, as though making himself comfortable for a show. She rounded the foot of the bed. Keeping her legs tented in the skirt of the gown, she crouched down by the cluster of suitcases. Blocking his view with her slender frame, she peeked into each one as though affirming their contents. Feeling his watchful gaze she swiveled on the balls of her feet to glare up at him. "You could leave me alone."

Not if she was going to be snappy about it, he decided, insulted. His shoulder ached, his big toe throbbed, all because she'd behaved like a dope. "This is *my* room."

She surveyed the feminine decor with a false grin. "And what lovely taste you have. I especially like the rosebud wallpaper and the silver brush set on your dressing table."

He smiled tightly. "Smarty-pants. This is an inn. I am a guest in this room. And that in turn, makes you *my* guest."

Sara couldn't miss the wolfish curl of his mouth. As if he considered her in his care, under his thumb. Or even worse, was he perhaps insinuating something had indeed transpired between them in bed? Her heart jackhammered at the notion. Her head spun with images of how tantalizing such an encounter would be. *A bigger mistake than mishandling the car.*

She closed her night case with a decisive snap and popped

up to full height, which in Alec's estimation, was about five foot three. Spotting her leather handbag on the highboy, she began checking the contents of that as well. "Look, I know nothing happened last night," she said in an uncomfortable mumble, keeping her back to him.

Alec's eyes widened. She should damn well know nothing sexual went on. He could see her reflection in the wall mirror and her expression was distressed and stubborn, genuinely a trifle unsure. The idea that she could even wonder rankled him. He'd fully expect her to remember *that*. How blind of her not to see that he was fishing for another kind of credit, for doing a special something before he did the gallant omission thing? He was a hero here. "You do know I saved your very *life*, don't you? Left my warm bed and braved the treacherous outdoors—"

"Yes!" She bowed her head and swallowed. "If you want thanks...then consider it done."

That was it? She might have thawed on the outside, but she was still running on ice water. Alec clenched his fists between the sheets, all the more challenged. After the way his cage had been rattled, he so badly wanted to see her squirm a little. A little misbehaving would serve her right.

"You're right," he crooned. "We're square. More than square." He made a lusty *ahhh* sound as he stretched his arms above his head.

"What are you doing?" she asked, trying to catch sight of him in the mirror.

"Stretching."

"That's a pretty satisfied sound."

"I'm a pretty good stretcher."

She pulled a small brush out of her purse and pulled it through her hair with fervor.

"*A-a-hhh...*"

"Okay, enough of the taffy pull." She tossed her brush back in the bag and closed it with a snap.

"Funny you should say that. Mrs. Nesbitt, the lady in the

sleigh last night, was talking about having on a taffy pull this week."

"I won't be around that long."

"Oh. Well, you did tell me you have no husband or lover waiting."

"When did I say that?"

"Last night. In this room. Don't you remember?"

"No. But I know we didn't make it."

He smiled innocently. "But you don't seem sure, so I'm just trying to help."

Her chin wobbled in the mirror. "Well, uh..." She looked down at her gown, then whirled to face him triumphantly. "I am sure."

"Oh, really? What's nailed it down? Something deep inside, an emptiness, a hunger, a curiosity still unsatisfied?"

"Nope. I'm convinced because of you."

He pressed his hand to his chest, mockingly aghast. "Me? You've wisely figured out I'm too fine a gentleman to take advantage? That I can have my pick and like 'em willing?"

Her mane gleamed like rich maple syrup as she shook her head. "Gee, no. It's how you're wrapped up in two layers of confining clothes, as tight as a mummy."

He fingered the striped cotton collar at his throat, feeling bested. "Not necessarily an impossible trap to escape."

"With a trapdoor in the rear of the long johns and in the front of the pajamas, I'd say you're lost in a hopeless maze."

"We'll just see about that." Alec swung his powerful legs over the side of the bed, quickly unbuttoning the front of the red one-piece suit. With swift movements, he stripped off the woollies and tossed them in the air. They landed in a heap beyond the edge of the braided rug.

Sara folded her arms across the ruffled bodice of her gown. Her expression was wry as she surveyed his ill-fitting striped pajamas. "Bravo."

"You don't seem truly impressed. Yet." With a flourish, he

began to unbutton the flimsy top straining across his broad chest, delighted with her gasp of dismay.

She raised a halting palm, her gray eyes frantic. "What are your terms for a truce?"

He smiled broadly. "Guess."

"Okay, I'm impressed," she said hastily. "You're a quick-change artist extraordinaire."

"And?" he urged.

"I'm sure I'd remember if something had happened," she added. "Is that what you want to hear?"

Needed to hear. For no discernible reason.

Alec stopped the striptease right there, letting the shirt hang open a couple of inches to display his hairy chest. Luckily she'd cried uncle on cue. The last thing he wanted to do was remove it and reveal his badge of retirement, the scarred flesh of his left shoulder. To cover up any traces of vulnerability, he stayed on the offensive. "Of course if you want to claim something *almost* happened, I won't argue."

She was stunned. "Why would I do that?"

He wiggled his thick black brows. "You do seem extremely familiar with my woollies."

She squealed in exasperation. "How could I not know the layout of those long johns, after a night plastered to 'em?"

He made a mocking, clucking sound. "Around these parts, that adds up to a marriage proposal."

She squinted at him in shrewd assessment. "You're no country boy. City talent with a shady background is my guess."

"You want my life story?" he asked eagerly.

"No," she snapped. "I want my baby."

"Of course you do," he said matter-of-factly, soberly. He couldn't help but admire her protective motherly instincts. But even so, he felt they had ground to cover now, before she got away. He sat on the bed once again and patted the side of the mattress she'd vacated. "Come back here for one last minute. Please."

There was a new confidence in her step as Sara moved toward the bed. This man was not unmanageable, after all. He wouldn't be a problem unless she let him. And she believed his story about this being an inn and that Rosie was safe and sound. She'd humor him a moment longer, avoid the kind of scene he could so obviously stir up.

She inched onto the white sheet, ignoring the way her gown was riding up under her seat, offering him only her profile as though only half-interested. Her aloofness made his hand on her cheek a surprise. It took all her cool to remain calm as ever-so-gently he drew some silken auburn strands away from her face and tucked them behind her ear. It seemed like a come-on. And it seemed to be working if her jumpy pulse was any indication.

"I don't know what you have in mind," she began haltingly. "What you're trying to do—"

"I'm clearing your ear so you can listen and listen good," he said sternly.

"Damn you!" She attempted to pop up again, but he clamped a hand on her bare thigh with a smacking sound.

"Look, I just want to tell you privately, before we join the others, that you put too many people at risk last night, out on the road at that hour, on a joyride, dressed for the tropics."

"That's my business, and mine alone!"

"Not anymore," he said seriously. "Mrs. Nesbitt and I have a stake, for starters, after braving the elements to save you."

"I told you I'm grateful—"

"You should be especially grateful to her," he clarified. "I want you to understand that it was she who initiated the rescue."

Sara turned her head sharply, her glittery gray eyes meeting his serious indigo ones. He sure meant business when it came to the innkeeper, which was kind of sweet. "Okay, okay."

"She's the most wonderful woman on earth," he went on

to explain, "the kindest, most generous—people probably take advantage of her."

Yeah right. Who was taking advantage? Seemed as if he was calling all the shots here, with his fingers burning streaks along her bare inner thigh, a place where only a select few had ever reached, and only when invited. "I will thank her profusely and sincerely and be out of her way as soon as possible. Satisfied?"

His fingers squeezed her leg as she tried to rise. "Not so fast. There's also a hard-and-fast rule about a guy saving a girl's life," he said. "Means he's got a say in her affairs from then on. A right to some answers."

"Oh, sure, like the brandy rule. The rescuer takes the first swig."

His brows rose. "Ah, so you remember that, do you?"

"I do, *Alec*. And I think your rule book is a self-serving bunch of hooey. Just wanted to tell you in private," she mimicked sweetly, "before we join the others."

He brightened. She remembered his name. Deep inside he knew he shouldn't feel a lift over it, but this whole encounter was the most stimulation he'd had in months. "C'mon, Frosty, give. What were you doing out on the road with a baby this close to the holidays, with no doting husband to do the driving?"

"I had hoped I'd imagined the 'Frosty' part."

He shrugged. "Had to call you something. And you're evading the question."

Sara returned his steady gaze with a sweet smile. He didn't know the meaning of the word evasion yet!

A single rap on the door startled them. Alec snatched his hand back with lightning speed and Sara tugged the ruffled flannel hem over her pink thigh. A moment later Mrs. Nesbitt entered, carrying Rosie in her arms. The innkeeper was already dressed for the day in a zip-front housedress of floral cotton, her steel-gray braids wound in a coronet on her head;

the baby was bright-eyed and struggled against the confines of the white blanket wrapped round her.

"Ah, so you're awake," the old lady chirped. "And getting to know each other already." She approached the bed and set Rosie in Sara's lap.

"We were just going over last night," Alec explained, reaching to tickle Rosie's double chin, sending her into giggles. "Told you the baby was fine, Frosty."

"I didn't doubt it," Sara said, her tone snappier than intended as she tried to keep the flailing child in check. "I'd appreciate it if you wouldn't get her excited."

Alec couldn't help noticing that Frosty was ill at ease as Rosie stretched and bobbed from side to side, trying to wiggle free. Maybe it was the setting that made Sara nervous, in his bed, with Mrs. Nesbitt hovering. Certainly baby Rosie was of sturdier stock than her delicate mother, and along with her paler complexion and corn-silk hair, he thought absently, no one would ever think they were related.

Suddenly his senses sharpened; these oddities didn't seem to add up to an innocuous mother-daughter picture. But that had to be his FBI training, always looking for the chink in the armor. Not a fair weapon to use against a stranded motorist with the loveliest gray eyes and shapeliest tanned gams he'd seen in a good long while.

At least not yet. Not without further evidence.

Mrs. Nesbitt clapped her hands together, her voice crisp with authority. "Breakfast downstairs in the dining room in thirty minutes. Come along now, Alec, and leave the ladies alone."

He gave her a hangdog look. "What about my breakfast in bed? The very reason for these hideous pajamas?"

"And deny the others the details of our derring-do? Nonsense!"

Sara politely promised to be down soon.

Mrs. Nesbitt tried to haul Alec directly from the bed to the door, but he detoured to snatch up his clothing, fresh underwear and shaving kit.

"Men," the innkeeper huffed, playing sentry at the open door.

"Women," Alec teased as he brushed by her into the hallway. "Always getting a guy in tight jams."

"Or jammies." Mrs. Nesbitt tittered.

The door thumped shut behind him and muted laughter filled the air. He whirled around to find he was all alone. Mrs. Nesbitt was still on the *inside!* With a heavy sigh, he padded down the hall toward the community bathroom. Being putty in one woman's hand was tough enough. But three?

A wave of nostalgia poured over him at the thought of being surrounded by females again, full of secrets and laughter. There was never a whole lot of fun in his boyhood apartment back in Chicago, but tying him in knots had been cheap fun for his two little sisters Dana and Sarah. And when his alcoholic mother was sober, she too could be cheery. Unfortunately the late Sheila Wagner's efforts were always fleeting and not to be trusted.

All three Wagner children had in consequence grown up slow to trust, finding loopholes in relationships, deftly managing to escape commitment. Characteristics that made it easy to recognize the symptoms of sneakiness in somebody else. It sometimes took one to know one, and Alec was sure that there was a whole lot more to little Frosty than met the eye.

3

THE KITCHEN WAS ALIVE with the inviting smells and sounds of breakfast as Mrs. Nesbitt ushered Sara and Rosie inside. The musical clang of pots, the aromatic sizzle of bacon, the homeyness of it all brought Sara's senses alive and her defenses down. She was hungry and lonely, no two ways about it.

The cook, bustling from cupboard to stove in a navy blue gingham dress and sensible shoes, greatly resembled Beatrice Nesbitt. Both were scarcely more than five feet tall, were pleasingly plump, and wore wire-rimmed spectacles. She appeared to be about five years older than Beatrice, however, had a pointier nose, and short curls rather than a gray coronet of braids.

"Sara Jameson, I'd like you to meet my sister Camille Parker."

At the sound of Mrs. Nesbitt's voice, Camille turned away from her heavy black skillet, holding a large fork in the air. "Good morning! Didn't know we'd picked up new guests." Her smile broadened as Rosie made a chirpy sound. "Such a lovely baby," she enthused. "What's her name? Is your husband along? The baby must favor him."

Sara grimaced. So much for lowering her defenses. Determined to weigh her every word before speaking, she cleared her throat. "No, we're on our own."

"Just wanted to know how many plates to set," Camille claimed. She turned back to the skillet. "Start the eggs, will you, Beatrice?"

Mrs. Nesbitt pulled out a bow-backed chair, took the

quilted diaper bag off of Sara's shoulder and set it on the round oak table. "Here, now, Sara. Sit down. Rosie must be heavy."

Sara graciously thanked her, slid onto the chair and propped the animated child on her lap. Rosie gleefully began to pat the tabletop with her chubby hands. Sara took in her surroundings, amazed at all the furnishings of a bygone era. The small, rounded refrigerator, the nickel-plated stove, and the freestanding sink were all porcelain-coated antiques in mint condition. There was a grand old spice chest on the wall, and a large step-back cupboard housing blue and white ceramic pitchers, labeled canisters and a full set of dinnerware behind glass doors.

Just when Sara was wondering if they ever dared risk breakage by using any of the pieces, Mrs. Nesbitt swung open a cupboard door and took hold of the sugar bowl and creamer in careless haste. Sara's mother had one pitcher of similar style that no one was allowed to touch! But that was understandable; the market value of the turn-of-the-century pieces was rather high. She made a mental note to watch Rosie's frisky fingers every second.

"So young to be traveling on your own," Camille remarked in unmistakable query.

"A lot of women travel alone."

Camille pressed a hand to her heart. "My stars, do they really? Is this a long trip you're taking?"

"She's traveling all the way to Miami, Camille," Beatrice reported impatiently. "She has no man of her own, so she has no choice about her arrangements."

"I figured she had no man, with her left hand bare," Camille said with dignity, turning the bacon in the skillet.

Sara touched the inside of her ring finger with her thumb. There had been a ring there, a modest diamond set in a raised silver setting. But she'd removed it in a deliberate attempt to set aside the sadness of the past.

"So how do you manage financially?" Camille pressed.

Sara sighed. "I'm a hairstylist."

Camille sighed wistfully. "Oh, how nice. Always wanted to be a hairstylist. So much information passes through Elm City's salon. Why, on any given Saturday, you can find out everything about everybody!"

Mrs. Nesbitt cast Camille a stern look. "Now there's a fitting reason for a career."

"Harmless fun, Beatrice."

"Sisters are such a trial," Mrs. Nesbitt huffed in apology.

"Have one of my own," Sara blurted out. "Though Julie's certainly the more sober of the two of us." Too sober to know what her big sister was up to, for instance. She gently stroked Rosie's pale head like a worry bead. Both Mrs. Nesbitt and Camille seemed to mistake interrogation for normal conversation. How naive of her to assume that just because Alec was sterner and more direct, he'd be the toughest to deal with. These mother hens were worse, picking away at her story with warm reassuring clucks.

It seemed wise to keep track of the information she'd been handily dealing out like cards from a deck. She'd been fairly clever under Alec's bold interest, not discouraging the sensual direction their banter had taken, letting his hormones fog issues surrounding her. But she'd been on high alert every second, nervous around the raw power of the man. And so relieved to have Mrs. Nesbitt bounce him from the room, she'd immediately let her guard down.

Thinking back to the scene in the bedroom, Sara had to concede that the innkeeper had cut through her treasured reserve like a hot knife through butter, drawing her into conversation, subtly taking over. As Sara picked through her open suitcase, the matron had strongly suggested that she wear the warm black slacks and emerald turtleneck sweater that would bring out the gemstone flecks in her gray eyes. Then she had chosen a loose, crawling-friendly, royal-blue corduroy romper and red shirt for the baby.

Before Sara knew it, she and Rosie were dressed in those

very outfits and she'd revealed her Miami destination, as well as the name Sara Jameson. The latter slip meant she couldn't use a credit card to pay for the room, an idiotic blunder. She couldn't afford many more of those.

It was definitely time to step into the shadows, aim the spotlight somewhere—anywhere—else.

"Eggs are a popular item around here, I see," Sara noted as Mrs. Nesbitt bent over a slatted blue crate full of them. "You must have the market cornered at the grocer's."

The sisters laughed merrily, Mrs. Nesbitt straightened up with three eggs in each hand. "They're a staple on the menu because we keep fifty chickens out in the barn."

"Really?" Sara smiled self-consciously. "Should've realized."

"Not at all," Mrs. Nesbitt protested.

"Natural mistake, especially if you're a city girl," Camille said, again with an inquiring inflection.

"Slept like a country girl last night," Sara said simply. "Needed the rest more than I realized."

Camille eyed her indulgently. "Still, you are from the city, aren't you?"

Would it do any harm to admit it? "I'm from Seattle," she said. "Where Rosie keeps me up more nights than I care to count."

Mrs. Nesbitt took a blue bowl out of the cupboard and set it on the table, safely out of Rosie's reach. "Hope Alec didn't disturb you too much, Sara," she said quietly.

"Disturb me?" Sara whispered back.

Mrs. Nesbitt cracked an egg on the edge of the bowl with an efficient flick of the wrist. "Tossing and turning," she clarified in a louder voice.

"Tossing and turning?" Camille parroted from across the large room. "Saturday's no day to experiment with the eggs. Everyone will be at the table. Just scramble as usual. We'll try Sara's city way on Monday."

Sara chuckled along with Mrs. Nesbitt.

"You were so very cold and I didn't know what else to do with you," Mrs. Nesbitt went on to say softly.

"He was the perfect gentleman all night." The statement was the truth as far as it went. But the dawn was a different story entirely. Reflection on their repartee brought her blood to a disturbing simmer. It was as though he felt she owed him personal information in payment for his body heat. She found it impossible to be completely angry with him, though. Behind his gruff exterior, his macho striptease, she'd caught traces of intelligence and depth. Most revealing was the vulnerability in his eyes, which suggested Alec harbored intriguing secrets of his own.

She shrugged off these speculations with a sigh. She couldn't afford to involve herself. Still, like the sisters, she couldn't resist nosy questions. "So, is Alec here alone?"

"Oh my, yes," Camille promptly replied, suggesting that she was in the habit of passing on the information she collected. "Grumpy, keeps to himself, hates to answer even the simplest questions. No mystery as to *why* he's alone."

"Ca—mille!" Mrs. Nesbitt was clearly annoyed.

Sara was mulling over these fascinating bits of information about Alec when she was snapped out of her reverie by Mrs. Nesbitt rummaging through Rosie's quilted diaper bag.

"See you have baby bottles in here."

"Yes, and formula. I'll mix things up once you're finished with your cooking."

Mrs. Nesbitt beamed, tapping Rosie's small nose. "Very well, dear."

"So you aren't nursing, then?" Camille piped up.

Sara pressed her lips together, hoping her distress wasn't obvious. "No, I'm not...anymore. Rosie's perfectly healthy," she added defensively. "Past the six-month mark."

The ladies crooned in complete agreement. A needle and thread, that's what Sara needed for her lips. Much more of this and she'd be cracking, falling into their arms, telling them her woes. But as she closed her eyes it was Alec's strong arms she envisioned catching her, pictured as she'd last seen them, sleeved in those dreadful striped pajamas!

THE DINING ROOM was humming with activity when Alec entered with a bounce in his step. This was the first breakfast he'd taken out of bed since his arrival and he found himself looking forward to it. Frosty, after all, couldn't be let off the hook so easily. It seemed his duty to make sure that she'd properly thanked Mrs. Nesbitt for initiating the rescue.

As for pulling out his best plaid flannel shirt and black twill slacks for the occasion, why, it was a few scant days until Christmas. It was time he got into the spirit of the season.

A round of greetings welcomed him as he sat down at the head of the old rectangular table, the place of honor while Mrs. Nesbitt's husband Jim was on the road selling shoes. He acknowledged everyone separately, going clockwise around the table.

On his left sat Martha Doanes and her ten-year-old boy Timothy, frequently left on their own by Mr. Doanes, an army major currently stationed overseas. Martha sometimes joined her husband, but Timothy was settled here at the inn with the sisters year-round, enrolled in the Elm City school.

Camille and Beatrice followed respectively, their seats closest to the door leading to the kitchen. Coming down the other side sat eightyish Lyle Bisbee, a handsome dandy of a bachelor with a sweep of oiled white hair and a handlebar moustache. He always smelled of peppermint and boasted a wardrobe of dark pinstripe suits straight out of the late-show gangster movies.

The chair at his right remained empty for the moment.

Whenever they were brought together like this, Alec was reminded of the brochure he'd gotten along with the gift certificate. It advertised this bed-and-breakfast as a thoroughly modern asset to the quaint tourist town, a magnet for adventurous guests seeking Christmas revelry.

In truth, the Cozy Rest was an old twenty-acre farm several miles off the beaten path, lacking in appliances as common as a dishwasher and television set. As for the guests, they were all as permanent as the changing of the seasons, with nary a revel between them, beyond the popping of corn on the parlor hearth.

A setting that should have sent him packing within twenty-four hours.

But who could have predicted how much he'd enjoy moping around here? Who could have foretold the sheer pleasure of having one's mind totally free of all distractions for an uninterrupted run of self-pity?

Nevertheless, Frosty was a welcome diversion here in the frozen tundra, he thought, as he accepted the platter passed to him, and piled his plate high with eggs, bacon and toast. Mysterious enough to talk circles around simple questions, attractive enough to make a flannel nightgown as tempting as a G-string. He found himself hoping that she'd claim the empty chair at his side.

"Our hero is hungry, I see." Mrs. Nesbitt's round face beamed with approval as she splashed coffee into his blue ceramic cup.

"Hero?" Voices chorused in surprise, eyes pinned him down.

Alec tensed at the attention, dabbing his mouth with his napkin even though he hadn't touched a bite yet. He was so accustomed to breakfasting alone. He'd acquired the habit after years of hustling round to get himself and his sisters off each morning with lunches and schoolbags.

"Would've thought you'd have hashed it all over by now," he said evenly.

"But it's up to you children to tell the story, Alec," Mrs. Nesbitt insisted, elbowing him in his good shoulder. "Sara!"

Alec decided things were looking up as Frosty came bounding through the swinging door, Rosie cradled in her arms and sucking on a bottle of milk.

"Everyone," Mrs. Nesbitt announced with pleasure, "this is Sara Jameson and her daughter Rosie."

As Sara moved toward the empty chair beside him, Alec jumped to his feet. Swiftly, he exchanged his armchair for the sidechair.

Sara stood by in bewilderment. "What are you doing?"

She couldn't guess? He patted the wooden arm. "All the better to brace the baby."

Her fine brows arched. "Oh, sure. Thanks." Self-conscious under his suspicious look, Sara took her time getting comfortable on the pale blue sateen seat. Mrs. Nesbitt set the stainless-steel coffeepot on the table and hovered beside Sara, serving her generous helpings of each dish.

At the opposite side of the long table, an incensed Camille was making a clinking sound with every scoop of her fork. "What is this 'hero' business? I can't believe the things that go on around here behind my back!"

"Surely you always get to the bottom of things, eventually," Sara said consolingly, leaning away from Rosie as she took a sip of coffee. The cup was from the antique set, so she was extra careful as she set it back in its saucer.

Her innuendo concerning Camille's natural nose for news brought faint, knowing grins to all the guests' faces, making Sara feel a bit more at ease. And Mrs. Nesbitt, true to her take-charge nature, went on to relate the whole story of the rescue without as much as a word from either of the other participants.

By the set of Alec's sharp features Sara suspected that he was still mourning the loss of his breakfast tray. She was completely empathetic. Mrs. Nesbitt didn't need either one of them to flesh out the tale.

"Well, it's no wonder Sara got a little flustered on the icy road," Camille declared with a raised knife. "Being from Seattle. Lots more rain in those parts than snow."

Sara from Seattle. Alec sipped his coffee slowly, conceding that her roots excused the poor driving, lightweight clothing and foolish decision to brave the outdoors. A Pacific-coast resident wouldn't have experience with slippery roads and windchills.

But Sara the clumsy baby handler was definitely tougher to explain away. For the third time, Alec adjusted her elbow where it was braced on the armchair, intent on raising Rosie's head just a fraction as she drank. Sara seemed to resent his interference, but didn't resist. True, the baby had to be fairly heavy for such a slight woman. But surely a mother's biceps strengthened over the course of six months on the job, didn't they?

Alec buttered a half slice of toast and munched on it. His suspicions were probably totally unfair, fallout from his years as an investigator.

Besides, he wasn't into that kind of thing anymore. He was retired.

If he didn't watch out, he'd end up like Camille, a nosy old gossip in a country boardinghouse.

Still, something about ole Frosty wasn't settling quite as well as his delicious eggs and bacon.

He bit into the other wedge of toast, his eyes narrowed to slits. Then he had it!

Sara Jameson. *S.J.* According to her monogrammed cases she was a K.H., a Karen, Kris or Katrina. So where did the truth lie? He thought she'd winced a little when Mrs. Nesbitt announced her as Sara. It could've been simply the strain of her precious cargo, he supposed. Cargo that wouldn't have been that much of a strain to a real mother.

Damn, seemed no matter at what angle he viewed things, the picture rested a little crooked. And he was just a little too agitated over it for his own good.

WHEN MRS. NESBITT encouraged Sara to use the front parlor later that morning for her own needs, Sara was enormously grateful. The room was cozy and inviting, with flames licking in the tile-bordered hearth. A huge tapestry rug covered much of the polished pine floor, and the pale yellow plaster walls were full of old black-and-white photographs and small oils. The only sounds were the occasional crackle of the burning logs and the rhythmic ticking of a rosewood clock atop the upright piano.

There were glitches in this perfect setting, however, in the form of holiday reminders. The huge Scotch pine adorned with silver bulbs and golden tinsel and surrounded by bright packages, most of which were the shape of shoe boxes; the red-flannel stockings hanging along the mantel, each with white cuffs bearing a resident's name, including Alec's.

It appeared they were a family of odds and ends, not all related, but blending to make it work—the kind of Christmas magic she was accustomed to. It tugged painfully at her heart; it was just what she needed right now.

All the more reason to get back on the road, put this sentimental trap behind her.

Feeling tremendously pressed for time, she worked as quickly as possible, spreading a blanket out on the rug as a temporary playground for Rosie, smoothing out her road map beside the blanket. Placing the child on her back within easy reach, she sat cross-legged on the rug, studying her itinerary.

Sara traced her finger down the purple hand-drawn line from her Washington home base to her stops in Idaho, Montana, South Dakota, Minnesota, and here, near the outskirts of Madison, Wisconsin. Next stop was Bloomington, Illinois. What she needed now was her car and a better idea of exactly where the Cozy Rest was situated in reference to the Interstate.

Rosie, in the meantime, was doing her tricks, turning over from her belly to her back, gurgling and kicking her bootie-clad feet.

Distracted by the small miracle child, Sara rubbed her belly with a giggle and dug through the diaper bag for a plastic ring set Rosie was particularly fond of.

"Looks like quite an operation."

Alec's rich voice made her jump. Sara hadn't heard him enter the room. But he was hovering directly overhead, the tips of his scuffed brown moccasins edging over the map, one toe on Saskatchewan, the other on Ontario. He immediately crouched to her level and took the plastic rings out of her pinched fingers.

"Planning strategy, Sara?"

She forced herself to meet his gaze with calm forthrightness. She didn't care for the mocking way he said her name. Did he wonder about it? Had she babbled something different on the chilly sleigh ride or in the warm cocoon of his bed?

"I, ah, am reaffirming strategy."

"Oh, yeah?" He seemed his indolent self as he sat down beside the baby and scooped her up in his lap. But an amazing transformation took place as he bounced Rosie on his thigh; the hard planes of his face melted and his steely voice softened as he crooned to the delightful child.

Great. A closet baby-lover. Sara was better off with the cold, distant hero who scorned tennis-shoed damsels. "Surely Camille has mentioned to you by now that I am on my way to Miami," she said flatly.

"So she did," he confessed. His gooey look included her for one fleeting moment, catching her off guard, making her pulse jump. The dark blue eyes that had seemed so ruthless earlier now twinkled merrily, rivaling the lights strung over the tree and across the facade of the house. As their sleeves grazed she noticed that the same shade of green in her sweater was threaded through his colorful flannel shirt. They probably painted a serene family picture, a couple who'd shopped together, who shared parental duties with pleasure.

A dream pathetically lost to her now.

"Is Mrs. Nesbitt around?" she asked forlornly.

Alec was holding Rosie under the armpits, nuzzling her

downy cheek with his nose, not paying the least bit attention to Sara.

"I say, is—"

"She's always around," Alec interrupted calmly. With a baffled frown he added. "All of them are...*always* around."

"Well, I can't afford to hibernate. I need to get my car up and running. Right away."

Alec sat Rosie down on his leg, his expression tinged with sympathy. "That's out of the question. Until Elm City's plow hits the frontage road, it's stuck out there in the ditch."

"Well, what's the weather forecast look like?"

Alec shrugged, the movement seeming to cause him some pain. "Don't know."

"So turn on the radio!"

"There is *nothing* to turn on," he reported unhappily. "No radio or TV or shortwave."

"You're joking!"

"I only wish. As much as I first enjoyed the isolation, I've come to miss updates on the news and the national hockey league games."

"How long have you been here?" she inquired, surveying him as one might a demented hermit.

"Hey, only a week," he protested. "It's not like I'm a regular."

"Honest mistake, being as there are several permanent boarders. Mrs. Nesbitt told me that much."

"Yes, that's right. But I got this trip as a gift. It's not like I believe this is the ideal Christmas vacation, Sara."

"I think what the people around here need most are some activities outside the inn."

"In their defense, it's been almost one continual blizzard since I got here. My airport taxi barely made it in and out before the gale picked up." He shook his head. "Man, was he glad to have found the inn so easily. The colored lights were a lifesaver."

Sara bit her lip. "Yes, they caught my eye, too."

A sound at the doorway drew their attention. There stood Mrs. Nesbitt in her floral housedress, her hands clasped in front of her. "My, my, what a pretty picture."

Sara was pleased to see that Alec's features sharpened once again. Ah, thank heaven, the man she had encountered this morning was back. The man she felt she could keep in check. The man who didn't threaten to shatter her protective shell.

She needed all the help she could get to keep him at a distance.

"I was just telling Sara about the roads, Mrs. Nesbitt," Alec said smoothly. "How we're at the mercy of the Elm City municipal services."

"Goodness, yes," the older woman confirmed with pursed lips. "Your car is especially trapped. We have a fine garage in town, but they can't send the tow truck until the road is cleared."

Sara's pretty face crumpled. "But when? How?"

"I think you should try to call the town hall," Alec suggested, more anxiously than he meant to. But Sara liked the idea so much she didn't seem to notice. She was on her feet in a flash. "Where is the telephone, Mrs. Nesbitt?"

Alec lingered on the blanket with Rosie, swinging her around, thoroughly enjoying her sweet, melodic laughter. His doubts concerning Sara's parental status seemed preposterous as he surveyed the healthy, joyous child. Keeping her tucked snugly in the crook of his arm, he crawled closer to the map, studying the route traced in bold purple marker.

Seattle, Washington to Miami, Florida. Hmm, the route appeared about as sensible as Sara's tennis shoes. Sure, she was heading down in a southwesterly direction, but it was in a zigzag fashion that looked illogical. Alec bemusedly drew a tissue from the diaper bag and swiped Rosie's spittled mouth. He could understand last night's detour, stopping for supplies, getting confused. But this impractical route had been mapped out with deliberateness.

Hearing the gallop of Timothy's shoes on the foyer staircase, he quickly rose. If Timothy noticed his interest in the map he would be full of questions and might alert Frosty to his curiosity about her indirect route.

Alec sauntered over to the decorated tree, hoisting the baby higher on his chest. "We'll just give the ladies a few more minutes to dig that phone number out of the inn's little green address book."

Rosie made gurgling sounds as he spoke in soothing tones, and rested her head against his chest in utter contentment. She liked him—really liked him! Alec kissed her soft, fair hair, inhaling her baby sweetness, realizing he was trembling a little. Her cuddly softness and scent had actually penetrated his reserve, stirring long dormant feelings of unconditional affection. Was there anything between heaven and earth so innocent, so joyful?

"I just may be jinxed where that telephone is concerned," he murmured lovingly in her tiny ear. "Maybe Frosty can tame it for both of us. Uh-uh, mustn't touch the tinsel, sweet thing." He guided her moist, fat patty away from the branches, only to have Rosie clap it against his cheek. "Hey," he crowed, "it's been awhile since a pretty lady slapped the heck out of me! Bet your mommy would like to. If she *is* your mommy, that is...."

4

"HELLO? HELLO? Can anybody hear me?"

Sara's strained voice echoed down the hallway from the kitchen to the parlor, where Alec was patiently awaiting his cue. This was it. Sara had apparently lost her battle with their only line to the outside world. Hoisting Rosie up on his shoulders, he headed for the kitchen.

Sara took one look at her precious charge atop the gruff giant's shoulders and sagged against the wide, varnished doorjamb, the telephone receiver still clenched in one hand. It just didn't seem safe, even though he towered over everybody with the sturdiest-looking frame she'd ever seen. "Hey, that's dangerous!"

"Not at all. She's smiling, isn't she?"

"Like Rosie knows what's good for her," Sara cried in disgust, slamming the phone back on its hook. "Give her to me right now!"

Alec lurched back as Sara moved toward him, sending a jolt of pain from his collarbone to the tips of his fingers. He froze with gritted teeth, keeping a secure grip on the child, waiting for the agony to take its course. Before the shooting, he could have carried a full-grown man a fair distance. Now he couldn't even give a baby a ride. Pain, physical and mental, twisted his face. This kind of weakness was unacceptable. He was determined not to give in to it.

Nothing is really wrong with me. I just need a bit more time to recuperate.

"Alec? You okay?"

Sara's strong voice pierced his fog. Her hand touched his

flannel sleeve. There was no mistaking the energy in her fingertips. He was certain she was ready to climb his back herself, if necessary, to reclaim Rosie. Ever so carefully, he lifted the cheery baby over his head and down into Sara's outstretched arms.

"You are hurt, aren't you?" she asked.

"Was hurt," he corrected shortly. "But Rosie was safe every second. I guarantee it. I have some experience with kids, carried my sisters all over the place just like that." It took some effort on his part, but he added a heartfelt admission. "I miss it more than I realized."

Sara, frustrated by her futile attempt to call Elm City, was not sympathetic. "May I suggest you beat the bushes for a baby of your own if you so desire one."

His large mouth thinned. He only hoped the advice wasn't from personal experience. "Won't kill you to share *your child* while you're here," he said evenly, with an ingratiating smile for Mrs. Nesbitt.

Sara shifted in discomfort as Alec and the innkeeper rested longing eyes upon Rosie. They just didn't understand that she couldn't get enough of Rosie's company herself. In the wake of last night's accident, it was all the harder to let go.

With mounting tension, Sara realized she'd been shortsighted to view this trip as a piece of cake. But she'd only been trying to do what she thought best for Rosie. How badly she needed some unconditional support. But that wasn't possible with this merry band of shut-ins. Any inkling of her present emotional state would only bring on a barrage of questions.

Darn that Alec, staring her down like a prosecuting attorney!

"Oh...you have spit in your hair," Sara finally snapped, then turned her back on him and moved closer to the table where Timothy was playing solitaire. "Red two on the black three, buddy."

"Don't spoil it, Sara," he whined. "It's the most exciting thing happening around here."

Nobody argued.

Alec dabbed his head with a tissue, then waited several beats before rubbing his hands together with forced nonchalance and inquiring about the phone call. "So I take it you didn't manage to reach the town hall?"

"The line was a jumble of static," Sara reported unhappily. "As you knew it would be. Mrs. Nesbitt told me you've had the same trouble. What were you trying to do, make me look like a fool?"

He was quick on the defense. "Of course not. True, I did use you as a test pilot. But only because I thought I was jinxed."

"So sorry, my dears," Mrs. Nesbitt sang out as she went about serving Timothy a glass of lemonade and some frosted Christmas cookies. "It could be that the town hall is closed, on this the Saturday before Christmas."

"It might have been ringing," Sara conceded. "But the sound was too distant to be sure."

Mrs. Nesbitt smiled apologetically at her. "The lines are terribly unreliable at this time of year. Alec's taken it far too personally."

Alec was tempted to argue that all the tenants seemed to use the thing successfully. Except for little Timothy Doanes, who seemed far more interested in his Hardy Boys novels and cardplaying.

Alec gazed over at the kid with the bright red crew cut, hunched over his lone game, his freckled face earnest. He didn't look Alec in the eye much anymore. But that was probably because Alec had been too brusque with the youngster during the past week and had even fallen asleep during the boy's parlor readings of his prized mystery books. Timothy liked to chatter and whine, pester the daylights out of everybody, and it had made the already edgy victim of early retirement all the more irritable.

A close look at Tim's situation was enough to put it into perspective for Alec, though. He was a pest because he was lonely. His father was away on a military mission and school was closed through the New Year. The kid was hungry for companionship and would probably calm down if Alec made the effort.

Alec couldn't help but marvel at how Sara's and Rosie's presence had pulled him out of his dark shell overnight. He barely recognized himself.

Naturally, rising out of his blue funk had a price. It drove home the fact that he desperately missed his task force at the Bureau, and it still hurt like crazy that he no longer qualified for field duty. But he wouldn't allow himself to sink back into the zombie-like state of the past week, sitting in the parlor window seat, watching the snow fly.

Miraculously, perhaps fatefully, he found himself with a puzzle to solve. The elusive Sara Jameson. Any dedicated FBI man, retired or not, would feel an obligation to get to the bottom of her story. She was too guarded to be completely genuine, and there were inconsistencies concerning her name, her clumsiness with the baby, and her strange route down to Miami.

There was only one hitch to his analytical approach. Despite her strange behavior, Alec found himself desperately wanting to believe every single word she uttered!

During his musings, Sara had with some reluctance handed Rosie to an eager Mrs. Nesbitt and wandered over to the window over the sink. Seeming to be in a rigid trance, she was gazing out through the lace curtains and the red straw wreath similar to the ones that adorned every pane in the house. Under the flag of investigator, Alec closed in and clamped his hands on her shoulders. Instead of protesting, she simply sagged a little. It gave him the nerve to console her.

"Are you all right? Anything I can do?"

She curled her fists, crossing them against her chest. "I can't believe this is happening to me, after coming so far."

Alec stood over her, frowning. *So far?* If she meant distance in miles, she had most of the trip ahead of her. What if she meant something else? Whisking off Rosie, changing her name? The very idea twisted his stomach in knots. "The claustrophobic feeling is bound to upset you today," he said gently, careful not to betray any doubts.

"Just wait until tomorrow," she grumbled. "That's when you'll begin to see some real alarms sounding off."

"Why, Sara?"

"Because I have a set timetable! I have to get word—" She clamped her mouth closed then, as though she had said too much.

Alec didn't make the conscious decision to massage her shoulders, but he needed to do something with his hands as he thought things through. If she was in such a hurry, why the roundabout route?

Unless she's trying to ditch somebody, throw them off the scent.

Could anything else account for the facts? He wanted to believe there was a reasonable explanation for everything, but he couldn't put his finger on one. And he wouldn't be satisfied until he could.

It was Timothy's voice that broke the silence some moments later. "Play cards with me, Sara. Please?"

Sara turned round to face both males with a forced smile. "I need some time to unwind, Tim. Maybe later." She touched Alec's arm. "But I bet Alec would be interested."

"He's never interested," Timothy said dully.

"Hey, don't give up so easily," Alec said heartily.

"Really, Mr. Wagner? Jeepers, guess there's a first time for everything."

Sara clearly got some satisfaction out of the self-conscious flush that crept over his sharply defined features. "I think I'll go rest in your bed. If you have no objections," she murmured on a husky note. "My being your guest and all."

Alec brightened in boyish hope. "You remembered."

She smiled falsely. "You stated your case pretty plainly."

Something quite wonderful and erotic stirred Alec's libido

as he gazed down into Sara's effervescent gray eyes. She might be annoyed with him, unsure of him, but she too was affected by the sparks flying between them. "I've been known to take an early-afternoon nap around here myself."

"Yeah, just like old Lyle Bisbee," Timothy confirmed flatly. "Only he's eighty-three."

Alec sighed hard as the electric moment died, falling from champagne fizz to false teeth and stewed prunes.

As Sara made her exit, Timothy hastily gathered up his playing cards and pushed them into a stack. "Wanna play poker?"

"Sure. And call me Alec." He scraped back a chair directly across from the boy and sat down, watching patiently as Timothy shuffled the cards in undersized hands.

"Five-card stud okay?"

Alec's brows lifted. "Fine. Too bad none of your friends can make it over," he said sympathetically.

"It *is* too bad." Timothy sent cards flying to Alec until they each had five.

"The snow will clear soon."

"But it's more than that! I can't— They can't—" His narrow chest deflated under his long-sleeved striped T-shirt.

"Why can't they come over, Tim?"

His small face screwed up. "Kinda hard to explain. But I'll see 'em back in school."

Alec couldn't help but wonder if the kid could get any action on that nutty phone. "Ever think of giving them a call?" he asked lightly.

He shook his head. "Naw, Ma doesn't want me bothering people this close to Christmas and that's that."

"Oh."

"Too bad it wouldn't work for Sara," Timothy said with surprising feeling.

"You like her?"

"She's real pretty and nice."

"Yeah..." Alec shared a man-to-man smile with him.

"Town hall probably is closed, but that other number didn't seem to ring at all."

Alec sat up straighter, staring over his fan of cards. "Other number?"

"Yeah, it was really long. I think she got it mixed up."

Or had been trying to make a long-distance connection. Alec encouraged Tim to go on.

"Not much happened. Then she tried to reach the operator. Mrs. Nesbitt told her that Loralee leaves her post sometimes. But Sara just kept sayin' she didn't need no Loralee. That it was very important that she check in."

"Check in?"

"Yup."

"Wonder if she meant a hotel."

Timothy shrugged a little, adjusting the cards in his hand. "I dunno."

"Then what happened?"

"Sara asked about phones in town, about taking the sleigh. Mrs. Nesbitt said old Sugar couldn't make it through the extra snow we got last night."

"And?"

"She tried to dial town hall again, and you showed up."

Alec hunched over the table, sinking into thought. What was she up to?

"We could play for pennies," Timothy suggested.

Alec waved his cards, inadvertently revealing them to his opponent. "Okay, okay, sure."

"Make that nickels," Timothy amended excitedly.

"Sure, sure."

"So you got any?"

"What, Tim?" Alec raised troubled blue eyes to the boy's expressive brown ones.

"Nickels, Alec. Nickels for the game."

Alec laughed out loud. It seemed he was going to have to pay more attention to everyone around here if he hoped to keep up!

SARA AWOKE FROM her nap two hours later to find Mrs. Nesbitt in the front parlor, nestled into her rocking chair, Rosie stretched out on her chest, relaxing after a bottle feeding.

The innkeeper greeted her with a serene smile. "Such a lamb, your girl."

"She certainly is."

"We had our lunch, but there are some cold sandwiches all made up in the icebox."

"Thanks. I'll help myself later."

Not wanting to disrupt the rocking pair, Sara began to gather up her things from the floor. It was strange, living in a home full of paying guests. She knew boardinghouses had been rather common in the old days, but it had to involve some huge compromises. For instance, she had no right to tie up this sitting room all day long. She was sure the residents spent many an afternoon in this cheery Christmas parlor.

She lifted the blanket from the fringed rug, folded it in a square, and pressed it to her chest with a pensive sigh. It wasn't like her to be so ruminative, but she had just awakened from a vivid dream about Alec and herself between the sheets. Unlike last night, there were no woollies and flannel barriers between them. They'd shared explosive sex, and he'd vowed to protect her from the cold, cruel world.

Is that what she secretly longed for right now?

She stuffed the blanket in the diaper bag disgustedly. She was an independent woman quite capable of taking care of herself. So what if she'd made some mistakes? Anybody could slide off the road. And she couldn't help it if she couldn't keep up her side of the bargain by checking in on time.

Was it so wrong to wish to lean upon a man for support, draw from his strength, support him in return in exclusively feminine ways? That was the foundation of any romantic relationship. She knew so firsthand. Alec found her attractive. And he was bonkers over Rosie. Despite his sternness and aloofness, he was appealing, the kind of man women fantasized about taming.

But the timing for involvement couldn't have been worse. She was committed to this trip and her itinerary didn't allow for any distractions. She was smack-dab in the middle of things, and there was no turning back.

It seemed wisest to keep her distance.

But it was bound to be no cinch. Alec was impossible to ignore. There was his overpowering masculine appeal to deal with, as well as his grand inquisitor's soul. She sensed a judgment call behind his every observation, and he was proving to be very observant.

The road map was a prime example. As she'd rested on her knees, patiently folding it back up, she'd spotted a fair amount of saliva wetting the Atlantic and parts of North Carolina. It was Rosie's work for sure, suggesting that she'd been dangling over the map for quite some time, while Alec studied it. So he was determined to dig out facts she held private. She simply had to find out more about him if she hoped to keep him in check.

Mrs. Nesbitt seemed the perfect source for such information. Though she looked half-asleep, Sara sensed that the old woman was watching her moves closely. She forced herself to relax and strolled over to the rocker.

"In the mood for a chat, Mrs. Nesbitt?" The question was a mere formality as she lit on the arm of a nearby settee. Perched a few inches higher than the rocker, she had a clear view of Rosie's soft, round profile, snuggled against the older woman's bosom. She hated prying, but she couldn't let that stand in her way.

"Of course, dear," Mrs. Nesbitt breathed.

"A private one?"

"Certainly."

Sara studied her gnawed fingernails. "About Alec..."

The innkeeper kept right on rocking, her expression serene. "He's only concerned about you, dear. And the map's nearly dry, no real harm to it."

Was there anything the innkeeper missed? "Of course," Sara said brightly, determined to forge on. "Being that he's so attentive, I can't resist wondering about him in return. What's he do for a living, for instance?"

"He's retired. Thought you knew. Talks of it incessantly."

"Seems rather young for it."

"Thirty-five."

"Then the retirement's nothing to brag about. Is it?"

Beatrice shook her head emphatically. "No, he talks about it all the time because he's trying to justify it in his own mind—in all our minds. I figure he's accustomed to group feedback. He's been behaving like a hermit, but I don't think it's a natural thing. I think he misses the interaction of his co-workers."

"But why then would he..."

"It's the wound, you see."

"Wound!"

"You notice how he favors his left shoulder?" When the dumbstruck Sara nodded, she continued. "Took a bullet in the line of duty."

"What duty?"

"He's an FBI agent. Or was one." Mrs. Nesbitt absently rubbed the baby's back. "Dearie me, you have been letting him ask all the questions, haven't you?"

"Well, it seems he's the pro at it."

Mrs. Nesbitt nodded, but said shrewdly, "Nothing you can't handle, surely."

Sara's smile was bleak. *Oh, yeah?* This news was the absolute worst. She was snowbound, with Mr. FBI, Retired. In her mind his current status made him all the more threatening. The man had absolutely nothing to do but play poker with a ten-year-old and dig into her business. She had to get out of here somehow!

"Why," Mrs. Nesbitt continued, "Alec was—"

"He was admiring your lovely wedding ring set, too?" Sara interrupted in a gush.

Mrs. Nesbitt's puzzled frown melted away as Martha Doanes sat down on a blue sateen sofa opposite them. As greetings were exchanged, Sara studied the newcomer with interest. Martha was a handsome woman of about forty, her long hair every bit as red as her son Timothy's. She had a trim figure, which seemed wasted beneath out-of-date clothing, a plaid woollen skirt that fell to midcalf, and a cream-colored sweater trimmed in some kind of animal fur. Sara couldn't help but think that a beauty makeover in a city like nearby Madison would do wonders for the military wife. Admittedly, Martha did seem content. She was digging through a roomy canvas knitting bag, and eventually pulled out a skein of pink yarn and two midsized needles.

"What a lovely shade of yarn," Sara said admiringly. "Have a project in mind?"

"A matinee jacket for Rosie," Martha announced excitedly. "So fun to knit for a baby girl. The major and I probably won't be having any more children of our own."

Panic squeezed Sara's chest. "But we'll be gone before you finish it!"

"You'll be here for Christmas, won't you? And it's only right you have gifts under the tree." She winked at the horrified Sara. "Luckily Rosie's sleeping. I can measure her without giving away the surprise." Martha giggled over her joke.

"I'm so sorry," Sara hastened to say, "but we'll be going. Very soon."

"Well, you won't be leaving this afternoon, surely," Mrs. Nesbitt put in. "Where were we? Oh, yes, my rings." She held out the aged hand bearing the gold bands boasting diamonds and ruby chips. "My Jim chose it himself. Bought it on the road. Sells shoes, you know. Adores me, he does."

Sara understood that Mrs. Nesbitt was trying to calm her down, but her hammering heart was nearly out of control.

Trapped through Christmas? It took all her might to speak calmly. "He sounds wonderful. Must be hard for you when Jim's away."

Mrs. Nesbitt patted Rosie's bottom with a wistful sigh. "Oh, no question. But a man should use his skills and my Jim, he's born to sell shoes. Me, I'm the homebody type who likes to make folks comfortable."

"I agree about one's calling," Sara said. "I love doing hair. It brings me a lot of pleasure."

"You know, Camille would be tickled if you'd do hers," Mrs. Nesbitt said excitedly.

"Mine too, please!" Martha Doanes chimed in.

"What a fine idea," Mrs. Nesbitt declared with finality. "How kind of you, Sara. How clever of you to think of it. Perfect Christmas gift."

Sara stared at her dazedly. "No trouble at all. How about tomorrow morning?"

"Say, can anybody join this hen party?"

As Alec sauntered through the doorway Sara shot up like a bullet, FBI flashing behind her eyes in jumbo letters.

Alec took note of her reaction, suspicion pinching his heavy black brows.

"Run out of nickels?" Martha piped up.

"Uh, yes," Alec replied, tearing his eyes from Sara to address the redhead. "Timothy is a real cardsharp."

Martha returned to her knitting, looping yarn around her needles. "Thanks for playing along. Tim's so fascinated by you, and his father's been gone quite a stretch this tour of duty."

Sara flinched as he sat on the sofa beside Martha. He was staying!

Alec rubbed his hands together. "What's the topic of conversation this afternoon?"

"Jobs," Mrs. Nesbitt announced with pleasure. "Goals. So important for a body to do what they love. Right, Alec?"

"If they're allowed to," he said staunchly.

"Sometimes dreams need tune-ups," Sara added.

Alec bared his teeth, looking particularly dangerous. "So you've heard my tale, *Sara*?"

Again, the ironic inflection on her name. It caused a tremor along her spine. "Yes, I have, and I suspect you're finding probing into other people's affairs a challenging habit to break."

His job had never been defined with such pat ignorance, but he let it slide. "I disagree," he claimed airily. "I'm retired. On to other things."

"Your course all *mapped* out?"

He was about to launch another zippy reply when he realized she didn't really want answers about his future, that she was indirectly complaining about his invasive questions, his study of the road map. He'd been so engrossed in her route, he'd forgotten to wipe Rosie's drool off the Atlantic.

"Perhaps not every detail of my path is set in my mind yet," he finally said.

"That's good. Because I'd say that a paycheck is what makes the difference between being an agent and a Paul Pry." Sara stood, keeping her chin high, her smile steady. "If you'll excuse me, I believe I'll have some lunch."

His jaw slackened in wonder as she strolled out of the room, like a leggy boxer leaving the ring. In a few concise words, she'd managed to reduce his job description to paid snooping, his concern for her to overzealous meddling!

Once he'd stabilized his ego and looked at the situation carefully, he realized that she'd most likely put on her sparring gloves because his old job had struck a nerve with her. There was no way he could let it rest. And if that meant he was a snoop, they could just start calling him Pry for short.

5

"HOPE YOU DON'T mind giving up your bedroom, Alec."

"No, no, Sara, it's fine. The only space left is pretty drafty, and smaller."

"But all the trouble of packing and unpacking. I mean, it hardly seems necessary when I'll probably be on my way sometime tomorrow." Sara paused at the dressing table to drop some cosmetics on its glass surface, conscious of the plaintive strain in her voice. She watched him out of the corner of her eye, lounging in the scarlet chintz club chair beside the bed. Several times she'd almost tripped over his extended legs. He'd moved them every time she passed, only to stretch them out again.

Making a game of it, she decided, if his glittery blue eyes were any indication. Trying to trip her up any way he could, get a rise out of her, force a revelation. Trouble was, she was close to cracking, pouring out her heart.

Dare she? He really had been very kind, and perhaps what she had interpreted as nosiness was no more than concern for her and Rosie. He appeared to be enjoying her company; his stern features were almost tranquil and she sensed she might be able to make him understand her position. He would have sound advice, surely.

But what if such an attempt backfired? What if he pulled the plug on her charade?

How could something so right be happening at the worst of times? The idea of losing herself in this winter wonderland where everybody was full of joy and affection and the goodwill of the season was tempting her till she ached to the toenails. The answers to all her needs were right here for the taking. Still, she didn't dare indulge herself.

Christmas at the Cozy Rest was an impossibility!

"Hard to say when the plow will come through," Alec remarked, piercing her reverie with this gloomy speculation. "Wouldn't get my hopes too high." Alec could hear the fatigue in his own voice and marveled at how deeply relaxed he'd become watching Sara move around the comfortable room. The skirted bed they'd shared last night was presently taken over by Rosie, a cuddly dream in a pale blue sleeper. Surrounded by a square of protective pillows, she was up on her hand and knees, rocking back and forth and making babbling sounds at her tiny white teddy bear. The coiled heater was blasting the room full of heat at noisy intervals, heightening the feminine and baby scents. Inhaling deeply, Alec felt drugged with a sense of serenity.

The ambience of the Cozy Rest Inn.

A tender trap for a fallen man.

If a man wanted to walk into it.

But would the woman be there waiting? Sara's message to the contrary hit him like a cold splash of common sense, keeping him from entirely going off the deep end. The lady herself, the centerpiece of this comfort zone, couldn't wait to make her getaway. She'd stuck to her agenda all day long, without a hint that she just might be a little interested in him, at least enough to keep in touch.

The truth was that she was growing more edgy around him by the hour. But why? Because she considered him a bozo? Or because her future was one she couldn't share?

He was certain she felt the sexual fireworks between them, that instantaneous, unexplainable something that struck two people like lightning.

A smart man would see no future in this chance holiday meeting and would be distancing himself right now, marching next door to his new digs, keeping his head straight. But here he sat, stubborn as an old mule, mystified by his own behavior.

The way he was totally captivated by her was pure magic, something he couldn't rationalize, a state of mind he was un-used to, for Alec had never been the stardust, maudlin type. He'd known intimacy with more than the average guy's quota of women, most of whom shared his law-enforcement background, his career-centered life-style.

Sara went against the prototype. She was probably *break-ing* the law!

Perhaps his interest only seemed romantic because his bat-teries were on low charge.

Part of her allure was surely her obvious need for a strong hero, and being a hero was Alec's life work. The sleigh res-cue had jump-started all his old field-agent cylinders. She was so ripe for protecting, a fragile contrast to his bulk, seeming even smaller when she was holding the chubby Rosie.

He had to face it, a part of him missed being needed. But he was accustomed to winning the trust and respect of those in his care. At this point there was a feeling of suspicion brewing between them; each seemed to be waiting for the other to cross the line with a sexual overture.

Rosie rolled over on her back with a discontented cry. Sara turned away from the dresser, appearing unduly distressed. "What's the matter, honey?" she crooned in bewilderment.

"I'll hold her," he offered, rising quickly to his feet.

Sara brightened with relief. "Okay. But please keep her at a reasonable altitude this time."

"I won't sit her on my shoulders again, I promise." Grasp-ing the baby under the arms, he lifted her up in the air, stared into her sober blue eyes and rubbed his nose against hers. "I know you wanna fly, jingle-bell baby, but we're grounded. Orders."

"Jingle-bell baby?" Sara repeated in surprise.

"Sure, took a ride on a jingling sleigh, didn't she? Jingled all the way, arriving just like a Christmas present, all wrapped up just for me." He beamed from Sara to Rosie. "Frosty and Jingle."

Sara tossed her head in affront. "She's the present. I get the chilly name."

"You *were* chilly. A foolishly unwrapped present."

She leveled a finger at him. "Don't even go there!"

"I won't," he said cheerily. "But you can be sure nobody's going to let you loose out on the road again without a decent jacket!"

"Huh." Tucking her silken auburn hair behind her ears, Sara surveyed the rosebud-papered room with furrowed brows. "Wonder what kind of baby bed Mrs. Nesbitt made up last night?"

"I asked. A dresser drawer."

Sara was visibly impressed. "Oh, how clever. I'll remember that for—"

"The road?"

"Yes, for the road. Don't you think *my* jingle-bell baby has a dandy crib back in Seattle?"

He raised a palm in a conciliatory gesture. "I'm sure she does."

She pulled open the top drawer and her mouth pursed in disapproval. "Your stuff is still in here. Thought you were moving on."

Feeling stung by her wish to dismiss him, he strolled over for a look. "Those woollies belong to the absent shoe salesman extraordinaire, Jim Nesbitt."

"Oh." She opened the next drawer. Finding it empty, she slid it out and carried it to the braided bedside rug.

"There are some extra quilts on the closet shelf." He moved across the room and turned the closet door's glass knob, then stepped aside with the yawning Rosie as Sara bustled over in a businesslike way.

"These will be fine," she judged confidently.

"You may want to build a nest with downy layers, then

cover it with her own blanket, things she's used to." He tapped Rosie's pug nose. "Give the old sniffer something to latch on to."

"Well, of course!" Sara whisked by him with a patchwork bundle, her lower lip extended huffily, and for the first time Alec could see a resemblance to Rosie.

Did she protest too much? Alec wondered, watching her as she dropped to her knees beside the drawer. There'd been a flicker in her pretty gray eyes as the idea had registered, as though it were valuable and new. Unfortunately, her face was now lost behind a curtain of auburn as she cushioned the roomy drawer. Knowing full well that he'd be stirring up trouble, he leaned over the bed close to where she crouched, causing her to tip back with a squeal and land squarely on her tight little bottom.

Alec now had some idea of what he himself had looked like when Mrs. Nesbitt had bounced him out of bed last night. He'd taken a bigger fall, but the state of dishevelment had to be a match. "I was just reaching for her teddy," he said with a chuckle.

"Well, sure! I didn't think—"

"You thought I was going to plow onto the mattress and drag you along. Something like this." Holding the baby close to his chest, he pushed aside the fence of pillows and eased onto the mattress.

"Fat lot you know." Struggling to her knees again, she went back to work on the maple drawer with a cool determination. It was a difficult front to keep up, though, not knowing what either Alec or Rosie would do next.

The difference between them was that Rosie was a treat and Alec a threat. His interest in her was undeniable at this point. It rattled her, flattered her, and left her wishing for the impossible: comfort and safety, with just a dash of hot romance.

Never before in her life, however, was it more important that she be alone. She was worried enough that she'd be caught with Rosie. And if *he* somehow found out what she was doing, he'd undoubtedly interfere, making matters a whole lot worse.

She shivered underneath her sweater and jeans, fervently wishing he'd go away now. Maybe if she fiddled long enough he would. That was when she felt the first plop, right on top of her head. He'd thrown a pillow at her!

"Hey, knock it off!" She glared up at him, rubbing a spot above her right ear.

"Got her, didn't we, Jingle?" Alec clapped the baby's hands together. "Score one for the bed team."

"And what team am I supposed to be?"

"Oh." He screwed up his whisker-shadowed face in thought. "How about the droopy-drawers team?"

"Well, if that's the way it's going to be, I'd say you'd better hand me a couple pillows, and Rosie. Nobody's drawers droop more than hers."

Strands of dark hair fell over Alec's brow as he shook his head. "Oh, no, we're in place, our strategy planned." He picked up the white teddy bear and shook it at her. "Here, take him. Then we'll be evenly matched."

The teddy landed in Sara's lap. She stared up at man and babe with a mean squint. "The pairing is all wrong, Alec. It should be the girls against the bears, the stuffed and should-be-stuffed." With that she lunged onto the mattress and pulled Rosie toward her. She rolled over on her back then, adjusting Rosie on her chest. "There, Alec. You see."

Alec raised himself up on one elbow and stared down into Sara's face. It was his first close-up view since the rescue. The sight was striking. Her face was animated, her complexion flushed from excitement rather than the wind, her eyes wide open and sparkling. Her hair, recently brushed to a bright sheen, framed her classical features in rich mahogany hues, reminding him of a fine portrait. A true masterpiece. In all his adventures over the years, Alec had never been so tempted to lose himself in a woman, to press his mouth against the pulse point at her throat and count the beats.

Sara tensed. He was going to make a move, and she wasn't going to stop him. All the warning signals flashing behind her eyes were lost in the drumbeat of her blood. It had been so long since a man had regarded her with such raw desire. Too long.

His finger hooked the high, ribbed neck of her sweater, gently tugging it away from her skin. He kissed her throat tentatively, stamping it with a trail of small nips. Pleased by her groan, he captured her mouth and kissed her deeply, thoroughly. Ever so gently he worked around the baby, kissing Sara on and on, gliding his tongue into her mouth with a loving caress.

When he felt her soften helplessly he dared to slip his hand up beneath her sweater, to stroke the smooth length of her belly. When she responded, he climbed higher to massage her breasts through the minuscule cups of her bra. With further encouragement he slipped his fingers inside the wispy band of satin and rolled one nipple, then the other, between his fingers.

The love play was so simple, so tame, but had a profound effect on Sara. She lolled with desire, enjoying every sensation, the grinding burn of his evening shadow, the pinch-pull on her breasts. It was the stuff kids did in parked cars. But to Sara it was so much more....

A rap on the door eventually interrupted them. Sara quickly sat up, sliding the baby onto her lap. "Come in."

The door bounced open with a creak and Timothy ambled inside. His freckled face absorbed the scene on the rumpled bed. "You still here, Alec? Thought you had a new room."

Alec raked his fingers through his tousled black hair, his voice a little sharp. "I do. I'm getting there." He swung his legs over the opposite side the bed and got to his feet.

"Your moccasins are over here," Timothy said helpfully,

pointing to the floor before he climbed up on the bed in Alec's vacated spot.

Alec hitched his pants a little higher, rounded the spindle footboard, and jammed his feet into his shoes.

"Look, Rosie likes to rub my head." Sure enough, when Timothy leaned over the baby, she patted his orange crew cut. Her fingers flailed as she desperately tried to fist some of the short hair.

"She isn't hurting you, is she, Tim?" Sara asked, struggling to regain her composure.

"Jeepers, no, Sara." He gave the baby's chubby cheek a kiss. "I like having our own jingle-bell baby."

"How'd you know about that jingle stuff?" Alec asked.

The boy's skinny shoulders lifted underneath his stripped T-shirt. "Aw, somebody heard you say it. Now everybody in the house calls her that."

"But I don't..." Alec trailed off, puzzled. He must've mentioned it downstairs, but for the life of him he couldn't remember when. Such lapses frightened him, made him wonder if he was as unfit for duty as his Bureau superiors thought. But the tricks of eye and ear had only started after he'd arrived here. It was several months since the shooting, and he had been back at the Bureau for part of that time, behind a desk, using his brains to full capacity. It had to be this place. He was wandering around here in a fog.

"So, do you want anything particular, Tim, or are you just visiting?"

Sara was patient with the boy, her smile genuine. Alec had to admire her fortitude. They'd been about to pick up some real steam there on the mattress. Her own hunger had matched his, all right.

"Mrs. Nesbitt says it's a good time for Rosie's bath. She's got the kitchen all warm from baking bread, and the sink's as clean as a whistle."

"Wonderful!" Sara scrambled off the bed and gave his cheek a pinch. "I'll just gather up our things."

Alec hovered, planning to assist the caravan downstairs. But Timothy stood stubbornly in his path, gallantly offering his services. Clearly, it meant the world to the boy. His rail-thin frame held dignity and a smile split his small face in half. The kid obviously had a miniature crush on Sara. Certainly understandable to the smitten Alec, whose own feelings were a king-size version of the same.

Still, most things about Sara weren't as cut and dried as her appeal. Lost in abandon only minutes ago, she was back to moving cautiously about the bedroom, approaching her set of sinfully expensive Gucci luggage with the stealth of a thief.

"I could hoist those on the bed," he offered, gesturing to the three hard-sided pieces clustered around her.

"So could I," Timothy countered, a competitive gleam in his eye.

"No!" she quickly exclaimed, dropping to her knees. "No, thanks, I mean. You both just stay right where you are—keep an eye on Rosie."

Both males automatically looked to the bed where Rosie was lying peacefully on her back, chanting a sweet string of *Ma-ma-ma-mas*.

Completely distracted, Timothy moved over to rub the child's fair head. Alec wasn't so easily put off. Why would Sara not jump at the chance to have the cases hoisted up on the bed where they could be opened more conveniently?

Alec put his keen peripheral vision to good use to keep an eye on her. She was opening each one halfway, peering inside, fishing things out. The overnight case seemed especially touchy. She extracted a yellow rubber duck from it and clicked it shut again so fast that she almost pinched her thumb off! Again he fretted over the K.H. monogram. Was that the reason for her nervousness? She certainly didn't want him touching the pieces, and she kept them tipped on their sides, with the initials facing the wall.

She'd have let him fondle her breasts all he liked, but he

wasn't to lay a finger on the handle of her suitcase. Weird. And strangely enough, rather insulting.

Within minutes Sara and Tim were exiting the room, Sara's arms full of wiggly baby, the boy with the diaper bag on one shoulder and a large bath towel draped across the other. She waited patiently in the hallway until Alec had cleared the threshold as well.

"Sure you don't want me to carry something?" Alec asked, pretending he didn't notice how firmly she closed the door in his wake, her nod of verification as the lock clicked into place.

"Whatever Tim thinks," Sara said. "He's the one with the burden."

Tim's round, brown puppy-dog eyes spoke volumes to Alec. The kid, bored stiff, surrounded by old fogies, was having the time of his life. "Ah, go on without me," Alec insisted. "I have some unpacking to do."

Alec watched them move down the narrow creaky hallway to the staircase, Timothy jabbering on a mile a minute about a Hardy Boys adventure he'd just finished, how everybody loved his readings in the parlor by the fire, when Camille didn't insist upon playing her old piano, that is.

It wasn't until Alec was turning on his heel, planning to go next door to his new hovel, that he noticed something white on the hardwood floor near the stairs. It was one of Rosie's squeeze toys, a squishy baseball. His first impulse was to chase them down to the kitchen and toss it into the water with a playful plop.

Alec took the first stair, then paused. The baby had a bag of such things, and a house full of indulgent overseers. It wouldn't be missed.

The best place for this toy, it seemed, was safely back in a suitcase, where it wouldn't be misplaced. On the wings of that feeble excuse, Alec dashed for the locked door, jamming the toy in his waistband so it wouldn't interfere with his real mission.

He felt a tiny nostalgic rush as he stood at Sara's darkened door, preparing to pop the lock. He produced a Swiss Army knife from his pants pocket and slid the steel toothpick out of the knife's red plastic case. This bedroom lock in particular appeared crackerjack simple—had to be, with Mrs. Nesbitt's intrusion last night. Sure enough, some pressure in the keyhole swiftly brought about the desired click of release.

Alec returned the pick to its proper slot, dropped the knife back in his pocket, turned the brass knob. The rubber ball pressed to his waist made a squeak, causing him to freeze in place. A squeak of protest?

Am I doing something wrong? The tiny voice of conscience came in loud and clear to verify the judgment call. But it was his habit to ignore most moral objections. Investigating was his job, his duty. Spying crossed many gray lines.

But I'm retired now. Didn't that make him little more than an apprentice to the busybody Camille? She'd argue that she wanted the best for everyone, just as he was doing.

This is different. A real case. A serious circumstance. Citizen or agent, he had to know what Sara was hiding. He'd never forgive himself if she caused harm to herself or Rosie. With that he slipped inside, closing the door behind him.

He clicked on the pink ceramic bedside lamp as he'd done so many times during the past week, causing familiar shadows to spring up in the soft light. Sara's and Rosie's personalities were already imprinted all over the room, a reminder of his trespass.

Wanting it over with, he headed straight for the suitcases. To his amazement, they too were locked! She'd managed to put that over on him fairly slickly, he thought, which bruised his ego a bit. Well, he'd just have to pick those locks, too.

The ball, still lodged in his waistband, was quickly forgotten as he rifled through the largest case. Among the clothing he found her small purse. A quick look in her wallet was a disappointment. She carried no identification whatsoever. She had some money, mostly tens and twenties. But a trip like this took a wad of dough, and usually a credit card. Could be she was hiding her credit card elsewhere. Some people did. He doubted he'd come across it in this hurried fishing expedition.

He rummaged on to find the drool-smudged road map, as well as a journal outlining her itinerary. Between them, he ascertained that she had indeed been making stops in all the towns marked on the map. Names of hotels behind her were checked off, and expenses logged in, receipts in order. The list was long. A breakfast in Butte, Montana, had been 5.95, including tip. A dinner in Buffalo, Wyoming, fifteen dollars even. Mileage and gas prices were recorded as well.

Everything was in order. Running his finger down the entries, he checked the stop for last night. The Super 8 Motel in Madison. And bless her efficient little heart, there was a phone number for the place. Grabbing a pen from the nightstand he wrote the number on his hand, along with the number of tonight's scheduled stop, a TraveLodge in Decatur and tomorrow's destination, an inn somewhere near Nashville, Tennessee. She'd make none of them, of course; even if she had her car back this second, she was way behind schedule.

Hot damn, all he needed was a telephone! Hard to believe that could be a problem in this electronic age.

Alec moved on to the midsized case, and found it full of Rosie's clothing. It all appeared brand-new—a sign that she might not have been in Sara's care for long. There was another answer just as reasonable, of course; living in mild climes, the baby would have needed warmer clothing for the trip.

The sound of approaching footsteps on the hallway's pine floor gave him a start. It was too late to escape, so with swift, practiced moves he shut the cases, switched off the lamp and locked the door on the inside. With only a second's hesitation he chose the closet as his refuge, easing inside and closing the door to within an inch.

Please don't be Sara. Please pass on by.

Just his luck, a key was clinking in the lock. His mind raced frantically. What could Sara want this soon? It was a long shot, but he had nothing to lose. Just as the door began to creak open he rolled the squishy white ball out into the center of the braided rug. The overhead light flickered on then and she entered, her green sweater, presumably damp from the bath session, clinging to her torso.

The image was pure erotica to the reluctant voyeur peeking through a crack between the door hinges. She was a sculptured goddess. How badly Alec wanted to touch her again, to mold the wet knit fabric to her breasts with his bare hands.

Suddenly his heart lurched in terror. What if she meant to change tops! Some of her sweaters were hanging in here, tickling his ears. Others were folded up in the largest suitcase—which he'd left unlocked! Either way he'd be in trouble. He held his breath as she scanned the room, her hands on her hips. He'd never noticed before how she thrust out her breasts when she stood that way. Good lord, much more of this tension laced with hot, perfumed oxygen and he'd surely pass out!

To his amazement, she bent over then, right in the center of the room, and picked up the squishy ball. With a satisfied nod, she retreated, turning out the light, setting the lock, and closing the door with a bit of a slam.

He counted to twenty before he left his hideout.

Taking gulps of air, he dashed back to switch on the lamp. He wouldn't be stopping at all if he didn't need to secure those suitcases again. Kneeling down to lock the bags, he prayed for forgiveness. Everything had a reasonable explanation. He'd had no right to snoop.

Nevertheless, he couldn't resist opening the small overnight case she was so protective of. As she should be. It was chock-full of cash, neat stacks of hundred-dollar bills.

6

TWENTY-FIVE THOUSAND DOLLARS, still fastened in bank wrappers. A payoff? A holdup? A ransom?

The choices were many. The excuses few.

Alec stopped in his new postage-stamp-sized room to change his shirt, then galloped downstairs. Would anybody comment on the change? The plaids were noticeably different. In any case, it couldn't be helped. The other shirt was heavy with intoxicating scents too disturbing for him to handle at the moment.

He paused in the foyer to gather his wits and breathed deeply of the cooler air, sharpened with the bracing pine scent of the holiday greenery. Warm laughter and voices wafted down the hallway from the kitchen. Bathing the baby was bound to be the night's most novel attraction, he reasoned. Camille's piano playing and Timothy's Hardy Boys recitations were no doubt a little timeworn.

About to explode with fury and frustration, Alec hunched over and began to pace hard and fast, until the pattern of octagonal white tiles struck with black diamond shapes nearly made him dizzy.

He couldn't have fallen for a crook. If she was one, he wasn't really falling for her. No, his fascination had to be totally rooted in suspicion. Yes, that was it! Any interest he had stemmed from his instincts. He stopped short, giving his nose a tap. The old sniffer habitually picked up the most devious con artists, sometimes before anything took root in his conscious mind.

A mirthless smile widened his lean, taut face. Damn, he

was good. Still had the old flair, a top agent's cunning. Now that the old cylinders were back in motion, he could see through the sensuous fog surrounding Sara. She'd pushed his masculine buttons one by one, had him playing the hero, the papa, the seducer. She'd certainly created enough distractions to keep most men busy until she could make her escape. Might have worked here, if not for the sluggish plow service.

Her plan was diabolical; she'd caught him at a low point in his life, and was capitalizing on it!

Why, the way she'd kissed him back with shameless abandon was frighteningly effective!

The annoying voice in the pit of his gut spoke up again for the second time that night, reminding him that he'd initiated the love play.

But had he really? Sure, he'd been on the bed, thrown the first pillow, but she'd wasted no time in taking countermeasures— Alec stopped short there, not caring to relive the hot exchange that had ripped his protective shield right off for a few exhilarating moments. Somehow, she'd steered his libido into that snare, for the express purpose of keeping him too sated to reason things through.

Well, the jig was up.

The heavy swinging door dividing the kitchen from the hallway was closed to keep down the draft. Alec's moccasin-clad feet made no sound as he stole down the hall and eased the door open, so Sara was quick to notice when it bounced in just a few inches. As she turned around to wipe some soapy water out of her eye, she caught sight of the movement.

What on earth was Alec up to?

Sara was sure it was him for the simple reason that every other resident of the Cozy Rest was present in the bright, steamy room. Old Lyle Bisbee was playing poker with Timothy Doanes at the table. Camille was seated beside Lyle, thumbing through her recipe book for Christmas cookie possibilities for tomorrow's bake-a-thon. Martha Doanes and Mrs. Nesbitt were flanking her at the freestanding cast-iron sink, playing lifeguards to the rambunctious Rosie, who was splashing around in the water like a lily-white dolphin.

All present except Sara were way too busy to notice the door opening stealthily. The unfamiliar plaid sleeve inching in threw her off for a second, but she did recognize the hand feeling for the countertop as the one that had recently crawled up beneath her sweater. It snaked in, clamped on to the heavy black telephone and pulled it out into the hallway!

Sara squinted warily. Who could he be trying to reach at this hour? Why even try when he was so sure the phone was impossible? Feigning trouble with her eye, she pinched it shut, and scooted to the counter near the exit. Under Mrs. Nesbitt's direction she took a fresh tea towel from the drawer to press against her lashes. The door was already open a sliver because of the black cord running through it. With the gentlest pressure imaginable she placed the toe of her tennis shoe against the varnished wood, giving it a bit more of a nudge. Leaning on the short side of the counter, she went through the motions of blinking and dabbing as she listened.

The rotary dial spun and whirred. Peeking from behind the curtain of cloth, she caught sight of him standing as far away as the thin black cord would allow, underneath an amber-glass wall sconce trimmed in berries and holly. Judging by his rigid profile, he was after something with a vengeance. He dialed and dialed, first a zero, followed by a pause. Then a string of numbers signifying long distance. Back to the zero again, whispering hoarsely into the wire, as though he wanted to be heard, but not overheard by the household.

"Hello? Is anybody there? You sound so faint. Please speak up."

Sara believed he was pleading with nothing more than a crackle, just as she had this morning.

Something must have set him off.

Something she had done.

She quickly reviewed the events of the past hour for possibilities. Nothing came to mind. If anything, it seemed they were closer, that they'd moved into that fuzzy emotional zone where feelings took over with blazing force, nearly incinerating everything else.

Maybe he was a nutcase. Hard to say; she'd known him only on a couple of levels so far, angry and amorous. Perhaps the FBI had really put him out to pasture because he was ready to snap like a dry twig. Changing his shirt at this hour was certainly odd.

Rosie let out a screech then, followed by a series of *Ma-ma-ma-da-da-da's*. Not wanting to risk discovery, she quickly slid her toe back across the linoleum, letting the door fall back in the jamb.

Alec entered the room just as she was sidling up to the sink between the two older women. He set the telephone back on the counter in haste.

"Ah, looks like a pool party," he said jovially. The greeting rang false to Sara's ears, and also, she thought, to Mrs. Nesbitt's.

The innkeeper studied him carefully as she wiped her sudsy arms. "Don't tell me you were trying to call out again, Alec?"

"I was," he said with forced merriment. "No luck."

The innkeeper shook her gray head despairingly, her braided coronet tipping a little further to the right.

Uneasy lies the crown, Alec thought, thinking that Mrs. Nesbitt looked a bit like a frazzled queen in the midst of the chaotic high jinks. The baby was a handful, no matter how much one adored her.

Funny, the same applied to Sara. At least in his case!

Sara was in the process of lifting the wiggly, sudsy baby out of the shiny white sink. You could have heard a pin drop in the room as Rosie's chunky arms and legs flew wildly.

Alec automatically sprang back into protector mode, arms open wide.

He stood by anxiously as Sara tussled with the chubby infant, realizing that she was at a greater disadvantage this time because Rosie's skin was slick. Fairy godmothers, not unlike the ones featured on the child's towel, finished off the protective ring; Martha Doanes and Mrs. Nesbitt had also extended their arms in safety-net fashion. Sara blushed, self-consciously bundling Rosie into a snug terry-cloth trap. After wrapping her as tightly as a mummy, she gave her a loud kiss. "That's my snuggly girl."

Rosie, scrubbed pink and exhausted, yawned wide.

"I usually bathe her in a tub on the bed," Sara told them all, "in the morning, when she's not so difficult."

The women murmured their assurances as she looked around at her helpers. But it was Alec whose gaze she held. Waiting. Hoping. Longing.

Obviously she expected the man who had passionately made time with her upstairs to resurface. And rightfully so. No matter what excuses he gave himself for his interest in Sara, desire and compassion licked at his insides like a flame. He felt compelled to step closer, sweep Sara and her bundle into his arms for an all-embracing hug.

He inhaled deeply, this time overpowered by a sweet baby-soap scent. Even with his eyes closed, he could feel the fairy godmothers flanking the three of them. Then he felt their arms, urging them several small steps to the left.

"Look up, Alec," Mrs. Nesbitt whispered urgently in his ear. He did. They were standing directly under the overhead light fixture to which was tied the house's largest sprig of mistletoe. Alec stiffened as an expectant silence pervaded the room.

"Now, what do you see?" the plump old woman pressed, her arms folded beneath her bosom.

Alec saw that Mrs. Nesbitt was relentless in her quest to put some zing into his humdrum existence.

She was waiting for his response. They were all waiting. Especially Sara. He could feel the tremble of her body, transferred through the baby pressed between them. He raised and lowered his eyes a couple of times. "I see a crack up there the size of the Mississippi," he offered, regarding Mrs. Nesbitt with a deadpan expression.

"What else, Alec!"

"Well, I'd kiss her if you'd give me room," he blustered.

Exchanging a grin, Mrs. Nesbitt and Martha swept away.

Sara sighed hard, shifting the baby. "Can't say I'm in the mood anymore."

"Liar." Reaching past Rosie's sweet, round face, he cupped Sara's fragile jaw in his large hands and held it firm for a deep, delicious kiss. It was probably male-animal stupidity, but he couldn't help but delve into her mouth as thoroughly as he had upstairs, marking his turf with hot strokes of his tongue.

The paradox didn't escape him; this was the very same woman he'd desperately tried to report to somebody—anybody—only minutes ago.

Such unstable behavior wasn't like him. The trouble seemed to lie mainly in proximity. When she was within reach, he lost all power of reason. His emotions took over, squeezing every bit of common sense out of him. She was the sexiest, sweetest, most enticing woman alive. In turn, she made him feel alive too.

The idea of breaking apart and facing all the Cozy Rest residents kept the public smooch alive longer than necessary. Finally Alec broke free and faced their rapt audience. "So," he said haltingly. "Well."

"Merry Christmas. Everybody." Sara's voice was high and she moved swiftly out of mistletoe range.

"So who's next?" Alec rubbed his hands together as he looked over at Lyle, his only potential replacement, who was still seated at the table with Timothy. The old gent was always a bit stiff in his starched white shirts and pleated trousers with suspenders, but surely at this festive time of year he'd welcome the chance to kiss the ladies who took such good care of him all year long.

Lyle stared at Alec rather self-consciously. "Not up to it, Alec. You carry on."

"But that's not—" Alec realized then that he'd bungled everything. Still standing firm on kissable territory, his plea for a male replacement sounded more like an invitation to all the ladies. They were wasting no time gleefully lining up with lips smacking.

As Martha clamped her hands firmly to his cheeks, he saw crafty old Lyle slipping through the door. Sara's exit was close behind, punctuated by an announcement about calling it a night. Timothy was right on her heels, towing along the diaper bag and bath toys.

As soon as Alec could catch his breath and before the ladies could reassemble for a second round, he stepped out from under the mistletoe. "How about some brandy in the parlor, ladies? That's always such a nice nightcap. We can discuss the state of the union, and perhaps count the gifts. I swear there's a few more shoe boxes under that tree."

Sisters Beatrice and Camille exchanged a significant look. "Not tonight, dear," Mrs. Nesbitt declined. "Camille and I...have things to attend to."

Camille's lips pursed in sympathy. "We completely understand how you hate to be alone with your thoughts, though."

"I've been alone a lot since I came here!" he protested.

"Yes," Camille cooed. "Hating every blessed minute of it."

Mrs. Nesbitt turned to dry the edge of the sink with a towel. "Certainly natural, so accustomed to working with your team back at FBI headquarters."

Alec's heart jumped as he thought about how he'd even formed a separate team with Sara and Rosie. The sisters were right about him. He did his best work while interacting with a group.

They watched him now, surreptitiously, as they set about clearing the table of a scattering of candy wrappers and glasses. He was tempted to confide in them what he'd found out about Sara so far, but he sensed he was interfering with something important. Aprons were being slowly untied, lights dimmed.

With a sense of emptiness he made his goodbyes. As he leaned into the swinging door, Mrs. Nesbitt spoke up.

"Perhaps you'd like to take some brandy to your room, Alec. Might help you sleep."

"No, thanks." Alec trudged down the hallway, through the foyer and up the staircase. Drinking alone didn't appeal to him much anymore. He'd done his share of it, back in his Chicago apartment.

But here he'd been surrounded with people all over again, replacing the ones he no longer saw on the job. As much as he'd thought he was merely tolerating the binightly parlor get-togethers of last week, it seemed they'd become mighty important to him. He hadn't fallen asleep during Timothy's readings and Camille's piano recitals because he was bored. No, it was because he'd been completely relaxed, safe in his surroundings.

What on earth would happen to him once the holidays were over? He couldn't bear the idea of going back to his cramped, lonely hovel. He was tired of moping around, and more than ever wanted his old job back. He was fit, nearly a hundred percent again. Perhaps if he tried, he could appeal the Bureau's decision.

It was a stupid thing to do, but he couldn't stop indulging in a fantasy built for three. Sara and Rosie, waiting for him when he came home from his job. No crummy apartment for them, either. It would be a suburban home, the kind he always wanted as a kid.

That suitcase of money would make a sweet down payment. If it was clean.

The idea jumped out of nowhere, reminding him that his emotions for Sara seesawed madly. One minute he didn't care what she had done, was willing to spirit her off, begin anew with a clean slate.

The next moment he cared big-time about her actions and wanted to know everything. It was his nature, after all, to collect the facts, study them, act on them.

One way or the other, she was bound to drive him insane.

ALEC TOSSED AND TURNED into the night on his new and unimproved narrow bed. Everything about his new quarters was smaller, from the mattress to the closet to the floor space.

Adding to all his inner turmoil was the distant rumble of voices. He'd heard them in his former room, too, but had convinced himself it was his overactive imagination. But here, in this new space, the sounds were clearer—right over his ceiling. Definitely real.

There had always been times he could hear a pattern to the drone. It was only audible on those evenings when the residents didn't gather in the parlor for entertainment, on those nights when the sisters scurried off with one excuse or another, leaving Alec by the fireside with his snifter and maybe Lyle or Martha.

With so many mysteries swirling round him, Alec was bound and determined to get to the source of at least one of them. He rolled out of bed, tugged his jeans over his striped pajama bottoms, slipped into his ever-ready moccasins and silently slipped out the door.

He'd been up to the attic a couple of times before, fetching Mrs. Nesbitt's needlepoint from the sewing room, or boxes of tree ornaments from the storage nook. The sewing room boasted a treadle sewing machine that surely was already antiquated as far back as the fifties, and an ice-cream churn that had to date back to the turn of the century. He worried that the ladies didn't understand how valuable the contents of this place were and might end up in trouble with the wrong guest some day. He'd tried to caution them, but they'd seemed only mildly amused by his concern.

The space was small and cramped, though the sewing room did extend out into the pentagonal tower that with its long, leaded windows gave the structure its Victorian charm. The tower was put to good use by the sisters, he imagined, for there was some well-worn furniture there: an easy chair and ottoman, a lovely walnut cabinet, and two very comfortable brown velvet recliners with a pole lamp set between them. It was understandable that the sisters would want some privacy, a harbor away from their guests.

The staircase to the third level was more practical than beautiful, plain wood, painted white, with a simple pole serving as a banister. As he climbed, the sounds became stronger. They were coming from the sewing room which was just above his new quarters. It probably wasn't fair to invade this territory at this late hour, but he had to know. He walked purposefully down the creaky hallway and rapped on the white enamel door.

Silence followed.

"Who is it?" Camille's query was unusually alert and cheery for the hour.

Alec felt like an intruding nitwit as he cracked open the door and poked his head inside. "Evening, ladies." The sisters were seated in the recliners in the pentagon, eyeglasses perched on their noses, busy with needlework. Both of them had a flannel Christmas sock in their robed laps, identical to the ones hanging from the mantel downstairs.

"Change your mind about the brandy, Alec?" Mrs. Nesbitt inquired.

"Uh, yes."

"Suppose you tramped all the way down to the parlor first, poor boy." She gestured to a small table in the sewing room which held the familiar house decanter and circle of stout glasses.

Alec didn't correct her misconception as he poured himself an extra-large shot. Then, realizing he must look as ridiculous as he felt, paused to tuck his pajama shirttails into the waistband of his pants and raked a hand through his tousled hair. Picking up his glass, he ambled closer to the pentagon, lingering with ill-concealed need.

"Did you wish to speak to us?" Mrs. Nesbitt chirped.

He lifted his shoulders, straining his already tight cotton pajama top. The old ladies looked so cute dressed in their chenille wraps. Mrs. Nesbitt looked especially charming, her long braids dangling down her arms like a schoolgirl's. He did want to talk to them. Very badly.

"Couldn't sleep," he admitted. "Thought I heard voices up here. Male voices."

The sisters leaned forward in their chairs to stare at each other. "Why, Alec, just look over there in that corner."

Alec whirled on the fringed rug to discover Lyle, slumped in the easy chair, his feet propped on the purple satin ottoman with gold fringe. He too was dressed for the night, in a black smoking jacket and loose pajama slacks, with an ascot at his throat. The guy was posh around the clock, Alec thought with some affection for the old duffer.

"But ladies," he turned back to say, "this man is sound asleep. How could he—"

Camille reared back in her chair with a smirk. "He wasn't asleep all the while, Alec. He wouldn't come up here for that express purpose. Would be silly, having a fine bed of his own."

"I just heard the sounds outside the door seconds ago."

"You've been in here more than seconds," Camille pointed out.

"He's a bit of a snorer," Mrs. Nesbitt whispered, crinkling her face in distaste. "That's what you heard at the door."

"But a very dignified snorer," Camille said, rallying to his defense.

Alec predicted a shift in conversation that would set them sailing off in directions he'd rather not go. It was clear he wasn't going to get a better explanation out of them, so he took a long draw on his brandy and tried to steer them his way.

The socks they were embroidering with Sara and Rosie's names seemed like a good lead-in. He stood between their chairs, resting an elbow on the handsome round-cornered walnut cabinet. Oddly, it seemed warm to the touch, heating his skin through his pajama sleeve.

Mrs. Nesbitt stared up at him, a faint trace of disapproval bunching her soft gray brows. "Mustn't slouch. Not good for your shoulder." She pointed to the fringed ottoman not far from her feet. "Sit down there, so we can see your dashing face."

He obeyed, and perched on the edge, careful not to disturb Lyle's feet.

"About those socks...I wonder if they will upset Sara."

"Why should they, Alec?" Camille asked.

He laced his fingers around his brandy glass. "She is anxious to be on her way."

Camille sniffed and jabbed her needle into the sock's white cuff with even little stitches. "But she may be here, after all. And how awkward it would be if she and the baby aren't included in our circle. Definitely better to be prepared."

"Do you agree, Mrs. Nesbitt?"

Beatrice dazzled him with one of her trademark motherly smiles. "I have faith they *will* be joining us for Christmas. Wouldn't you enjoy that, Alec? Sara and Rosie for Christmas?"

"Yes! Of course..." He sputtered into silence. "I do like her a lot."

Smug murmurs passed between the sisters.

"It's just that Sara may not be who she says she is. May not be the kind of person she appears to be."

Both women stopped sewing; their hands sat limply on their respective armrests.

Camille arched a cottony brow at him. "Perhaps you'd better explain yourself, Alec."

Alec flexed his hands, and breathed through his teeth. "I don't know... Maybe you should forget I said anything."

"Oh, Alec," Mrs. Nesbitt clucked. "You're accustomed to an audience for your theories. You miss the nonjudgmental bantering of your co-workers." She lifted her fleshy chin confidently. "I'd go as far as to say that you've had your best thoughts in chatty sessions. Don't let your retirement hinder your confidence. Start talking."

Alec shifted uncomfortably. Her insightful look pinned him down with no means of escape. "Okay, but part of being on the team means keeping an objective point of view. We'll take the facts surrounding Sara and Rosie with an open mind. We'll draw conclusions without jumping to conclusions."

Lyle snorted from his chair, causing Alec to jump a little himself.

"My dear," Mrs. Nesbitt prompted. "Get to the point before *I'm* ready for retirement."

He did. He began with the K.H. initials on the luggage, and the quality of the luggage, which defied its cheap contents. He touched on the map, the impractical route made all the more impractical with a baby in tow. Sara's clumsy handling of the baby. Once he'd laid the groundwork for his suspicions, he went on to report his shadier deeds—finding the money, checking her wallet for identification. He topped it off with her desperation to get an outside telephone line.

"But Alec, you too are desperate to make outside calls."

"I know, but—"

"Maybe she borrowed the luggage."

"I know, but—"

"Maybe she has friends at some of these stops."

"Maybe. But," he continued firmly, "I intend to keep a close eye on her, make some sense of all of this."

The sisters exchanged the sort of look that has efficiently divided the sexes since the dawn of time.

"Don't you let her out of your sight, Alec."

"Indeed not!"

Self-conscious red splashed his cheeks. There was a titter in their voices that suggested they saw a budding romance whirling at the center of everything. Some team. He drained his brandy, stood up and returned his glass to the table. He spoke with his back to them. "Good night, ladies."

"Alec?" Mrs. Nesbitt said softly. He half turned with a tight smile. "We understand your points. Still, we prefer to give Sara the complete benefit of the doubt."

His mouth curled wistfully. "I was trained in direct opposition to blind faith."

"How fortunate you're retired, then," the innkeeper enthused. "You can drop all that mechanical thinking right here and now."

"But I can't do that! Can't change my whole way of thinking."

"How about meeting us halfway on this," Camille suggested.

He stared at his shoes. "Well, I do *hope* she's innocent."

"Yes, but why not trust that she is, approach this whole mess with faith in her?"

It was no use insisting that wasn't the way his former team worked. Mrs. Nesbitt was doing it again, he knew, turning his redundancy against him, challenging him to decide where he stood in this new life of his. It was too much to sift through right now. He was consumed with desire and doubt, struggling to hang on to the dignity offered by his agent status, his ability to crack tough cases.

"I'll try," he finally said with a polite nod. "As always, you've given me something to think about."

7

DAYLIGHT WAS SPILLING into Alec's new bedroom—which he fondly called the closet—the following morning when somebody rapped on his door. It was probably his routine breakfast in bed. A glance at his gold watch on the nightstand confirmed that it was nine o'clock, well past the hour for dining-room service. Pushing his pillows up the narrow wooden headboard, he issued a gruff invitation.

Another knock followed. Alec hopped out of bed and padded across the woven scatter rug and cool wooden flooring, grumbling under his breath. He swung the door open to find Timothy standing there with his food tray, dressed in another striped T-shirt and coveralls.

"How was I supposed to get in? The door was locked!"

"Well, I figured it was Mrs. Nesbitt, and nothing seems to stop her."

"Well, guess I don't have all her powers yet."

"You don't need 'em, boy. One magician per house is enough."

Timothy shrugged off Alec's attempt at humor, his freckled face sober. "I want to be a doctor when I grow up."

"That's great, kid."

"Yep, I'm gonna live right here in Elm City my whole life. Never leave."

Alec took the heavy tray and climbed back into bed. "I suppose it's tough having your dad gone so much."

The boy hung his carrot-topped head. "I miss him. He won't be here for Christmas. Again."

"We'll have a good time, anyhow. I promise."

Timothy's mood brightened again. "That's swell. I sure hope Sara stays, too."

"Maybe together we can convince her." Alec drove his fork into the generous helping of scrambled eggs on the blue-and-white plate. Without looking up, he asked how the community breakfast was.

Timothy sat on the edge of the mattress. He was wearing a shrewd look when Alec did finally meet his gaze. "*She* was there, all right. Kept staring at your empty chair, too."

Alec hated the way his heart leapt. Pathetic. "Anything else happen?"

"Camille went out to the barn for some more firewood. Lyle went along, saying it was for his constitutional." Timothy stole a triangle of Alec's toast. "I think they like to go out there and kiss."

"Lyle wasn't in a kissing mood last night in the kitchen, though, was he?"

Timothy laughed, his brown eyes twinkling. "I think he would've stayed if he'd had some of his peppermint candies with him. Always has a peppermint before he kisses Miss Camille. Yep, I always know when it's comin'. He drops a peppermint in his mouth and calls her his spoony lamb. Yuck."

"He must have an endless supply of candy, considering he never shows any desire to venture out."

Timothy pressed his lips together, dropping his eyes. "Must have, I guess."

"So, anything big happening today?"

"Sure hope the plow comes through. So the mailman can bring a present from my papa."

"Me too." Alec poured some coffee into his cup from the small, steaming pot. "Have some more toast."

"Okay! Put some jelly on it, will you, please?"

Alec laughed and obligingly dipped a knife into the jar of homemade marmalade. "Think there's a good chance of the road clearing today? Last week it seemed like only a day or two before the plow showed."

Timothy took the toast. "The service is pretty good. And it's nicer out. In the twenties."

"Well, let me know first thing if you see that plow."

"Oh, yeah, you don't sit in the window seat every day anymore, do you?"

Alec flushed. "Feeling better, if that's what you mean."

"I'll keep a lookout, but Miz Beatrice is doing cutout cookies this morning. I'm helping her. You can too, if you want."

Alec hadn't tasted a freshly baked Christmas cookie in thirty years, since the days when a neighbor in his apartment building brought him and his sisters a small paper plate of them. The memory moved him to scary depths. "I, uh, don't think so, kid."

"Sara's helping."

"Oh, well, then maybe..."

Timothy laughed, amused by the trap he'd set for the man. "I think you're going to need a tin of peppermints all your own."

ALEC APPEARED in the kitchen a half an hour later, dressed in a blue cable-knit sweater and worn jeans, as bright-eyed as he'd been since his arrival. The ladies were in the throes of a cookie-assembly procedure, and Timothy was gliding around the fringes of the action with the bubbly Rosie in his arms, feeding her a few crumbs at a time.

Mrs. Nesbitt greeted Alec pleasantly and inspected him from head to toe as she took his tray. "Must've slept soundly, Alec."

"Eventually." It was clear from her guileless smile that she did not intend to acknowledge their conversation last night. He was grateful for her discretion, even if he wasn't sold on her advice. Deep inside, he wanted Sara to be his dream woman. He just wasn't willing to accept her blindly, as a schoolboy might.

Hooking his thumbs in his belt loops, he took in his surroundings. This was the storybook version of the Christmas season. Women with dabs of flour on their faces fussing around the kitchen in aprons. Canisters and measuring spoons, bowls and cookie sheets scattered over the table and every counter surface. Merry chatter and numerous traffic jams.

The door to the service porch opened on the opposite wall near the refrigerator and Lyle tromped inside, dressed in one of the inn's green jackets and matching hats, carrying an armload of firewood.

"Can I help you, sir?" Alec offered.

"No, no, I'm fine." He nodded to everyone as he passed through. "I'll just take these on in to the box in the parlor." Timothy dipped through the swinging door with Rosie, asking Lyle if he thought there were enough ornaments on the tree.

"Feeling a new sense of peace, aren't you, Alec?" Mrs. Nesbitt surmised with quiet smugness.

He smiled broadly to take the edge off his answer. "What do you mean?"

"Oh, just that your life has taken on all sorts of new shapes during your stay, like a kaleidoscope."

It had. Miraculously, sad old memories of lonely holidays were at that very minute evaporating, like melting layers of frost. These new memories would be his foundation in the years to come. All holidays would be compared to this one at this wonderful, safe, cozy place full of love and goodwill.

Mrs. Nesbitt obviously liked what she was seeing in his expression and it irritated him a little. He rocked on the soles of his moccasins, feigning shyness. "You have every right to fish for credit, I guess. Kissing all you ladies has made me more worldly by far."

The remark caught the other women's attention. Camille, Martha and Sara all favored him with coy smiles. The kind only Sara had a right to wear, he thought, since she alone had felt the soft edge of his tongue, while the others had received chaste pecks.

Sara strolled over to the table, took a tree-shaped cookie from one of the cooling racks, and held it up to his face. "Better chomp down on this before you devour something bigger."

Alec closed his hand around hers and drew the cookie to his mouth. He took a nibble of the warm crisp dough—and her tender fingertips.

An electrical current surged through her veins. He hadn't changed his mind. Despite his suspicions, he was extremely interested, infatuated even.

But yellow caution signs flashed through Sara's mind as she stared into his fathomless sea-blue eyes. She could easily find herself in over her head if she didn't watch out. In over her head and spilling her guts.

A fine thing that would be, considering that she knew next to nothing about him, aside from the fact that he was a quiet, reserved loner with no place to go at Christmas.

Suddenly she realized how badly she did want to know his story. But if he didn't want to write it down in a letter for the road, she probably was going to have to pass.

"Hey! Everybody!" Timothy bounced back through the door with a firm hold on a squealing Rosie. "The plow came through! While we were baking the cookies, it snuck right on in, getting the driveway and all."

A little nervous over Timothy's exuberance, Sara gently took hold of Rosie. "How clever of you to notice so quickly, Tim," she said admiringly.

"There was the tow truck, too, dragging your car away."

Sara tore through the swinging door, Alec on her heels. She swooped into the parlor where Lyle was on his knees at the fireplace, patiently stacking logs in a knotty-pine box. He nodded his gray head at the newcomers. "Thought I'd wait with the fire, being as how the kitchen stove's been going for a couple of hours."

Alec courteously agreed with the plan as he watched Sara climb onto the cushioned window seat facing the front yard, his favorite hangout not so long ago. She sat Rosie on the cushion, then tipped the red straw wreath hanging in the center pane and craned her neck to get a glimpse of the tow truck in the distance. Alec braced a knee on the seat, touching her shoulder. The softness of her pink sweater contrasted with the taut muscle underneath. She was breathing heavily, furiously, as though contemplating battering her way through the glass.

"Sara..."

She whirled around with an indignant cry. "Don't use that patronizing tone with me. My car is gone! Get it? The only wheels in this place are gone! To lord only knows where."

"I know where," Timothy piped up.

"I think we all know where," Alec said reasonably. "There was only one garage in town that I could see, the Pump-U-Serve. It's on a corner, a block off Main Street."

"The tow truck was from there, Sara," Timothy said gently. He looked as though he wanted to squeeze her hand, but took the oblivious Rosie's instead. "The station's always had a green truck, so folks can spot it from a distance."

"Why would they do a tow without stopping in here?"

Lyle turned away from the hearth and met Timothy's eye. They shared a long, helpless stare.

"I think I can explain that," Alec said, garnering everyone's attention. "In small towns like this, everybody knows everybody else. Neighbor helps neighbor automatically." He deferred to Lyle. "Wouldn't you say so, sir?"

"Indeed, indeed." Lyle turned back to straighten the brass fire irons.

Timothy came to stand between Alec and the old man. "So, do you think we can stand a few more ornaments, Mr. Lyle? Miz Bea says she has some more in the attic."

Lyle's deeply creased face was thoughtful. "I'll study the

idea. First thing after lunch." With a groan he rose to his feet and headed for the staircase. "Yessir, directly after lunch."

Timothy snapped his fingers. "Dang it!"

Alec took hold of the boy's arm. "Never mind, I have another game we can play together for now." He turned to Sara's sagging form in the window seat. "Don't get all shook up. I'm going to get news of your car."

She arched on delicate brow. "How, Alec? Smoke signals?"

He lowered a calming palm at her. "Patience, Frosty, patience. I have a hunch about a better way."

"You say the heater isn't working in your new room, Alec?" Beatrice Nesbitt and her sister Camille were in the midst of tidying up the kitchen when Alec and Timothy returned minutes later. The sink was piled high with baking utensils and Mrs. Nesbitt was just about to run some water over them. To Alec's relief Timothy's mother Martha was nowhere in sight. Only two to contend with.

"I was referring to my old room," Alec clarified. "The one Sara's taken over."

"Oh, my."

"Oh, dearie me."

"Not that she's complained, mind you," he thought to add. "Maybe if you could just check it out on the sly. Ease our minds." He smiled faintly in concern. To his delight, the sisters tore loose their aprons and charged off.

"What are you up to, Alec?" Timothy asked in wide-eyed wonder.

"I want you to do me a great favor."

"Huh?" The boy's brown eyes were huge. "You *need* me?"

"More than I can say." Alec quickly steered him over to the corner of the counter that held the black pedestal telephone. "I want you to make a call."

Timothy turned around and stared up at the towering man. "I'm not supposed to."

"You're not supposed to call your friends this close to Christmas, I know. But this is different. I want you to call the garage."

Timothy waved his arms. "I tell ya, I'm not supposed to call anybody!"

"Look, it won't inconvenience anyone. And it will mean so much to Sara."

"Sara?" His voice was as gooey as warm bubblegum.

"She needs her car back. And for some reason, neither she nor I can get an outside line."

Alec held his breath as the boy turned back toward the telephone. You'd have thought he'd asked the kid to rob a bank for all his hesitation. "Okay. I'll do it. But no matter what happens, will you tell Sara I tried for her?"

"Sure."

"And don't tell anybody else," he added in a reedy voice.

Alec felt like hugging him, but was more comfortable giving him a sock on the arm. "It's a promise. And all my responsibility."

Timothy shook his orange head mournfully. "Yeah, but I'm the one that hasta live here."

Alec quickly took Mrs. Nesbitt's green address book out of the narrow drawer directly underneath the telephone. "Let's see...under P for Pump-U-Serve, I bet." He flipped through the index, finding the number without trouble. He read it to the boy, who spun the rotary dial with a shaky finger.

"Hello?" Timothy said in a squeak. "Is this the service station?" He cleared his throat. "No, I'm not playing a prank. This is Tim Doanes from the Cozy Rest. Oh, uh, Ben. Sure, Mother's just fine. No, Papa won't be home until January 15th. Everybody's just fine here. A guest would like to talk to you. Okay?"

Alec couldn't believe it! The ploy had worked. But there was no time to applaud his own cleverness, or analyze the reasons why. He took the receiver, mouthing his thanks.

Timothy scampered off as fast as his short legs would carry him, as though abandoning a sinking ship.

"Hello. Ben! Yes, my name is Alec Wagner." Alec pressed the heavy receiver tightly to his ear. Why, Timothy had listened normally, as though he could hear this fellow loud and clear. Damn, the line was a bunch of fuzz—almost as bad as before. But there was a real live voice present this time, a man who was responding—at least to some degree. "Ben," he shouted as loud as he dare. "Can barely hear you." Alec cringed then, certain he heard the telltale spit of a tobacco chewer.

"Hello? Hello?"

The line crackled some more. "Ben, your tow truck just picked up a car from here. A black Lincoln Town Car. Yes, a Lincoln." Alec thought for a minute that he'd lost the connection, but apparently Ben was speaking to someone in the background.

"Nope. No Lincoln here."

"But it still may be on the way."

"Tow truck's here." Spitting sound. "No Lincoln."

"But that can't be so!"

"'Tis so, sonny. We don't do a lot of work this close to Christmas. Folks save it for after Christmas."

"What about emergencies?"

"Ain't hearda one today. No such car here today. Good day to you, sonny."

The dial tone was fuzzy too, but it was unmistakable. Alec dropped the receiver in disgust. He'd thought it would be so simple if he could just get through. Sara would be furious when she learned of the conversation. Alec decided he wouldn't tell her at all. This Ben character simply had to be mistaken. Tim would recognize the town's tow truck when he saw it. And nobody else would be out in the boondocks in the middle of the morning looking for stranded vehicles.

Alec decided the best thing to do would be to take a trip into Elm City. With the winds calm and the temperatures nudging the freezing mark, the three-mile or so walk would not only be practical, but pleasant. He could have a look around the shops, buy a few Christmas gifts. Stop by the garage, speak to the tow-truck driver.

He could also find a pay phone and run a check on Sara and Rosie. There were too many questions about Sara that could no longer go unanswered. Of course, until he knew better, he was inclined to believe that Sara had a right to Rosie, and deserved respect for the way she cared for the child.

Until he knew better.

"I'M GLAD TO HEAR the heater's fine." Alec murmured in the face of the sisters' lofty report soon thereafter. He stood quietly in the center of the kitchen as they did the dishes and rambled on about how he was so accustomed to playing hero to mother and child that he had panicked, pure and simple.

"Pure and simple," he agreed, stepping out into the service porch.

Mrs. Nesbitt followed in bewilderment, drying her hands on a tea towel. "What are you doing out here, Alec?"

"I'm planning a walk into town," he replied, sifting through the gloves in a cedar chest beside the canned goods. "Hope you will lend me Jim's gear."

"Certainly. But I wish you'd stay put, until it's a bit warmer."

Alec found the gloves he'd worn during the rescue. He reached for them and turned to face the innkeeper. "The weather's as good as it's going to get before Christmas," he reasoned kindly, but firmly. "And I'll be leaving after that."

"Don't talk of that day, Alec. I shall miss you more than I can say."

Alec melted at the sight of her round cheeks bunched in distress. "We'll have a wonderful Christmas. I promise." He couldn't believe the turn of events; Alec Wagner, the rogue agent with a heart of beef jerky was promising somebody a fine holiday.

"OF COURSE I'M going with you!" Sara was waiting outside Alec's bedroom door when he emerged, fully dressed for his trek in the olive-green jacket.

So much for getting away undetected, he thought grimly, squeezing the gloves in his hand. She was dressed for the weather too, in a red cloth coat with fur collar and matching hat that just had to belong to the slender Martha Doanes.

Sara stared up at him spunkily. "What are you thinking, Alec?"

"That your ensemble brings out the red highlights in your hair." With a faint smile he sidestepped her and started down the hallway.

"Oh, c'mon!"

"I *was* thinking that." He sighed as she trotted up on his right. In some ways Sara seemed as spontaneous as a teenager. Hardly the type to be involved in any illegal activity. "Is it Martha's?"

"Why, yes. So are boots. How'd you guess?"

"Process of elimination." He suspected she was trying to keep him talking, right out the door and down the road. A shallow trick that amused him. "The sisters are a little plump for such a tailored garment. Timothy's too short and Lyle doesn't seem like the fur-collar kind."

"It's not exactly my style, either, but I didn't want to hurt Martha's feelings. She—and everyone else—have been so nice."

He turned as he grasped the handrail at the top of the staircase. "They are extremely fond of you, too."

"The fur collar is a nice touch," she chattered on as they descended the staircase. "Bound to be warm when turned up."

He reached the foyer and turned to her. "Don't see much

skunk on clothing anymore," he said, controlling his features with mighty strength.

"Skunk!" she shrieked. "You lie! I couldn't..."

He could no longer contain his laughter. "I'm sorry I let the rodent out of the bag. It's the truth. Now wouldn't it be simpler for you to stay right here? You can slip out of the skunk, back into your tennies—"

Sara stamped her foot. "Shut up, you beast!"

Mrs. Nesbitt ambled out of the arched parlor doorway opposite the staircase. Alec sobered immediately when he caught sight of Rosie in the innkeeper's arms, bundled up in her pink snowsuit, a white scarf at her chin.

"This really, really, isn't going to work! Carrying a baby down a slippery road!"

Mrs. Nesbitt tore her eyes away from Rosie. "I expect you to take the sleigh, Alec. Didn't Sara tell you?"

"No way."

"No, she didn't, or no she isn't welcome?" Mrs. Nesbitt asked impatiently.

"Both!" he thundered, his sense of humor spent. Jeez, how was a guy supposed to spy on a lady with cold objectivity if she was hanging around him, all pretty and sexy and needy? Not to mention carting along a child who pulled the strings of his heart like a seasoned puppeteer?

"Oh, tish-tosh," Mrs. Nesbitt scoffed, handing the baby over to Sara. "Better get a move on if you hope to have some lunch at the café."

"Lunch!" Alec gaped as both Rosie and Sara extended a pouty lower lip at him. "Okay, okay." He threw his arms in the air. "Let's go."

The foursome wended their way along the path to the barn. Mrs. Nesbitt led the parade, dressed in olive-green clothing like Alec's, carrying a wicker basket meant for eggs. Sara followed in skunk-trimmed hat and coat, carrying Rosie. Alec brought up the rear with the quilted diaper bag.

Nursemaid Alec, trailing after three of the most conniving

females on earth. Especially that little Rosie, bouncing on Sara's shoulder up ahead. Her cherub face was pure delight, peeking out of her pink hood, making goo-goo faces at him.

The baby had a way of melting his temper like butter in the sun.

He already pitied the young naive lad who would court her someday.

But he'd better be a good lad, whoever he was.

Responsible, with a decent education and some ambition.

"Think you can handle the sleigh yourself, Alec?"

Mrs. Nesbitt's challenge brought him back to the problem at hand. "This was your idea," he called out.

She fluttered a mitten over her head. "Just double-checking."

Right. He grimaced in the brilliant sunshine, the lines deepening around his eyes. "You didn't have to put yourself out at all. I could've gotten the rig going."

Mrs. Nesbitt paused near the barn, lifting her basket. "Told you we needed some extra eggs. Used so many in the cookies."

Alec stepped up to open the huge double doors. Unlike their emergency visit in the dark, everything was clearly defined in the daylight. Stalls on the left, large animal pens on the right. The chickens were in their wire-mesh cage in the middle of the building, some swooping through the air, others perched on rows of dowels.

Sara watched with fascination as Mrs. Nesbitt entered the cage and edged past tin feeders holding seed and water, up to the tin box full of compartments. Each compartment had a hole and she reached inside several, extracting eggs for her basket.

Alec lingered by the pen that held Sugar and Spice, stroking Sugar's curly blond mane. He was sorely tempted to make a run for it, mount the chestnut-colored horse and gallop off.

"Not Sugar, Alec," Mrs. Nesbitt called out as she emerged

from the mesh door. "Spice is the better choice for a trip into town. He won't be as skittish around the traffic."

"Spice it is," he called out agreeably. How did she know what he was up to in this wooden pen, a hundred feet away? Not only could she pass through locked doors, she could also read his mind. It seemed she possessed powers that broke down all barriers!

Alec and Mrs. Nesbitt worked together as before, hitching the horse to the sleigh. He hoped she'd forget the bells, but of course she didn't. The bells on the bellyband jingled merrily as she adjusted the strap around the draft and buckled it.

Then Mrs. Nesbitt stood up to her full five-foot-four height like a round wobble-doll and dusted off her mittens. "Such a nice sound at this time of year, don't you think?" She touched the leather strap, drawing Alec's attention to the round brass bells, which were two inches in diameter on the top, but grew progressively smaller near the horse's belly. "The larger the bell, the deeper the tone. The different sizes make for splendid music."

"So we heard the other night, Mrs. Nesbitt," Alec reminded her. "Very jolly."

Sara, already nestled in the front seat of the sleek black sleigh with Rosie in her lap, listened to the sound and felt an awkward tingle course along her spine. The bells did indeed bring back the rescue. The lifesaving jingle in the distance, the wall of long johns against her chilled face, the frosty cover on Alec's face. She couldn't remember everything, but those details were vivid in her mind.

Grumpy old St. Nick, with a bum shoulder.

Every time he favored his left side—as he was doing now as he climbed up on the bench beside her—Sara wondered what caused his pain. What a joy it would be to focus on his secrets for a while, watch him dance as she fired questions into the dirt at his feet, sort of like a modern-day Annie Oakley.

Mrs. Nesbitt stood back after giving the horse one last pat.

"Remember, Alec, a light touch of the reins is enough. Spice knows exactly where he's going."

"Lucky Spice." With those farewell words and a small salute, Alec tapped the reins and they were off down the winding drive.

8

IT WAS A GLORIOUS DAY for a sleigh ride in the country. The bright sun reflected off the snow cover, giving the land a dazzling diamond-chip sheen. The air was cool, but not cold. They headed along the frontage road, Spice trotting at an easy clip. There wasn't another soul in transit by foot, car or sled.

"There *are* a few other farms to the west," Sara noted, pointing in that direction.

Alec spared her a glance. "I know what you mean. Seems like the Cozy Rest is adrift from civilization, doesn't it?"

Sara laughed huskily. "Ah, you do know my mind."

He only wished!

"That night—the other night..." She faltered, squeezing Rosie closer. "It did seem like I was all alone in the world. Except for that brightly decorated Victorian house standing in the middle of nowhere."

"It does get extremely dark around here. No one else seems to have decorated the way Mrs. Nesbitt has and there are no streetlights. Driving these country roads at night sort of reminds me of crawling into a coal bin." He paused. "It's very understandable how you got turned around. Could happen to anybody."

"Really think so, Alec?"

"Know so."

Suddenly Sara's mouth lifted in a dazzling smile. Her shield had fallen away, her eyes were wide and luminous, her mouth parted. She seemed so incredibly vulnerable and grateful, it set his heart to fluttering like one of the inn's chickens. Made him want to say anything that would keep that smile in place.

"I mean, a similar thing happened to me. I took a cab from the Madison airport, stopped in town for a few supplies, then set off again. It was snowing like crazy by then and the roads were pitch-black. We got lost in no time—or thought we were lost. Suddenly, there was the inn in the distance, all aglow with those golf-ball-sized bulbs. I hoped it was the place, and sure enough, the sign confirmed it. Cozy Rest Inn. Welcome."

"Yes." Sara nodded happily at Alec and patted the gloved hand clenching the reins. In his own clumsy way he was telling her, "We're equal, we're together, we all make mistakes."

A comfortable silence settled between them, broken only by the clop-clop-jingle of Spice's trotting.

The calm before the storm? Alec hoped not. He desperately wanted to believe every word the woman uttered. Sara probably had a generous neighbor with the initials K.H., who'd lent her the luggage. She probably was trekking to Miami to visit a rich, newly retired uncle—an eccentric uncle—who'd asked her to clean out his Seattle bank account and bring it all to him in cash.

A string of nutty probabilities to cling to. And why not? He'd believed in a lot of less likely things on the job over the past twelve years. But not once had there ever been a lady like Sara to fret over, pine over, lust over. If she needed his protection, he wanted to provide it. He was capable. He was! The shoulder was getting better by the minute. The more he ignored it, the better it felt.

Their arrival in Elm City proper drew some attention. Slow-moving cars honked, pedestrians waved from the boulevards. None of the ruckus disturbed Spice, who clopped on without a care.

To the couple's mutual delight, Spice headed straight for a small public park on the fringes of the main drag. It was a lovely spot, clustered with evergreens and oaks, dotted with park benches, with a bronze statue of George Washington in the center. It was done up nicely for Christmas, with tiny lights strung on the trees, garlands hung on the street lamps, and a Nativity scene nestled in a curve of small pines. Even old George was holding some mistletoe in his outstretched hand, suggesting that this might be a lovers' rendezvous.

"Spice has been this way before," Sara wagered. "Must be all right to stop."

"Should be no harm in it," Alec agreed, his voice full of amazement. To think he thought he'd done it all, seen it all. This was a new one, a horse was showing him the ropes!

Sara noticed his uncertainty. "Mrs. Nesbitt wouldn't have sent us on the sleigh if it wasn't allowed, Alec. Everyone in town must know her."

"No doubt," he conceded. "I'm surprised she's not mayor." Alec alighted from the sleigh and turned around to aid the ladies. Before Sara could protest, he'd stripped off his gloves, clamped his hands around her middle, and swung her and Rosie to the ground.

The agony etched in his handsome features was graphic.

With a gasp, she raised a gloved hand to her mouth. "Alec! You shouldn't have!"

His voice was as terse as his expression. "Do what I want."

"But the pain in your shoulder..."

He mumbled something about a pain in the ordinance as the sheriff rolled up in the turnabout near George Washington.

The sheriff seemed full of the Christmas spirit as he approached in his uniform blues, taking the curb with a jaunty step.

Alec took Sara's elbow and guided her toward the sidewalk.

"Bet his collar's not skunk," Sara joked. She hoped her anxiety wasn't evident in her voice. But he was the law and she didn't care to explain the enigma of her identity to a man with a holding cell.

"Welcome to Elm City, folks. I'm Sheriff Walters." The sheriff tipped his hat, surveying them with some curiosity. He was a big man, with a clumsy gait and oversized features full of cheer. There was a shrewdness in his eyes, however, that suggested he ran a tight ship within the city limits.

He certainly closed in fast. Though he had nothing to hide, Alec wondered why their arrival had created a stir.

The agent was accustomed to being looked over, but Sara didn't take the inspection as calmly. She crowded against Alec with unmistakable tension.

"Oh, let me hold the baby for a while," Alec said solicitously, implying that she was off-kilter because of her load. He took Rosie before Sara could react. When their eyes met for a split second, raw pools of fear stared back at him.

What on earth was she hiding?

And why was he so all-fired determined to protect her? That was just as mysterious.

Alec trembled a little himself. There was no escaping it, he was falling for Sara Jameson, alias Frosty, alias "K.H." Whatever her name, whatever her crimes, he wanted to cuddle up with her forever for a nice long thaw.

The sheriff shuffled his feet in the dusting of snow on the cement path. "Staying at the Cozy Rest?"

"Yes," Alec replied with a smile. "The horse give it away?"

The sheriff stared back at the spot where they'd parked the sleigh. Stared hard. "Honestly, I'd have to say it was more Mrs. Nesbitt's sleigh. Fine old sled, isn't it?"

"Mint."

"Lovely town, Sheriff," Sara ventured to say, a crack in her voice. "Must attract a lot of tourists."

He beamed at the compliment. "A lot more in the summertime. We have our apple orchards in the north, which hawk everything from cider to pies to jams. Run a craft fair along Main Street every weekend from May to October. And then there's the farm museum." He clamped his mouth shut then, as though embarrassed by his own rambling. "But Christmas is nice, too. The Cozy Rest, especially, has a fine atmosphere."

"Oh, yes." Alec nodded. "Must say though, their brochure is a little misleading. I expected the inn to be more...modern, I guess."

Sheriff Walters shrugged. "Having a good time? I mean, you two look like you are. And the baby's as happy as a lark." He tweaked Rosie's cheek with thick fingers. Alec and Sara assured him they were satisfied, that Mrs. Nesbitt was simply charming and completely attentive. The man finally turned to leave.

"So, Sheriff," Alec called after him. "Is it okay with the city to leave our sleigh parked here for a couple of hours?"

The sheriff turned back on the blacktop circle. "Ah, sure. Just wanted to wish you a happy holiday."

"You don't think somebody will come along and take old Spice for a joyride, do you?" Sara asked.

The sheriff barked with laughter as he opened the driver's door of his squad car. "No, ma'am, you can rest easy. Bye now!"

Alec urged Sara to wave as Walters rolled through the turnaround.

Her smile was stiff. "His behavior is mighty strange."

Alec hooted. "Look who's talkin'."

She balled her fists and squinted angrily at him. "Oh, give me my baby back!"

He sobered, but it was impossible to control the gleam in his eye. "Okay, okay. Right after we cross over to the main drag." The light was green at the intersection, so they moved quickly. It didn't escape Alec's notice that Sara's anxious gaze was all over the place, scanning the cars stopped at the light, the pedestrians passing by them in the crosswalk.

How badly he wanted to know what was wrong!

Once safely on the other side, Alec handed over Rosie. If the baby hadn't been between them, he'd have been sorely tempted to give Sara a shake and insist that she confide in him. But it was essential not to spook her at this point. It would be so awful if she ran. He'd spoil everybody's Christmas at the inn by having to track her down.

Oh, how he hated the unknowns. How could he hope to help her without answers? How could he get the answers without slyly checking up on her? He hated to leave her side for a moment, but he felt he had no choice.

It took self-control, but he managed to keep his voice even. "So, do you want to part ways for a while?"

Her face, pink from the cold, brightened. "Yes, Alec, that would be great."

He kept his smile even, though it was clear that her longing for some private time matched his and overrode any fears she might have. "Aren't we eager," he couldn't help remarking.

"I just want to relax for a while on my own," she said slowly, as though talking to an imbecile. She tipped her head toward the row of quaint shopfronts, all decked out in holiday splendor. "And I'm sure you don't want to start off with a stop at the beauty shop on the corner."

Alec stared over at the pink stucco structure with Curly Q stenciled on the window, wondering if he'd misread her tense, watchful demeanor moments ago. "Your hair is perfection," he raved, fingering the auburn strands peeping out from beneath her hat.

"I want to buy a pair of salon shears," she explained, fighting the urge to tip her chin into his hand, enjoy the feel of his fingers once again. But she couldn't think very well under his touch. And it was imperative she keep her head. Things were so out of control already. "My gift to the ladies is going to be new hairdos." When he stared blankly, she added, "I am a stylist, remember? It's my job, when I'm not trudging across the countryside."

He couldn't wait to see her prove herself with a snip or two. Any confirmation of her story was a ray of hope that she wasn't a complete fake. "Let's meet in about forty minutes for lunch. First thing I'll do is check on your car," he added, determined to pounce on the opportunity. "The station's a block away behind some big banks of snow."

Sara considered the offer, far too carefully in Alec's estimation. His heart thumped in his chest and he jammed his bare hands in the pockets of the green parka, shifting from one foot to another. The thing to do was take control of her wheels. Without them, she was stuck. And he very much wanted her stuck right now. At least until he could get to the bottom of her story. Until he could properly diagnose his feelings for her.

"I suppose it would be tough to drag Rosie over there," Sara finally decided.

He fought to contain his delight behind a frown of concern. "The sidewalks aren't even shoveled."

"But I should be dealing with the owner. It's my responsibility."

"I don't mind," he assured her. "Unfair as it is, men usually have better luck dickering over prices and all. And I *am* a man," he added on a teasing note.

And how. Sara sighed wistfully. How easy it would be to lean on him just a little bit. How much she missed having a man for this sort of thing. "Okay, thanks. But I'm treating you to lunch at Leslie's Fine Café there. Whatever they're serving smells great."

"We'll just see who pays. It'll give us another thing to bicker about." He could tell she was debating something more. He paused for a few seconds that seemed like an eternity.

"If you, ah, don't mind, Alec, I need something from the car."

"Oh, like what?"

"It's a plastic puzzle of Rosie's. She isn't very good at it, of course, but she likes the colors and can get a good grip on the pieces."

Alec exhaled in relief. She didn't want a pistol or a vial of knockout drops, she wanted a child's toy. As any concerned mother would. "Will do," he guaranteed merrily, with a pat to Rosie's padded backside.

Then Alec swiftly crossed Main Street. The gratitude in Sara's eyes made him feel like a heel. But in his own defense, he really did want to help, even if all his motives weren't altruistic and aboveboard.

"HELLO? ANYBODY HERE?" Alec sauntered into the Pump-U-Serve station, and paused at the counter holding the cash register. It was a classic small-town operation, handling everything from gas to engine repair. The place was a little chilly and a little dirty, but efficient-looking and modern. There was a desk behind the counter holding stacks of work orders, sales brochures, a push-button telephone, and miraculously, a fax machine.

Through a partially open door behind the counter Alec could see into the back repair area. Tools were arranged neatly on pegs over a long work bench and there were two cars up on hoists.

No work just before the holidays, eh? Isn't that what old Ben had claimed on the telephone? If nothing else, it gave him hope that Ben had been wrong about the Lincoln as well.

"Hi there, mister." A man emerged from the back, wiping his hands on a rag. He was tall, with dark blond hair cut short around his large ears. Alec judged him to be in his late forties. The name tag sewn onto his greasy striped coverall read Hal, which he confirmed as they exchanged introductions.

"You happen to bring in a black Lincoln Town Car?" Alec inquired pleasantly.

"Sure did. Just this morning. I sometimes follow the city plow into the countryside, help out where needed. Figured the car belonged to somebody at the inn and knew they didn't have the equipment to pull it out of there."

"Well, the owner is mighty upset that you didn't stop in to consult her."

"The owner of the inn?" he squawked. "I doubt—"

"No, the owner of the car."

"Oh. I see. Sorry about that. Willie, the snow-plough driver, hadn't gotten to the inn's drive yet, and I didn't want to wait around till he did."

"What shape is the car in? I had a look at it right after the accident and it didn't seem too bad."

"Naw, it's nearly right as rain. I gave it a thorough going-over. C'mon through, I'll show you." Hal led Alec through the high-ceilinged work area. The Town Car was near the big doors, parked beside a badly dented pickup.

As Alec circled Sara's vehicle, Hal pulled a small notebook out of his top pocket.

"Beautiful machine. Must be a lady of means driving it."

Alec's heavy black brows joined over her nose. Between the car and the case of dough, the evidence pointed to it. But then he thought about how Sara and Rosie's clothes didn't seem especially extravagant in quality. Certainly a contradiction to the wheels.

"There's a few dings in the fender that I can hammer out," Hal continued. "And the oil in the engine was too heavy for our harsh weather." He looked up from the page, gesturing at the license plate in the rear. "I'm sure it was all right for Seattle, but you have to be careful when you're travelin'. The owner in a hurry? Promised the sheriff I'd tune up the squad car this afternoon, being he's heading up to Stevens Point tonight for the holidays."

Alec memorized the plate number as Hal rambled on, thrilled with how everything was clicking. Hal was obviously an honest, law-abiding businessman who had great respect for the sheriff. It stood to reason it would extend to an FBI agent. With Hal's help, it would be a cinch to slow Sara down. Alec would have to lie to her, but justified it easily, convinced that there was no safer place in the world for her right now than under his wing. He sighed, preparing to make his pitch. "Actually, Hal, there's no rush on this job at all. As a matter of fact, I'd like you to hem and haw your way through this job until further notice."

"But I shouldn't do that. Not without the lady's approval."

It felt so good to reach into his back pocket for his wallet, flash his FBI identification with a practiced flick of the wrist. Hal's eyes grew with interest and excitement.

"Always glad to help out the authorities."

Alec launched into a brief explanation about how Sara was temporarily in his care and that it was in her own best interest to stick around town through Christmas. He assured Hal that he probably wouldn't even hear from Sara personally. All he had to do was sit tight on the car and find he was just too busy to fit it into his workload.

Hal was hooked. An upstanding citizen prepared for a little intrigue. He looked a trifle wary when Alec reached into the back seat of the Lincoln and pulled out a fishnet bag holding Rosie's clown puzzle, but relaxed as Alec kept his tone briskly pleasant, inquiring about the location of his pay phone.

Hal led him back up front to his business phone on the desk behind the counter. "Pay machine is outside. But feel free to use this one." Hal wheeled back the old springy office chair for his guest.

Alec extracted his wallet again and produced his phone card. "Thanks a lot. Won't cost you a cent."

"I figured I could trust you, Mr. Wagner."

"Call me Alec."

"While you're taking care of things, I'll just write up the work order for the car." Hal took hold of a pen and order tablet and started to move away. On impulse, Alec stopped him. "Say, just wanted to ask, you don't have a fuzzy connection here, do you?"

"Huh?"

"The line at the inn is impossible."

Hal chuckled, rubbing his pointy chin. "Everything is a hundred percent up-to-date here in town."

Alec clamped a hand on the smudged white receiver with a frown. "I don't mean to cause anyone trouble, but I did try to phone you earlier."

"And couldn't get through from there," Hal said matter-of-factly. "Heard the complaint about the inn circulating through town."

Alec forged on, not to be dismissed. "Well, young Timothy Doanes dialed out for me and he did manage to raise somebody here at the station."

Hal's hands trembled, the pen and pad slid from his fingers to the desk. "Hang on a second." He rushed to the doorway and hollered into the garage. "Dad? Dad!"

With regret Alec braced himself for a confrontation as a faded version of Hal shuffled in from the garage in the same kind of coveralls, a little grayer, a little heavier, swollen knuckles curled around a wrench.

"Alec, this is my dad Frank. Dad, this is Alec Wagner from the Cozy Rest. Says he spoke to somebody here this morning. *From the Nesbitts' Cozy Rest,*" he added when the older man looked blank.

Alec felt rather foolish. "Oh, this guy's name wasn't Frank."

"Course it wasn't me!" Frank bellowed.

"It was a man named Ben," Alec explained, wishing he'd kept his big mouth shut.

Frank was staring curiously at his son. "He serious?"

Hal nodded. "The little Doanes boy got ahold of the telephone and called here today. This fella really spoke to Ben."

Alec leaned forward in the battered cushioned chair. "Don't mean to get Ben in trouble."

Frank sank onto a wooden stool by the register. "Nobody ever has had control of Ben. Always done as he pleased. Part owner of the place from way back."

"Well, thought you'd like to know he claimed the Lincoln wasn't here. Said not much repair work is done this close to Christmas."

Frank sighed, his aged face gentle. "Ben always did see it that way. Pretty stubborn about it. Why, even in his heyday he wouldn't show up at the garage at all this close to the holiday. Rather pay some of the teenagers to pump the gas and clean the windshields."

"Don't mean to make waves," Alec assured him.

"No, no, so glad you said something," Hal insisted. "How did he sound?"

Alec's face lit up. "Feisty."

"Tell us the conversation word for word," Frank requested, poised in anticipation.

Alec did so, looking around every so often, sure the old coot would charge in any minute to give his own version.

Hal read him accurately. "Ben's impossible to pin down. Chances are we won't be hearing from him today. Right, Dad?"

Frank sighed, eyeing an old, yellowed photograph of the station on the wall. "Pops leaves the day-to-day business to us now. As much as I'd like to see him pick up a wrench again." He picked up his own wrench and ambled off.

"Pops?" Alec repeated. "This guy didn't sound much over sixty, younger than Frank."

"Everybody calls Ben 'Pops,'" Hal explained in a rush. "Get a nickname in a town this size and it sticks." Retrieving his pen and paper, he disappeared through the doorway.

Alec sighed, feeling as if he'd missed something. Probably Ben had been passing through and had taken the call just to be a pest. That made the most sense. He was just overly suspicious because Sara seemed to have so many secrets.

Sara. A glance at his watch told Alec that twenty minutes

had passed since he'd parted ways with her. If he fell behind, she might come looking for him. He took a list of numbers out of his wallet, scooped up the receiver and tucked it beneath his right cheek. Ah, a clear, sweet dial tone.

Alec called the hotel Sara was supposed to have stayed in two days ago, the Super 8 in nearby Madison. Without a second thought, he paved the way with the day manager by again identifying himself as a representative of the FBI. Some checking on the hotel computer confirmed that there was no Sara Jameson registered that night, or any other night. Alec tossed the initials K.H. at him. That brought results. There was a Kelly Hutton on the books and she was a no-show. She'd used a credit-card number to book the room and she'd been charged in full because she hadn't canceled in time. In fact, they still hadn't heard from her.

Alec jotted Kelly Hutton onto his paper, confusion creasing his forehead. Who was Sara, really? He hadn't found any identification in her things, yet she was able to charge under the name of Hutton.

He went on to the next stop on Sara's itinerary, a Trave-Lodge in Decatur, Illinois. They put Alec on hold. Absently, he took Rosie's puzzle out of its fishnet bag. It had five large pieces. The one on top was the clown's head, the two beneath that formed his midsection, and the two bottom pieces made up his huge shoes.

Funny, it seemed rather an advanced toy for the babe. The pieces seemed hollow and had sharp corners, nothing like Rosie's other things. He decided he'd tell Sara the toy might be a hazard.

His contact at the lodge returned to the line. The story was the same. No Sara Jameson, a no-show Kelly Hutton. Their reservation policy was less strict and they hadn't charged the room to her.

Alec took more notes and forged on to the stop Sara had earmarked for tonight, a Whistle Stop Motel outside Nashville, Tennessee. He gave the same spiel, made the same inquiries. The answer stalled his heart with an electric jolt. Kelly Hutton had called the Whistle Stop only moments ago to cancel her reservation. She'd tried to make one for three nights down the road, but they were booked through New Year's Day and had to turn her down.

Alec jammed the receiver back in its cradle, fury building inside him.

Sara was someplace in town, on the blower just as he was, posing as Kelly Hutton, rarin' to be on her way.

No wonder she'd jumped at the chance to get rid of him! He banged an angry fist on the desk and sent the puzzle skidding to the concrete floor. He scrambled to pick up the pieces, not wanting the garage attendants to catch him this way.

That conniving little Frosty! The fact that he'd initiated this separation for the express purpose of spying on *her*, manipulating *her* future, didn't lessen his sense of betrayal. It was his job to be a low-down sneak!

Damn if the puzzle pieces hadn't popped apart on impact. He examined them on the desk, all the while wondering how Sara could allow it near the baby. Then all at once knew she didn't.

This wasn't one of Rosie's playthings. It was a hiding place. For what had popped out of one of the long, curved clown shoes was a credit card. Kelly Hutton's credit card.

Just when he thought he might be getting to know the real Frosty. Just when he'd begun to believe that Sara was her real name. After all, she answered to it readily enough. Enjoyed the husky way he said it sometimes.

He tapped the square of plastic with his thumbnail. Whoever she was, she'd be waiting for him. Time was running out, but he had one last call to make. To his old FBI unit back in Chicago.

"Hello? Jennifer?" Alec settled back in the springy chair, his mouth splitting in a wide grin at the sound of his former co-worker's voice. He was so grateful she was in. After the years she'd served on his team, he knew he could trust her implicitly. "Sure, it's Alec. You sound surprised. Is it because you knew the Cozy Rest doesn't have a telephone that works?" He grimaced as she babbled her ignorance. "No, I'm not kidding. But never mind. I have a plate number I want you to run. Yes, I'm serious. No, obviously I'm not bored to tears. Look, quit grilling me like my doctor. I'm fine. Perfectly fit. I'm also in a damn hurry." He read off the Lincoln's plate number. "Well, can't you just pretend I'm *not* retired? What do you mean you will if I will? C'mon, honey, the meter's running on my personal phone bill. Yes, yes, I'm hanging on."

Alec rapped his fingers on the desktop, and examined the cluttered wall space while he waited. There was a calendar bearing a sketch of a jolly Santa holding up a bottle of Coke, some Christmas cards tacked to a bulletin board. Alec's gaze eventually settled on the faded photograph that Frank had stared at earlier. There was a man standing in front of the station between a couple of tall old-fashioned gas pumps. Behind him was a DeSoto sedan, a vintage '30s model with a rounded body, sloping side windows and a running board. The fellow wore coveralls like Hal's and Frank's, and certainly resembled them in size and features. Alec half raised himself out of the chair in an effort to read the name embroidered on the man's chest, but couldn't make it out.

"Hello? Yes, I'm still holding." Alec sat down once again with a firm grip on his pen. "Lincoln's registered to a Kelly Hutton, huh? Tell you the truth, Jennifer, I need you to do some more digging for me. Doesn't matter if I am retired. You owe me big-time. I could give you a list a mile—" He inhaled as he stared at the fax machine on the corner of the desk. "Hang on, that gives me an idea." Alec cupped the receiver and shouted for Hal. He appeared in the doorway almost immediately.

"What's up, Alec?"

"All right if I have a fax sent here?"

"Suppose so." The mechanic scratched his blond head, eyeing the puzzle spread across the desk. "Take 'em for the flower shop and the bookstore, so why not?" He discreetly disappeared again.

Alec slid his palm away from the mouthpiece. "Look, Jen. There's a fax machine here. No, of course not at the inn. As if you didn't know that! But never mind. What's most important is a background check on this Kelly Hutton. Her credit, any babies." His voice caught a little on the latter, but Jennifer didn't comment. "I mean the works. Down to the fillings in her teeth. I've got a credit-card number you can start with. See if it's on the level."

Alec gave her the station's phone and fax numbers, and signed off. Then he began to reassemble the puzzle. The front and back sides of each piece snapped together easily and he carefully planted the credit card back in a shoe. He couldn't remember which shoe, but surely she wouldn't either in all the commotion.

He exhaled as though carrying the weight of the world all of a sudden. Things didn't look so good in light of this development. If Frosty was Sara Jameson, mother of Rosie, it was highly unlikely she'd have a valid reason for using Kelly Hutton's credit card.

It seemed far more likely that she was Kelly Hutton. So why was she keeping the fact a secret? Why was she so nervous?

He was startled to find Hal had joined him again.

"Everything okay, Alec?"

"Absolutely, Hal." Alec slipped the toy back in the fishnet bag, scrambling for conversation. "Neat DeSoto," he said, gesturing to the framed photo on the wall.

"A beauty, all right."

"Family member?" Alec asked, stuffing his phone card back in his wallet.

"The DeSoto?"

"No, I mean the attendant. He looks like you and Frank."

"Oh. Yeah. A relative." Hal moved and his body blocked Alec's view of the photograph, but Alec doubted it was deliberate. Besides, he had no time to analyze the foibles of the station's owners. Though it was an interesting place, with old Ben's antics and all.

Alec still had his wallet open as he stood up. He peeled out a crisp hundred-dollar bill and handed it to Hal.

Hal hesitated. "Aw, Alec, this is way too much. I haven't done a thing to the car yet."

"Keep it that way," he said adamantly. "If anybody asks you, you're backlogged, working as fast as you can." He looked back at the desk. "As for the faxes, I'd appreciate it if you could get them out to me at the inn."

"Oh. I don't—"

"Please, Hal. You know the phone is a bust out there. And I can't keep trotting to town on maybes. I'm sure you can use this hundred for some extra Christmas cheer." He stuffed the bill in Hal's palm and closed his fist.

"Okay. For the FBI."

"That's the spirit. Thanks for everything." With a harried glance at his watch, Alec picked up his fishnet sack and left.

9

"I KNOW I was supposed to call every day—" Sara held the telephone receiver away from her ear as complaints spewed from it "—but I've been stranded!"

Sara had hurried to Leslie's Fine Café as fast as her errands would allow and was presently ensconced in the back booth closest to the wall-mounted pay phone, trying to reason with her employer.

She noted that she wasn't the first to use this dining area as a phone booth. There were numbers penned on the wall, as well as some half-moon dents where the receiver had swung like a pendulum on its armored cord.

She'd originally tried making her calls standing behind the seating area as the management had no doubt intended. But as she'd fumbled for a quarter with Rosie in her arms she quickly came to realize that the receiver could be reached from this very last bench. She'd been forced to give a couple of adolescent boys five dollars to vacate the space, but it had been worth it. Her back and arms were saved further wear and tear and Rosie had a lap to sit on while she chomped on a teething cookie.

"This isn't my fault," Sara reiterated. "Yes, maybe I was the wrong choice." She flinched as Rosie made a squealing sound. "The baby sounds? It's only natural—I'm in a café. Of course I'm alone. That was part of the deal." She gently clamped her hand over Rosie's mouth as the baby wound up again. Rosie bucked, and slobbered her palm like a puppy.

"Look, I have to hang up. As soon as the car's fixed, I'll be on my way. Yes, I'll start hitting the motels on the list as planned. I'll call again when I'm set to leave. No, I doubt anyone's smart enough to have tracked me here. I haven't charged a thing on the credit card. Yes, I'm watching for a tail. Nothing. Of course if someone gets real close they'll know I'm not you and that'll be the end. Watch out for who? He looks like what? What do you mean, be extra careful around a man like that? Hello...hello?"

The dial tone buzzed in Sara's ear. There couldn't be any real trouble involved. It was a case of the jitters on both sides. This trip was cut and dried. *Cut and dried.*

With new determination she tucked her arm under Rosie's armpits and turned, planning to kneel on the bench to re-place the receiver.

"Here, let me help you."

"Alec!" Sara squealed as his hand snaked out from behind and grabbed the receiver. "How...how—"

"How'd I do it? Came in the back door near the rest rooms." He gestured to an exit not five feet away.

She wondered how much he'd heard, but didn't have the courage to accuse him of eavesdropping. He was as taut as a bowstring as he sat opposite her in the booth. Oh, was he suspicious! Annoyed too. Why couldn't he leave her alone!

What she really wanted was his help with this cat-and-mouse chase across the country, but her desires were sec-ondary to what Rosie needed—a secure home with an atten-tive caregiver. It was so crucial that she and Rosie bond thoroughly, that she become more accustomed to handling the strong, sturdy girl. And have the income to support her.

She raised her eyes to find Alec engrossed in the menu. Was it as bad as she thought, that this ex-FBI agent was just looking for a challenging puzzle to assemble? That thought reminded her of the request she'd made of him.

"Did you get it, Alec? Rosie's toy?"

Alec bristled behind his menu. Rosie's toy, indeed. A lie for sure. He decided to return the favor in kind; lowering the

plastic-covered sheet to nose level, he pretended to have forgotten with a wide-eyed, "Oops."

"Alec!"

"Just kidding." He unzipped his parka and extracted the
fishnet sack. She quickly bypassed Rosie's reach and stuffed
it in the diaper bag.

"Aren't you going to let the baby have it?" he asked
mildly, easing out of the jacket.

She closed the bag and looked at him, trying to read his expression. Was he being sarcastic? It was impossible to tell
what was happening under that inscrutable mask.

"No, I think she has enough on the table right now."

"Yes. Don't we all?" He lifted his brows and returned to
the list of lunch entrées.

Sara licked her lips and took a sip of coffee.

He'd heard something.

He knew everything.

What should she do?

Wait him out. Divert his attention at any cost. Careful to
control her nervous hand, Sara set her cup down behind the
napkin rack. "So, how's my car doing?"

"Huh?" He met her gaze again, his blue eyes as untrou-
bled as the baby's.

"My car, Alec. You had to have found it to get the toy."

"Oh, yeah." He beamed encouragingly.

"Well?" she asked shrilly.

"It's there," he assured her calmly. "In the garage, all safe
and almost sound."

"When can I have it back? How much is it going to cost
me?"

"It's going to be cheap. But it's going to take some time.
There's a terrible backlog, you see."

She gasped. "In a town this size?"

"Yeah, go figure."

The waitress in a black nylon uniform with a festive green
apron strolled up to them with an extra mug and a glass ca-

rafe full of coffee. Alec clapped his hands together appreciatively. "Ah, you read my mind."

The waitress smiled and efficiently filled both their cups. "Didn't know you were expecting another party, miss. Uh, guess I should say ma'am, but you're so young."

Sara instinctively liked the waitress. She was in her midfifties, pleasingly plump and seemed to enjoy her job. "We all like miss a little better, don't we?"

The waitress threw her curly salt-and-pepper head back with a laugh. "I'll say so! I don't mean to be nosy, but now that I see you together, I have to assume you're the ones who came in on the Cozy Rest sleigh."

Alec poured some cream into his brew. "News travels fast around here."

"Well, the sleigh's kind of a novelty in these parts. All we hometowners like to see it. Gives us a nostalgic feeling."

"You grew up here, then?" Alec asked politely.

The waitress sighed with fondness. "Oh, yes. This is my café. I'm Leslie, Leslie Anderson. My husband and I were high-school sweethearts and we run this place together."

"I imagine things are really jumping in the summertime."

"Definitely. More responsibilities—" Leslie broke off then, blushing a little. "Here I am rambling, when I wanted to ask you how you're enjoying the Cozy Rest."

"It's charming," Sara gushed.

"And Beatrice? How's she feeling?"

"Strong as an ox!" Alec blurted that out before thinking, but Leslie wasn't offended.

"She can be spunky and bossy. Everyone in Elm City knows it."

"And loves her dearly, I bet," Sara murmured, shifting Rosie on her lap for some bottle-feeding.

Leslie nodded as she took her order book out of her hip pocket. "Beatrice is a respected mother figure to the entire town. Nobody's ever crossed her. She'd surely hunt 'em down and haunt 'em forever." Leslie took their orders for hamburgers and hustled up to the front of the café.

Alec propped his elbows on the table and watched the baby greedily suck milk from her bottle. "Leslie seems very nice."

Sara smiled and agreed. It seemed to Alec that she was trying to keep their little relationship afloat, on a friendly level. Why? Maybe because she was so very lost and lonely. Or maybe because she hoped to distract him from the facts.

In any case, Alec couldn't help smiling back. If they had to consort, he might as well enjoy the ride. She was so deep under his skin now that the pleasure and the irritations were all one jumble of confusion.

He hoped she wasn't in too far over her head. He'd heard enough of her conversation to have some very serious doubts.

"Leslie reminds me of somebody," Sara was insisting, unaware of the intense calculations behind his calm facade. "Can you guess who?"

"No."

She cleared her throat and stared over his shoulder to make sure Leslie was out of earshot. "Mrs. Nesbitt, silly."

"Silly Mrs. Nesbitt?"

She picked up her leather glove from the table and smacked his hand. "Oh, shut up. You just have way too much fun needling me."

He rubbed his hands together with a chuckle. "I see the resemblance, now that you mention it. Makes sense that a lot of the townspeople would be related."

"And Leslie did seem especially fond of her."

"Agreed. If you want to take the game a step further, there's somebody else in here who looks like somebody at the inn."

"Really?"

Alec nodded. "I saw him come in the front door when I was popping in the back."

Popping hardly covered the covert way Alec had snuck in and quietly eavesdropped when she'd been on the phone, but she let it pass. She'd have to pretend not to care if she hoped to avoid further suspicion. In the spirit of the guessing game she gazed over his shoulder to scan the café's patrons. It was something she wanted to do anyway. Could some pursuer actually be dangerous? She hadn't liked the tone of her phone conversation, the implication of danger. "A he, huh?"

"Uh-huh, a he," Alec teased. "Can I hold the baby for a while?"

"I suppose." Sara stood up and transferred the drowsy child to his arms. Rosie cracked open one eye and contentedly resumed sucking on the bottle. Alec's reference to the patron with a resemblance to one of the inn's guests was forgotten as Sara fretted over the call. If only she could get out of here!

Sipping her coffee and watching the scene between Alec and Rosie, Sara tried to relax. "She really likes you."

"You don't have to sound so awed," Alec complained, cuddling the infant against the softness of his flannel shirt. "Girls are crazy for me. Large and small."

Sara could feel the heat climbing her face as she relived their play on the bed. She'd felt so desired, so wanted. She couldn't help but imagine what belonging to Alec body and soul would feel like. Why did he have to show up in her life now!

"So have you seen your man yet, Frosty?"

Sara's heart slammed against her rib cage. "What man?"

Alec eyed her shrewdly. "The one who resembles someone at the inn, of course."

"Oh, yeah. Him." Hoping to divert suspicion from her outburst, she made a show of once again inspecting the tables at the front of the diner. "I dunno. Maybe he's gone."

Alec half turned and stared up the aisle. "Nope. Still there."

Sara rolled her eyes. There was only one other adult male in the place. Alec had to think her a real dope. "You mean the redhead?"

"He has to be related to the Doanes clan. Certainly, he gives a glimpse of what Timothy's going to look like in about forty years."

"Yes, I see what you mean." Sara wrapped her arms around herself with a little shiver. "There must be comfort in having such deep roots, people to automatically rely upon."

"I wouldn't know." Alec smiled shortly.

"Still, you know about children." She leveled a finger at him, recognizing a chance to take the heat off herself. "And don't tell me it's because you were once one yourself. That's no answer."

"Well, I'm afraid that's part of the explanation," he cautioned. "I had two little sisters to look after, and being a youngster myself didn't diminish the responsibility. Guess you could say it was on-the-job experience for the greenest kind of amateur."

Alec understood her motives. She was probing into his life to distract him from hers. But, judging from the soft lilt of her voice and the compassion in her gray eyes, it seemed certain that she really cared. He found himself drawn into her warm, inviting web. A weakness that was beneath him, certainly. But he justified it with the hope that she'd eventually trade confidences with him.

That was the excuse he gave himself as his past came flowing forth, over his protective, mile-high stone wall. "You see, after my father died, my mother started drinking and, well, sort of zoned out."

"How old were you?"

"Ten. The girls were five and six."

"Why didn't anyone step in?"

"Because I was too clever," he said, bitter and proud all at once. "I figured social services would've only made matters worse. The girls didn't want to be spilt up, and we did love our mother. It wasn't all that difficult to get her signature on Dad's pension checks and school forms. Guess I saw it as a family-honor thing. Family's very, very important to me."

"But looking back, do you think such a charade was right?"

Alec shrugged off the question. "I don't know. I'm eternally grateful that the girls grew up properly, that they are happy and settled—they share a nice bungalow in San Diego. My methods may have been wrong, but we made it through."

Leslie arrived with their food then, and another waitress brought a baby seat for Rosie.

Alec took a breather from Sara's intense scrutiny by making conversation with Leslie, inquiring about the redheaded man.

Leslie turned just as the gentleman in question was rising from his seat. He went about buttoning his topcoat, then reached down to a chair at his table and produced a fedora and a black bag. "That's Doc," Leslie said fondly. "He's our only town physician, like his father before him."

"I wonder...is he related—"

"Near everyone is related to someone around here," Leslie interrupted, gesturing to some customers at the cash register. "Excuse me, duty calls."

"People sure are closemouthed about their kin," Alec mused, thinking back to Hal and the photograph at the garage.

Sara, not about to be sidetracked from her intention of finding out more about Alec, asked, "Why aren't you with your sisters now, Alec? At Christmas, of all times?"

Alec stuffed a garnish of lettuce into his hamburger bun. "Because."

She leaned over the table earnestly. "I wish you'd tell me about it. What are you doing at an inn in the middle of nowhere, with no woman, no wedding ring—no job?"

He smiled thinly. This was tougher than he'd anticipated.

He'd already told her more about his childhood than he'd offered close associates. Besides, she was stealing his lines. More than anything, he wanted to know what *she* was doing here!

"Why do you want to know these things, Frosty?" He was having trouble calling her Sara now that he was so dead sure she was Kelly Hutton.

She met his gaze squarely. "Because," she gently mimicked. Then she added, "Because I care." She held up her hands in defense. "I know I shouldn't. You're a grumpy stranger who probably hangs around me for my baby, but I like you, Alec."

He smiled grimly. It took a gutsy woman to demand the truth straight up from a lion like him. The fact that she herself had made hypocrisy an art form made it all the more fascinating.

"I...don't want my sisters to see me like this," he blurted out quietly.

"Like what?"

"A man down. Betrayed by his own company. Booted out of active service for no good reason." He exhaled, reining in his mounting temper. "Naturally, my sisters have always viewed me as invincible and I don't want to risk spoiling it. They might mistake my setback for weakness. I don't know what Mrs. Nesbitt told you about me and my retirement—"

"Only that you were with the FBI, took a bullet to the chest."

"Well, losing my field status was a grave injustice. I'm fit as ever. My unit was—is—the best in the business. Our operations are unsurpassed. I put everything into it, you see. Everything. Then I get hurt and I'm chained to a desk on office duty."

"That wasn't enough for you?"

He shook his head adamantly. "No way. Hatching the plans was only the beginning of the process. The execution was the meat, the real thrill. It's all wrong what they've done to me, believe it."

Sara gave him full credit for talking a good game, but she could tell he wasn't in peak form. Maybe he was a sad and wounded warrior, in the throes of denial, staggering after his heartier comrades. He'd hate that image, she realized. Despise her for the notion.

As sympathetic as she was, Sara couldn't help but be increasingly annoyed with Alec. There was little doubt that he was using her situation as a distraction to keep himself in the spy trade. If only she could bring the man-woman chemistry to the forefront instead. She'd feel more confident under those circumstances. Unfortunately, mating dances normally took time and patience. She had neither this trip.

Her small, hard sigh betrayed her impatience.

"What are you thinking?" he demanded. "C'mon, tell me the truth."

"Only that...well...I'm sure it must have been awful being demoted. But to quit outright—"

"Not demoted, not demoted." He gritted his teeth in disgust. "Just on leave." He reached for the catsup and doused his burger. "They want me back—my team. I figure it's why they gave me a gift certificate to this isolated burg." He jabbed a french fry at her. "It was a crafty plan to bore me to death. They think I'll come running back from this slow-motion funny farm, dying to take back my desk job. But I won't!"

"Guess the last laugh's on them, isn't it?" she said with some sarcasm. "I mean, you aren't bored at all."

"No, I'm sure not," he agreed heartily.

They stared deeply into each other's eyes until Alec's fry went limp in his fingers.

"You haven't called me Sara once since you sat down," she complained softly.

He dropped his fry and curled his fingers. "That bother you?"

"A little. The name sounds so wonderful when you say it."

The lines driven so deeply between his raven brows softened a little. "It's my younger sister's name. Sarah with an *h*. You use an *h*?"

She tensed at the steel glint behind the silky inquiry. "Who wants to know? The FBI?"

He laughed shortly. "I do admit to being retired, remember? Not demoted, but not official either."

Who needed an official title to be an obnoxious beast? "No," she said flatly, "I don't spell it with an *h*."

Offended by that simple question, it was clear that Sara wasn't about to return Alec's confidence. He had intended to take care of business here, away from the sentimental aura of the inn; grill her about the money and the credit card. But, damnation, he couldn't. On edge about all the demons she'd encouraged him to dredge up, he couldn't do hers the justice they deserved. Like it or not, he was too upset to ask the right questions or to interpret her answers. Seemed he'd have to survive on his gut-level faith in her for a while longer.

On impulse Alec reached over and gently stroked the fragile curve of her jaw. Common sense warned him that she might be taking him for the biggest, most twisted ride of his life. But lord help him, he was in way too deep to put on the brakes.

The fact that Beatrice and Camille were so convinced of Sara's innocence certainly weighed on his decision as well. Although the sisters seemed much too cheery and understanding than any humans had a right to be, Alec respected them.

In the end he decided he'd keep collecting the facts with an open mind. True, he might very well be playing her personal chump. But what a way to go.

THE AFTERNOON SUN was fading as they emerged from the café, and began strolling down Elm City's main street for one last inspection.

"I should get Rosie back pretty soon," Sara said to Alec, who was carrying the baby like a prized trophy on his strong side. The sight shouldn't have made her throat swell, but it did. A new daddy was just what the child needed. Rosie seemed to fulfill Alec too. But a man who refused to face his future realistically was not in touch with his most urgent needs. Sara knew all about fresh starts, and if ever there was a man who needed one, it was Alec "Retired" Wagner.

"You get your scissors?" he thought to ask as they passed the salon.

"Yes," Sara said, impressed by his interest. "As well as a blow-dryer and curling iron. I'm now set for any and all makeover gifts."

"I thought I'd buy chocolates for everybody," Alec confided. "Except Timothy. I'd like to get him something unique."

"Do you think we should stop at a supermarket? They must have one."

"It's on the next street beside the service station," Alec reported. "But I wouldn't know where to start, would you? There seems to be food aplenty at the inn."

"Yes, now that you mention it. Sort of like the Biblical loaves and fishes."

Alec nodded. "I think Mrs. Nesbitt has her kitchen well in hand. I suggest we leave her to it." On that note, he steered her into a neat bookstore named Cabin Fever.

The shop resembled a cabin inside with its pale varnished log walls. Every inch of shelf space was lined with reading material, every aisle crowded with shoppers. With little trouble Alec found the children's section, and rows of Hardy Boys books.

"For Tim? What a thoughtful gesture," Sara commented. "His collection has such outdated book jackets."

"We'll give them as a couple if you like."

"Yes, please!"

Delighted by Sara's enthusiasm, Alec turned a little more

sharply than he meant to into the congested aisle. With Rosie hoisted on his chest he didn't see the man standing next to him. It was the doctor from the café.

"Oh, excuse me, sir." Alec nodded, noticing the old man's sparkling brown eyes, so much like the young Hardy Boys fan. Doc just had to be a Doanes relation.

"Wonderful series," the doctor remarked, picking up a volume for inspection.

"Yes, I know a little boy who loves them," Alec remarked, studying the titles.

Doc's smile grew with delight. "Leslie said you came in on the sleigh."

"That's right," Sara interposed cheerily, noting the resemblance as well.

Doc surveyed the threesome. "Hope you're enjoying your stay in our little mecca."

"Very much," Alec assured.

"Yes," Doc went on, "you make a nice little family."

Sara politely excused herself in a choked voice at this point, claiming she wanted to find a new storybook for Rosie. Alec stood his ground, flushing over the assessment. It was especially nice to hear someone else validate the tantalizing fantasy he'd been toying with in secret. Leave it to him to fall for a fugitive, probably in heaps of trouble!

Turning his attention back to the volumes, Alec tried to recall which books Timothy had. He was surprised when Doc sidled closer.

"May I suggest some of the newer titles at the end of the series? That's what I'd buy if I wasn't sure."

Alec thanked him for the wise advice. When he'd chosen a couple of potential volumes, he turned to ask the doctor what he thought. Unfortunately the older man had disappeared.

"Talking to yourself?" Sara asked, sidling up to him again with a volume of stories for small children.

"No—yes, I guess so," he admitted with a chuckle.

"Your latest case left the store altogether," she reported.

"Hmm, just when I was warming up to ask him some direct questions."

"Maybe people don't like to answer a lot of questions," Sara suggested.

Alec bared his white teeth. "Funny, coming from a grillmaster like you. C'mon, let's check out."

Alec left the store in a state of euphoria. Not only had the clerk gift wrapped the four books he'd bought for Timothy, but she'd come up with a box close in shape to a shoe box, like most of the others beneath the inn's tree. Alec smiled as he envisioned Timothy's delight over the surprise contents.

This holiday was so different from last year's. He'd been on the job in New York City, tracking down a money-laundering operation. He and Jennifer had grabbed a hasty brunch downtown, but it hadn't been memorable, for either agent. And it hadn't bothered him one bit, either, until this very moment as he compared it to this year's homespun Christmas.

Life's smaller touches—a baby's burp after a bottle, the teasing smile of a beautiful young woman, a new book for an earnest young man, were the center of a deeper, more meaningful holiday.

It was clear that something was upsetting Sara all of sudden. She shrank against him, as though trying to conceal herself from the street. Alec looked around into the sea of shoppers. But it was no good. If someone was stalking her, she would have to tell him.

How he wished he had his pistol on him. Unfortunately, he hadn't even brought it along on the trip.

"Alec, is it okay if I meet you back at the sleigh in about, say, ten minutes?"

He stopped right there in the center of the sidewalk. "Why? What's wrong?"

"I—" She gasped as a man in an expensive gray coat passed by them, and into the arms of a slender blond woman

dressed with the same kind of elegance. "Just a minute."
With a small false laugh she dug into her purse. "Never
mind, here it is." She extracted Rosie's pacifier. "Thought I'd
dropped it in the café. No problem. Now, about that candy
shop. I'm in the mood for some fudge."

Like hell. She'd mistaken the gray-coated man for someone
else, and it had scared the daylights out of her. It took all of
Alec's self-control not to grab a handful of her lush, auburn
hair, draw her face to his and force her to make a complete
confession. But that would spoil everything. She'd hate him
after that, and with every passing hour, he was discovering
he couldn't bear to be anything but her hero. Her unin-
formed, weaponless chump of a hero.

10

"YOU BOUGHT *ME* a Christmas present?" Timothy squealed delightedly, assailing Sara and Alec in the kitchen upon their return from town.

Alec had barely gotten his boots and parka off in the service porch before the boy was scrambling about on the floor, his flame-colored head dipping into their sacks.

"What a terrific day!" Timothy rejoiced. "A box from Papa and a present from you two!"

"There it is," Alec said, gesturing to the shoe-box-shaped package.

Timothy's freckled face clouded. "Gee, hope you know Jim Nesbitt gets everybody around here all the shoes they'll ever need."

Alec gasped. "You hear that, Sara? Have you ever heard anything so lucky? All the shoes a guy could ever need."

Sara, standing by in Martha's red outerwear, the baby in her arms, beamed with pure pleasure at hearing her name on Alec's lips. She ruffled the boy's soft crew cut. "Don't worry, buddy. We didn't pull a stunt like that on you."

Alec frowned. "Hey, what happened to our prank?"

"Timothy can't take it, Alec. Can't you see that?"

Timothy hugged Sara fiercely, capturing Rosie too. "You are the greatest, Sara."

"So are you, Tim. Just the kind of son I hope to have one day."

Alec lifted his heavy brows as he moved to the porch to stow his parka on a peg. Hmm, it was uplifting to know that

Sara wasn't intending to end up behind bars in a women's facility.

Mrs. Nesbitt strolled into the kitchen. "Why, Alec, I was intending to meet you out in the barn, help you with Spice."

"Camille and Lyle are out there and were glad to oblige," he reported.

"On one of their constitutionals," Timothy surmised, his chest puffing with knowledge.

Alec's and Sara's eyes locked across the room with shared amusement. They'd spotted some violet lipstick on Lyle's jaw while he and Camille were making a production out of setting Spice comfortably in his stall.

"Made stew for supper," Mrs. Nesbitt announced, moving to the stove to stir her bubbling kettle.

Alec joined her and put his hand over hers on the large wooden spoon. "It smells glorious. I swear you're the perfect woman. Nurturing, loving, honest and a darn good cook!"

Sara watched the tender scene rather sulkily as she laid Rosie on the table to remove her snowsuit. She wasn't jealous of Mrs. Nesbitt, she simply longed for Alec's approval and affection. Why, if he ever looked at her the way he was looking at that pot of stew...she'd strip off her clothes and dance around on his mattress!

The sudden erotic inclination startled her clear down to her toenails. How could she be falling for a conservative authority figure who'd griped about her tennis shoes even as he was saving her life! How could she lust for a has-been sleuth who was clinging to her predicament to make himself feel useful?

The reasons all seemed inconsequential in the wake of the tide of desire welling up inside her. Perhaps she was looking at the situation the wrong way. Perhaps it was fate that they'd met this way.

Perhaps he had been sent here to help her out of this jam. To put a stop to her journey.

But that would mean she'd have to return the money in

the suitcase. And she couldn't do that, not without an alternative financial source. Without that money she and Rosie would be destitute.

One thing was certain: Alec was steadily closing in on the truth about her life. Even now, as he stirred the stew, he was watching her pull Rosie's fat limbs out of the snug down-filled suit. Rosie was protesting and Sara was having a time with her. Sara figured he was wondering why she was so clumsy about everything concerning the infant. Maybe she was fumbling, but dammit, she was sincerely trying hard. The fact that she was with Rosie now was fate, for sure.

No man was going to upset this chance she'd been given. No man was going to come between Rosie's happiness or hers.

Even if he was the most irritating, fascinating, unforgettable man she'd ever met!

Unlike previous evenings Alec found himself thrilled over the prospect of another community get-together in the Cozy Rest parlor after dinner. Nothing was different, of course, except his own attitude. What he'd formerly looked upon as mild diversion for the long media-free nights, now took on new meaning due to Sara. He couldn't get enough of her voice, her scent, her teasing eyes.

Scooping Sara out of that ditch, offering her his body heat all through the night, fretting over her fat, squirmy babe as though she was his very own, had dislodged his heart from its state of frozen indifference. He felt genuine concern for his fellow man; his gestures of goodwill were more than just a duty.

The evening's routine was swiftly set in motion. A roaring fire was struck by Lyle, Camille parked herself at the upright piano to sort through her sheet music, Beatrice bustled around, setting out bowls of popcorn for stringing and munching. Timothy sat before the tall, tinsel-heavy pine tree, stacking his gifts with architectural flair. The package from his father wrapped in brown paper and twine, looked out of place in the colorful tower of shoe boxes.

Alec stood in the doorway, drinking in the warm, inviting atmosphere, then crossed the room with his red boxes of chocolates tied with shiny gold ribbons. He knelt on the fringed rug beside Tim, and stashed the additions amidst the clutter of bright paper beneath the branches. Fascinated with the box wrapped in the old-fashioned brown paper and twine, he reached out for a closer look. The postmark appeared to be German, but the date was smudged and illegible. He ran his blunt thumbnail over it, straining to read it.

"Rosie dripped on the box," Timothy explained. "She sure leaks a lot, doesn't she?"

Alec chuckled in affirmation, thinking what precise aim the child must've had, to distort just that postmark. Still, Tim spent a lot of time with the baby and the gifts, so it was certainly possible that it had happened that way.

Martha appeared as Alec was studying the postmark and suggested that Tim remove the outer wrappings of his father's box. Alec produced his pocketknife, remarking that one didn't see parcels tied with twine much anymore. Martha quickly took the brown paper, folded it and tossed it into the fire, ending all speculation over the postmark.

Alec fleetingly wondered about her hasty actions, but was quickly distracted by the red-flannel socks hung on the stone mantel. The sisters had finished embroidering the socks for Sara and Rosie and had hung them with all the rest. He wondered if Sara would mind. To him, it looked so right.

Having taken care of the fire, Lyle turned his attention to the liquor trolley beside the piano. With brandy snifter in hand he seated himself on the piano bench and smiled so dreamily at Camille beside him that he nearly doused the piano keys with brandy. Alec noted that these parlor occasions always meant his bow tie was knotted and his vest buttoned. Alec only hoped that he'd be half as classy in his advanced years.

However, Alec hoped unlike Lyle, his bachelor days would be long over by his eighth decade. True, his vulnerability concerning Sara made him nervous, but he couldn't imagine going back to a life without her warmth, her wit, her saucy attitude. Or her baby. Oh, lord, how he hoped that Rosie truly belonged to Sara—or Kelly. They made a dynamite trio.

Sara and Rosie joined the party in the middle of Alec's second brandy. Sara looked lovely in a gray corduroy jumper a shade darker than her eyes, over a blue knit top the color of his. Rosie looked sweet in some lemon-yellow pajamas, but her eyes were pink and teary. Apparently not up for company, she kept her head nuzzled in the hollow of Sara's shoulder.

"I would've expected her to be asleep by now," Sara said apologetically, sinking into Mrs. Nesbitt's favorite rocking chair. "But every night's a surprise."

"She's bound to be out of sorts on a road trip," Mrs. Nesbitt said consolingly, setting a brandy snifter on a small table at Sara's elbow.

"I'm not sure I should drink that," Sara halfheartedly objected.

"You slurped it right down out on the sleigh," Alec teased. "Seems to me it did wonders for you."

Sara could read his little mind from clear across the room. Sure, it did wonders, it made her drowsy and vulnerable. Oh, wouldn't he just like that. Tip her upside down and her secrets would spill out all over the place. At least that's what she assumed he wanted. But his eyes were so full of longing, his voice so husky, she wasn't sure of his intentions.

"You deserve a tipple," Mrs. Nesbitt encouraged. "It's the holidays, after all."

"Can't be a rock every second," Martha murmured, reaching over from her chair to pat Sara's knee.

Sara knew she should be a rock without fail, but took a swallow of the amber liquor anyway. It burned going down, bringing back vivid images of the other night on the sleigh. She'd felt so very safe then. Dare she feel so now? She kept thinking back to her phone call, remembering the dead silence on the line when she'd questioned her safety. If everything blew up in her face, she didn't know what she'd do!

Camille played some soothing carols on the piano and everyone sang along softly, as though delivering a lullaby. Rosie was fairly content for a while, sniffling and crying out only intermittently.

Mrs. Nesbitt took her turn with the child, giving Sara a chance to string popcorn with Timothy and Alec. Together they added their handiwork to the tree, while Mrs. Nesbitt rocked and cooed in Rosie's soft little ear about being her Auntie Bea. Cookies were served, along with more brandy, and lemonade for Timothy.

By ten o'clock it was clear that Rosie could stand no more frivolity. She was sobbing and stretching out like a board against Mrs. Nesbitt torso. It was clear that the innkeeper was distressed, though she tried to hide it behind a frozen smile.

Sara looked nearly as lost herself, but took hold of the fussy child, and hurriedly bid everyone good-night. Camille and Mrs. Nesbitt filled their snifters to the brim shortly thereafter and excused themselves, no doubt heading up to their third-floor hideout. Lyle waited a full three minutes before following with his own snifter in hand.

That left Alec with the Doanes. With his dream girl gone, Timothy appeared to be at loose ends. That was before Martha suggested he read a chapter from his favorite Hardy Boys adventure.

"Jeepers, yeah!" Timothy dashed over the window seat where he'd left the book after his afternoon break.

Too late for escape. Alec sighed in surrender, snatched a couple of Christmas cookies from the plate on the coffee table, and sank back into the room's most comfortable easy chair. He tipped his head back, hoisted his feet onto a fringed ottoman, and told the boy to skip over any scary parts. Although he fought against it, he was soon sound asleep.

ALEC WOKE UP all alone in the parlor some hours later. The fire was reduced to glowing embers behind the brass grate, the lights snuffed out except for the bulbs in the red straw wreaths hanging in the bay window. Ever so slowly, he swung his feet off the ottoman and hoisted himself up, using the chair's wooden arms as leverage.

He stretched his arms over his head with a mighty groan, then stole a look at his watch. It was nearly 1:00 a.m. Amazingly, during his slumber, somebody had tidied up. The popcorn bowls and cookie plates and glasses had all been taken away. His empty brandy snifter remained on the side table by his chair, however, and the crystal carafe stood in its rightful place atop a doily over on the small liquor trolley.

If ever there was an invitation for another bump, this was it. Alec staggered wearily over to the trolley and filled his snifter to the brim. If ever there was a night he wanted to fall into a dreamless sleep, this was it. He didn't even want to consider the new tidbits he'd uncovered about Sara, the credit card with the name Kelly Hutton, her apprehension on the street over the gray-coated man, the cryptic phone call that had upset her so.

Tipping his glass to his lips, he took the top off the brandy. After all, he had to get up the stairs without sloshing. Pausing to unplug the cord giving power to the wreath, he trudged on up to bed.

It was an honest mistake to pause at his old door. He'd entered it blurred with alcohol and weariness many a night last week. Naturally, he realized his mistake when he heard the whimper of a child.

He squeezed his eyes shut as emotion overwhelmed him. Rosie. Sweet little Rosie was having a rough night.

Alec's head fell against the wooden door. She wasn't the only one.

WHO'D BE KNOCKING at her door at this hour? Sara wondered. She set Rosie on the mattress where she'd been cradling the fussy child, and rose to answer the door. She was sorry Rosie was so darn noisy. But the baby wasn't content and nothing Sara tried seemed to help.

She opened her mouth to offer apologies as she swung open the door. "Oh. It's you, Alec."

"Huh?" He stumbled as he crossed the threshold, reached out and caught her shoulder to regain his balance. He sank his fingers into the soft fabric of her peach satin robe, noting that there was a matching shift underneath. "This isn't Mrs. Nesbitt's flannel."

She shut the door. "No, it's all mine. Just because I was driving around in tennis shoes the other night doesn't mean I have no nice clothing of my own." She gripped the hand on her shoulder that had begun to sink a little lower. "So, what do you want, Alec? Don't tell me you can't sleep either, 'cause by the looks of it, you've been out for quite a while."

"Sorry. Got confused in the dark. Guess my head fell against your door while...I was figuring things out."

Rosie made a squawling sound from the bed.

Sara stepped out of Alec's reach. "Look, I'm really busy right now."

Alec extended his snifter to her. "Here, take some of this." Sara took it to avoid a spill. Once his hands were free, he circled around her to the other side of the bed, where he barely avoided tripping over Rosie's makeshift drawer-bed on the floor. "We got some problems, Jingle?"

Rosie was startled by his deep voice and quieted for a moment as she stared up at his whisker-shadowed face. She made another noise, but it was half the volume, more of an afterthought. Alec leaned over the mattress and rubbed the pad of his thumb on the baby's creamy brow, humming "Jingle Bells" under his breath.

Sara set the glass down on the highboy and stormed to the

opposite side of the bed in a cloud of flying peach satin. "Are you drunk?"

"No." He enunciated the word with the disdain he felt her question deserved. "You're seeing me down, exhausted, confused and half-asleep right now, but not juiced."

She fluttered her fingers in the air. "Okay, okay!"

Alec edged a thigh onto the bed and captured one of Rosie's fat hands as he spoke to her mother. "Don't know why you've turned so huffy all of a sudden."

Sara frowned. "Meaning?"

Alec's mouth crooked as he turned back to confront her. "Why, you were delighted to see me a minute ago."

"I—I—" Exhausted herself, Sara was at a loss.

"Are you trying to tell me I'm a wish come true, but forbidden fun?"

"No, I was happy that it was *only* you because I thought maybe Rosie's fussing was upsetting one of the older folks."

"Well, glad to be of service for a second there in the doorway."

Sara chuckled, but remembering the hand that had been stealing toward her breast, sat down on the opposite side of the bed. "You saw how Mrs. Nesbitt got fidgety when Rosie started to really crank up. Couldn't wait to unload her. Understandably so!"

"Ah, but we're not the kind to fall to pieces over a little spouting off," Alec murmured. He cast Sara only the briefest glance as he scooped Rosie up in his arms. "Are we, Frosty?"

Sara popped off the bed again and began to pace around the room. Alec leaned back against the headboard, stretching the baby across his chest. Sara was lovely in the muted lamplight, a henna sheen to her tide of hair, her negligée highlighting the natural peach tones in her skin.

After spending the previous week in this room, it was easy to pretend this was his bedroom. And after the brief but intense lovemaking with Sara, it was almost as easy to pretend this was his own little family, too.

Alec inhaled in self-disgust, banging his head back against the bed frame's steel spindles. There was not one reasonable argument in favor of a relationship. Sara-Frosty-Kelly could be anything and anyone. But somehow she'd managed to do the impossible, strip away his shield, leave him aching for affection.

More than anything on earth he wanted to rescue her from her own mess. Make things right. Make her his.

Rosie was growing dissatisfied with the new distraction and was starting to whine and fidget on Alec's chest.

"See what I mean?" Sara hissed desperately from where she was standing in front of the highboy. "Nothing pleases her, not walking, singing, rocking, feeding. I even tried whimpering right along with her." On impulse she took a swig from Alec's snifter. "She refuses to go to sleep!"

"This happen a lot?"

"Yes! No!" Sara rubbed her temples, concealing her expression. "I'm not sure."

Alec frowned. Why wouldn't she know her own baby's history? But there simply had to be a reasonable explanation. Tears were springing to Sara's eyes now as one would expect from a frustrated mother. This was incredibly tough on her.

So Alec took charge. He sat Sara down with the snifter in a worn wicker rocker near the window and started walking with Rosie, across the area rug, over the hardwood flooring. Back and forth and back again.

It didn't work for him, either. Sara fretfully rocked herself in the creaky little chair, watching the process over sips of brandy. Eventually the brandy was gone and Rosie was louder than ever. Sara found herself torn between a triumphant *I told you so* and a disappointed *Just when I was beginning to see you as my invincible hero.*

She stood up and stretched her arms over her head. The bell sleeves of the her wrap fell from her slender arms like angel's wings, the sash holding it closed loosened and the garment fell open, revealing the empire gown underneath.

Alec was distracted over his failure with Rosie, but not enough to miss the provocative display, or the way Sara's breasts strained the gown's lacy peach bodice with every breath. The fancy negligée seemed such an odd choice for a solo trip across the country. Impractical, not particularly warm. He couldn't help wondering about it, as he wondered about everything else concerning Frosty.

"What shall we do now, Alec?" she asked, her gray eyes huge and distressed.

Alec tipped his head against the baby's, and took short, relaxing breaths. Sara had no idea what she was doing to him! And that made it all the more erotic.

Sara strolled over to the pair, and gave Rosie's head a pat. "If only she were older, we could reason with her, convince her to sleep."

"What's needed sometimes is a trick or two. Even I—" Struck with inspiration, Alec snapped his fingers. "Where is the storybook you bought today?"

Sara stared blankly. "You want to read to her now? At this hour?"

"I don't take any pride in saying so, but the drone of reading puts me right to sleep. Poor little Timothy has proven it beyond a doubt. I can't tell you how many times I've drifted off while he's pouring his soul into one of those Hardy Boys adventures of his."

"I'll try anything." Sara acted swiftly, moving to the largest Gucci suitcase, digging out the large picture book.

"Great. Now go sit in the chair again. I'll hand you Rosie. You can rock while I read."

"I could read if you like," she offered.

"No, it should be a male drone. I mean, I take it she's never fallen asleep during one of your stories yet."

Gathering the satin folds of her negligée close to her body, Sara sank down in the wicker chair once again. "No, Alec, she hasn't." Humor touched her eyes, making them shine. "I'm probably just too exciting to be boring."

Alec grunted and set the baby in her lap. Then he sat on the edge of the mattress and began reading aloud about an adventurous pig family traveling the world in a hot-air balloon.

Rosie cracked open one eye from time to time to make sure she still was snug in somebody's arms, but it was a losing battle for the baby. The gentle rocking motion coupled with Alec's soft tones, was too powerful a sedative. Soon Rosie's shuddering breaths evened out, her lashes stayed glued to her soft, round cheeks. Alec finished the story for the second time just to make sure, then went to ease Sara out of the chair without disturbing her bundle.

Grasping her under the arms seemed like the smoothest method. It worked too, Sara was on her feet without effort. But not without cost. As Alec's fingers were putting pressure on her rib cage to help her rise, his palms were squeezing her breasts, pulling the lacy bodice taut against them. Already heated from the brandy, Sara's body tingled. She broke free, rounded the bed and knelt before the quilt-lined drawer serving as Rosie's bed. She tucked the baby in cozily, pressed fingers to her damp brow, and crouched close by to make certain Rosie snoozed on.

"Hurray for you, Alec," she called out in a whisper from the floor. "You saved us. All over again."

"My pleasure."

Sara's heart tripped at the sound his voice, so husky, so near. He'd actually followed her! It was only a matter of steps, but he'd taken them. It would have been easier, less complicated for him to walk away from her and Rosie, but he seemed bound and determined to be a part of their life.

She knew he was keeping his cool as he took note of all the inconsistencies in her story, privately struggling with their meaning. The odd initials on her luggage, her cryptic phone call at the cafe, the credit card she'd found in the wrong foot of the clown puzzle. Even when it was an effort for him to call her Sara, he treated her with faith, hope and affection.

As she stood up to meet his simmering expression, she had no doubt that he longed for her, body and soul. No matter what she'd done.

His hands were under her arms again, this time from behind. Before she knew it, he was lifting her up and around and into his embrace.

She nuzzled into the softness of his shirt. "Thank you, Alec."

He cupped her chin in his hand, raising her eyes to his for loving inspecting. "For what?"

She faltered. "For just about everything, I guess."

"So happy to be here for you, honey." Threading his fingers through the tide of hair at her ear, he dipped to kiss her hungrily, and drove his tongue into her mouth for a long, satisfying taste.

She gloried in the feast until she could no longer breathe. "What are you doing?"

He chuckled. "Tasting my long-lost brandy."

"Liar."

"Takes one to know one, honey."

Valid grounds for a walkout, Sara thought. Instead, he kissed her again, with an urgent grinding passion to match his rough tone of voice. It was the most erotic moment of her life, right down to the near-punishing burn of his whiskers. His rough, raw strength was just the affirmation she needed right now. She felt alive, protected, desirable; she could love again.

With a shrug, she sent her wrap falling from her shoulders. It landed in a heap at her feet, tickling her toes. She moaned softly as his hands skimmed her throat.

"Do you want me to go on, honey?" he asked huskily.

"Oh, yes." Sara closed her eyes, desperately wishing he'd call her by name. But that would surely come later.

Alec took her consent with a groan of pure masculine pleasure. His hands moved down her back as he dropped to his knees, then he pressed his face into the lacy bodice of her gown. Cupping her breast he suckled it through the lacy barrier, causing the dark bud of nipple to harden against his tongue. Hooking his thumbs beneath the straps of her empire gown he tugged it loose from her shoulders and pulled it down to her waist. He assailed her bared breasts with a feverish hunger, savoring their sweetness with a grazing tongue, burying his face in their softness.

A heightened awareness of her own sexuality filled Sara as Alec's burning whiskers followed the path of her slipping gown. He left nothing unexplored as he kissed and nibbled her silken skin.

Even naked, she felt incredibly safe in his care. Several times she tried to unbutton his shirt, but he thwarted each attempt. He slipped his fingers inside her with expert care, asking nothing of her, expecting nothing.

She moaned as he drove her into a delicious spiral. Alec quickly scooped her up and onto the open bed. He unfastened his belt and pants and knelt above her on the mattress. Arching like a sleek animal, he entered her with a deep, swift stroke, followed by another, then another.

Soft panting sounds of endearment passed between them. Sara couldn't remember ever feeling so alive, so desired. Fears that she might not be as sophisticated as the women he was accustomed to, that she might not be as perfectly shaped as he'd expected, were washed away on a tide of hot, surging sensations.

How she wanted to please him, surprise him in return. As he withdrew and arched forward to kiss her throat, she gathered her courage and pushed him off. He fell beside her, stunned. His fear of rejection was banished as she wantonly slithered over his solid hair-dusted body.

They wrestled and stroked for what seemed forever. Several times she tried to push his shirt up off over his shoulders, but every time his fingers were there to reroute her touch.

Sara really didn't care at the moment. She had headier

things to think about as she rose to straddle him, to slip his rigid flesh inside her.

Alec thought he might black out as she squeezed him with her soft thighs and feminine muscles. How unselfish she was, how inventive.

Sara sat stock-still for a long moment, clamped hard to his hips, relishing the seamless bond between them. Their eyes met then, with understanding and heady pleasure.

A secret smile curved her lips. There were times when Alec's self-control could come in mighty handy.

The smile did him in. Alec flipped her over on her back on the sheets and mounted her again. He entered her with a fresh urgency. Soon they were lost in a pounding rhythm that shut out everything but their wild, heated coupling.

Alec did indeed call her Sara then, as the tension sizzled and escalated. It was a half plea, half curse. Enough to push Sara over the edge and take Alec with her, up into the mists, then tumbling down, down, until he lay quiet and exhausted, still buried inside her softness. If only they could hide here, never to return to reality, never to face the demons circling their cocoon.

Sara opened her eyes a short while later to find the bed empty and Alec's tall, erect figure outlined in the lamplight, readjusting his pants. He smiled as she watched him, and gallantly bent to retrieve her nightgown. "Considering the way locks seem to melt in people's hands around here, I suggest you dress for breakfast far in advance."

His distant tone made her suddenly uncomfortable with her nudity. She took the gown he held out to her and quickly tugged it over her head. "Don't leave me."

The words were faint and wistful, causing Alec to sag a little. He crawled back up beside her and gathered her close against his flannel shirt. "Don't leave *me*, honey."

She forced a saucy smile. "You're confused. This is my room now."

"You know what I mean," he said sternly. "Say you'll stay

for Christmas. Give up whatever you're doing and stay, dammit!"

"I'd like to—"

"Then do it. Make me the happiest man in the world. Make the other guests around here glad they knitted jackets and embroidered socks."

"I know about Martha's project, but what socks?"

"The ones hung by the chimney with care. Didn't you notice them on the mantel this evening?"

"No. With Rosie acting up, guessed I missed a lot." Sara brushed some silken strands of hair from her face. "How very kind everyone is. How accepting..." She trailed off weakly.

It was all Alec could do to stop from exploding. Never in his entire life had he so longed for someone's confidence. But he couldn't force her to confide in him, any more than he could force her to stay once she discovered her car could be fixed.

With monumental self-control Alec settled for forcing a smile as he tweaked her nose. "A stocking on the mantel means you and Rosie are officially on the holiday roster, you know."

"Oh, Alec..."

"Can you seriously be looking forward to taking Rosie on the road again now, a couple days before Christmas? What a desolate idea."

"I know. Everything here is so...perfect."

Alec seized her bare arms, turning her toward him on the bed. "Whatever's wrong, Sara, I know I can help you fix it."

She rapped a closed fist on his chest. "Oh, Alec, please don't pressure me."

"Don't you think I'm...fit enough?"

She rolled her eyes. "It isn't that at all. You're jumping to all kinds of conclusions."

"Then set me straight."

"I'd like to, but I have a commitment, one I must handle alone. It's not as wild as it seems. Honestly."

He doubted that. The snatch of phone conversation he'd overheard at the café sounded like real trouble to him. "I just feel... I haven't held anything back from you," he said quietly. "I would like the same favor."

"Eventually, Alec. Promise. Tell you what," she said impulsively, "I will stay on through the twenty-fifth. We'll go on as we are, enjoying the wonderful Cozy Rest atmosphere."

"All right." He sighed and gave her another kiss to seal the deal. "Now try to sleep. I'll stay here until you're as snug as little Rosie."

Sara snuggled deeper under the covers. Just as Rosie had, she opened her eyes every once in a while to stare up at Alec, half-sitting against the pillows with his eyes closed.

Had he really not held anything back? True, he'd let go a lot; been open about his childhood, and seemed to be genuinely trying to trust her. And his response to their lovemaking couldn't have been faked; he ground out her name like a man discovering the answer to an ancient mystery. But oddly, he hadn't removed his shirt during the whole encounter.

It could have been one of those things, an urgency to couple, a desire not to interrupt the magic of the moment.

But Sara suspected it had more to do with the bullet wound he'd earned on the job. How hypocritical of him to harbor his own secrets while fuming about hers. But how comforting to know he, too, was only human.

11

A SHARP RAP on the door awakened Alec the following morning. Unfortunately it was the wrong door. Damned if he still wasn't snuggled in beside Sara. The rosebud coverlet was thrown back, and she'd entwined her legs around his in a possessive, erotic position.

How he longed to make hot love to her again, awaken her with a long, wet kiss.

But it was a dream better left to the night. He hadn't meant to be caught in the act at sunup this way. Seeing no way to escape the situation, however, he gently disengaged himself, covered up his lady love, and went to answer the door.

"Ah, Alec!" Mrs. Nesbitt whisked by him merrily, a breakfast tray in her sturdy arms. As always, her hair was neatly wrapped in a double-braid coronet, and she was dressed in a floral housedress that was both pretty and practical. He gave her extra credit for not appearing the least bit judgmental.

"I must've fallen asleep in here," he hastened to explain, tugging at his shirt and pants as he followed her over to the bed. Sara was just coming to, struggling to sit up against a fluffy pillow. She greeted them with a self-conscious croak.

Mrs. Nesbitt unfolded the legs beneath the tray and set it on Sara's lap. It was then that Alec noted the two place settings. She couldn't have known he'd be here...could she?

The innkeeper noted his surprise. "I heard Rosie's fussing last night. Heard your rap on the door, and the pacing round." She raised a hand to quell Sara's apologetic gasp. "Didn't disturb me, dears. I'm just glad you sorted things out for the wee one."

Alec curved an arm around Mrs. Nesbitt's padded shoulders and planted a kiss on her rouged cheek. "You are a gem."

"You are right." Mrs. Nesbitt's round face beamed. "Now eat up, before the food gets cold."

"You're in here again? Already?" Timothy came racing through the door in a sweatshirt and dungarees, but stopped short at the sight of Alec sliding back onto the bed within reach of the tray.

Alec accepted coffee from Sara. "Yep, called in to calm Rosie."

The young redhead thrust his chest out. "I could've done that."

So true. Alec and Sara shared a knowing smile over their blue-and-white ceramic cups. Armed with one of his adventure novels, Timothy most certainly could have droned a lullaby equal to Alec's.

"I have good news for you all," Alec announced. "Sara and Rosie are definitely staying through Christmas."

"Hot dog!" Timothy yelped and tore around the room, waking up Rosie in her drawer nest. He promptly picked the child up and cuddled her close. "Oh, don't cry, sweetie. But you're gonna stay. Isn't that swell?"

Sara was about to intervene when Mrs. Nesbitt took over, relieving Timothy of his cranky little bundle. Rosie immediately quieted in the old woman's arms. "I'll just take her down to the kitchen. Tim can bring her diaper bag."

Sara swallowed a forkful of egg. "Are you sure?"

"Definitely." Mrs. Nesbitt headed for the door, herding Timothy along. "You just carry on—with breakfast, that is!"

Timothy stood in the doorway for a minute, his freckled face hopeful. "Anybody interested in making a snowman? It's a real fine day today."

"I am," Alec volunteered. "I'll be down soon."

"I'm afraid I can't," Sara apologized. "I'm styling hair this morning for any and all comers."

"You don't have to," Mrs. Nesbitt told her, but it was obvious she was excited.

"Oh, but it's my gift to all of you. And Christmas Eve is tomorrow, so there's no time to waste."

"Wait till I tell Camille!" Mrs. Nesbitt rejoiced then thumped the door closed.

Alec slowly buttered a slice of toast and sank his teeth into it. "Do, you really style hair for a living?"

Sara glared as though she'd like to sink her teeth into him! "Yes," she said evenly, inspecting his short, precise cut. "You'd be amazed at what I can do, even with that short mop of yours."

Alec gobbled up his egg and slurped his coffee, as nervous as she'd ever seen him. "No offense, but I have this barber back in Chicago. Runs a nice little place off Michigan Avenue. Why, he'd consider it an act of adultery to let anyone else loose on my head." He scrambled off the bed, reflexively checking his hair in the mirror over the highboy. "I'm going to bathe and shave before old Lyle takes over the bathroom. If you need anything...guess you'll find me outside."

Sara laughed him off, but grew pensive once he was gone. She set the tray aside and drew her knees to her chest with a thoughtful frown. It all seemed like a fairy tale, Alec wanting her so very much, adoring Rosie to boot! How many men would have begged her to stay in these circumstances, *after* she'd given in to his advances?

· Still, this stopover could spoil everything.

But she was already behind schedule, wasn't she? A few more days couldn't hurt. Then she'd be back on the road as Kelly Hutton, charging up a proverbial storm, from here to Miami.

"C'MON, ALEC!"

"I am, Tim, I am!" Alec stepped out onto the front porch an hour later and looked around in wonder. The scene was right off a Christmas card—the acres of rolling white land, the winding driveway, the split rail fencing, all bathed in the mid-morning light.

The boy, dressed in a navy blue hooded suit, with red mittens and scarf, was struggling to push a huge boulder of snow over the ground to make it even larger. Alec ran out to the yard to help, and suggested they build the snowman near the parlor's bay window, so everyone could admire it from the seat inside.

They worked feverishly but quietly for a while. It was clear to Alec that Timothy was having the time of his life and he was glad he'd been shaken out of his brooding mood to enjoy the boy's company.

When they had the snowman's body constructed, three nearly round blocks of snow stacked atop one another, they decided to take a break. Circling their handiwork, they punched each other on the arm. Soon they were wrestling in the snow like pups, making snow angels, tossing snowballs.

"Too bad Sara couldn't come out and play," Timothy said breathlessly, staggering over to pat the snowman. "But I 'spose this was a man-sized job."

"Yeah, and you could burp as much as you wanted," Alec teased.

"Yeah." Timothy laughed, then added. "But she's a dish, ain't she?"

"She is a dish," Alec confirmed with a nod.

"A fella could do worse."

Alec raised his brows in mild surprise. "Guess he could."

Timothy sidled closer. "That's what my mom said about you. Alec Wagner could do worse. Even if that poor little dame's on the lam, he could do worse."

"I agree." He cringed at the idea that the Cozy Inn residents were all watching the romance bloom, and were speculating about Sara's predicament just as he was. Oh, how this place needed a television—even a radio! "It's good to know that Martha—your mother—knows how to pick 'em.

Won't be long before you'll be ready for matrimony. What are you...ten?"

Timothy packed some loose snow between the snowman's rounded layers, serious despite Alec's jovial tone. "I'm not going to get married. I'm going to be a physician, a healer."

Alec asked him if the redheaded doctor he'd run into at the bookstore was a relation, but the boy claimed he didn't know the man. Alec was surprised, but didn't press the issue. Instead he offered to go back into the house for some vegetables to fill out the snowman's face.

The boy readily agreed, but cautioned, "Better go round back."

"Through the drifts?"

"Snow's not so deep between the house and the snow fence."

"It's pretty deep," Alec insisted.

"Mrs. Nesbitt doesn't like a mess tracked in her foyer," Timothy warned in a singsong voice.

It turned out Mrs. Nesbitt didn't want snow on her kitchen floor, either. The moment he entered the service porch, she briskly directed Alec to remove his boots before entering the kitchen, dust his pant legs, too. He meekly obeyed, then dipped through the kitchen doorway to find a hen party in progress. Sara was in the process of cutting Martha Doanes's hair in a short bob. Martha was seated on a stool with a towel draped over her chest and Sara was circling and snipping, sending tufts of orange hair falling to the floor.

Definitely a no-man's-land.

"My boots wouldn't have made as much mess," Alec joked.

Mrs. Nesbitt paused, with hands planted on her ample hips. "I will decide the kind of messes I want to clean up, Alec Wagner!"

Alec stripped off his gloves, watching Sara at work with scissors and comb. She certainly did know what she was doing. So her claim to being a stylist was the truth. He was very glad. It was one more fact to slip into his mental file, one less lie told him.

She was so delectable in her pale blue sweatsuit, with her auburn tresses tied in a high ponytail, that he wanted to scoop her up and off to bed that instant. Or at the very least steal a kiss. She was standing under the mistletoe, after all.

He was startled when Sara met his gaze suddenly, drilling him with shrewd, triumphant eyes, as if she'd read his thoughts concerning her hairstyling skill. But he was the one who'd been begging for the truth from the start. He was the one who could justify anger here—not her!

"So, Alec, what do you want *exactly?*"

It was Mrs. Nesbitt who finally asked, her face pinched in impatience. Alec quickly explained about the snowman's empty face.

Together they searched the contents of the old icebox, and decided on a carrot for the nose and two apples for the eyes. The mouth took more imagination. Mrs. Nesbitt rifled through the cupboard and came up with a licorice whip. Alec stuffed the produce into his pocket and extended a hand for the candy.

"Make sure Tim doesn't eat it," she warned, slapping the whip in his hand. "It's stale."

Alec gave his solemn word, tempted to eat the candy himself. He hoped lunch wouldn't be late because of this salon work.

The swinging door bounced open just as Alec was putting on his gloves and Camille came bursting through with her curls newly trimmed, a dressed and pert Rosie in her arms. "A visitor for you, Alec. At least I think it's for you...."

"Who?"

"Someone from the Pump-U-Serve. He's standing outside, by his truck."

Alec grimaced. If only he'd been outside, Sara wouldn't have even noticed Hal's visit. Now she'd expect news of her car. "Oh, yes," he said pleasantly, "that would be for me."

"What does he want?" Camille asked.

Sara whirled excitedly. "A report on the Lincoln, I bet. I should speak to him personally."

A round of protest rose from the ladies in the kitchen. Sara was busy, they objected. She couldn't stop now. Besides, she was staying for Christmas and didn't need the car.

Taking advantage of Sara's indecision, Alec flicked her ponytail and stole a kiss from her pursed lips. "I'll handle it," he said, then thinking of his boots and the trip back around the house, added, "It would be easier if he just came into the foyer for a minute."

The statement was a question posed to Mrs. Nesbitt. She smiled thinly at him. "Whatever you think best."

"You don't mind, do you?"

"No, dear, this is an inn, we welcome guests around here." The old woman swatted his rear end with her wooden spoon. "Now scram!"

Alec was propelled into the hallway on a chorus of mocking feminine laughter. Their teasing bruised his ego a bit, but their attitude was a lucky break. Sara was too tied up to corner Hal. And Hal wouldn't have news of her car, he'd have a fax all about her.

Alec opened the front door to find the tall, blond attendant keeping vigil by his green tow truck, dressed in his coveralls, a stocking hat on his head. "Hal! Come in!"

The man motioned for Alec to come over. "Naw, you come out."

Alec pointed to his socks. "*You* come in!"

Hal shrugged, gesturing to his soiled coveralls and snowy boots. Alec surrendered, holding up splayed fingers to signal five minutes. He rushed through the kitchen to more feminine laughter, rescued his boots and dashed back around the house.

Snow crunched under Alec's feet as he trotted up to the truck. He scanned the front yard for Timothy and caught sight of the boy charging through the drifts around the opposite side of the house.

"Looks like you've been busy," Hal teased, gesturing to the snowman and the batch of angels imprinted in the snow.

"Yeah, sure. You saw the boy. Doing it for his sake."

"Boy?"

Hal looked genuinely bewildered, but Alec didn't pursue the question. "Did a fax from Jennifer come through?" he asked eagerly.

"It did." Hal reached into his half-zipped coveralls and produced a white sheet of paper folded in two.

Alec snatched it away and quickly scanned its contents.

"Not too good, is it?"

Alec raised a sharp eye to the attendant.

Hal kicked some snow with the toe of his boot. "I mean, Leslie over at the café told me what a nice woman she is, and well, I hate to see her in this kind of trouble."

Alec's expression grew stern. "Did you tell Leslie or anyone else about this?"

"Well...only Leslie. We're pretty close. Lifelong friends. But nobody else, not even Dad."

Alec exhaled, reining in his temper. Hal was a good guy, no sense taking anything out on him. Naturally he'd be intrigued by the report.

So there *was* a Kelly Hutton, just as he'd feared. She was a jet-setter Seattle lumber heiress, spoiled and immature, habitually in scrapes. Her biggest mistake to date was involving herself with a mobster named Mel Slade.

Alec had heard of old man Hutton and of Slade. Hutton was clean, but Slade certainly wasn't. Prosperous land investor on the surface, Slade was a clever racketeer who ran a series of illegal investment schemes from coast to coast. The Bureau was presently building a case against him for bilking a group of speculators out of millions through some nonexistent land-development scheme. What mattered most right now, though, was that Slade went through women like bars of soap, wore them down to nothing, then threw them away.

He squeezed his eyes shut, tormented by visions of Sara with Slade. How *could* she? But those things happened all the time. Young, vulnerable women in the clutches of hoods.

Had Slade bought her that exquisite peach negligée? The mere idea was horrific torture. Slade's hands on her where his had been. And more. Much, much more.

The only sign of his faltering control was the twitch of his eyelids as he read on. Apparently Kelly was a unique case to Slade. According to Jennifer's probe, informants reported that after a two-year relationship, Slade wanted Kelly for keeps and she'd grown tired of him. Several days ago Kelly had disappeared, and so had Slade.

He wondered what the odds were that Slade was at this moment someplace in Wisconsin, too, closing in on his obsession? And her child?

Was precious Rosie Slade's child? The idea made Alec sick to his stomach. This report said Kelly had no children, though. That raised another question. Where had the baby come from? Bought for companionship, perhaps, in her new life? The rich sometimes thought money could cure anything.

The whole thing had to be a mistake! Could Sara really be Kelly, in cahoots with a creep like Slade for two whole years?

He thought back on her telephone call at the café. He hadn't heard much, but had gotten the impression that she'd been reporting to somebody. Somebody who was helping her run? Sounded like it. The twenty-five grand in the suitcase could mean a fresh start someplace. The Huttons were loaded, everyone in the nation knew that, with the patriarch a regular on the cover of all the business magazines. Perhaps Kelly had kept the money on her, intending to hide out for awhile.

But a man like Slade wouldn't go away, and twenty-five

grand wouldn't last long in the hands of an adventurous debutante like Kelly Hutton, Alec realized.

Despite this new information, Alec couldn't stop hoping for the best. Maybe Kelly had given birth to Rosie in secret and was trying to change her ways. That would be a noble beginning. Again he thought about the modest clothing Sara and Rosie had, her initial shyness in making love to him. Not Slade's kind of woman, surely.

Maybe he had it all wrong. He was a trained investigator, but he was so dazzled by the lady and child it seemed he couldn't think straight.

Alec's eyes fell to the paper again. Damn, Sara even fit Kelly's general description. Average height, blond hair, gunmetal-gray eyes. And the company credit card he'd found was on the level, issued through Hutton Enterprises. It had not been reported stolen. The bank was honoring all charges on it.

But was his saucy Frosty really this outrageous woman? His woman's eyes were more dove than gunmetal, with the prettiest green flecks. A question of semantics at best, he supposed.

If only she weren't so tough. If only she'd broken down in bed and told him everything. But no, she'd kept her wits about her; Rosie's fussiness was her most noticeable weakness. He crumpled the paper in his fist. It was possible to be too brave for your own good. She wasn't frightened enough of Mel Slade.

Or of him for that matter.

"Any reply, Alec?"

Alec started at the sound of Hal's easy midwestern twang. So lost in his troubles, he'd forgotten the garage attendant. "You got a paper?" Hal reached into the truck for his clipboard and adjusted a fresh sheet at the top. Alec carefully printed out a message of thanks to Jennifer and the directive to track Slade's present whereabouts at all costs.

"What about Kelly Hutton? Don't you want positive proof about her location?"

Alec heaved a giant sigh. "No, Hal, that doesn't seem necessary. I'd say it's more than clear that Kelly Hutton is right here with me at the Cozy Rest."

ALEC HADN'T BEEN the same since he'd barged in on their hairstyling session. Sara made the deduction later on that afternoon after settling in the parlor window seat with Rosie to watch him and Timothy build a second snowman. They hadn't even come in for lunch. She could understand the boy's gusto, but not Alec's. He didn't seem especially happy being outside anymore. And he refused to meet her gaze through the glass.

Had he changed his mind about her? Did he hope she'd leave after all? She could be a memory in short order. Give her her car in working order and she could be gone in a flash.

With a sigh, she cuddled Rosie close, revelling in her downy softness. It would be horribly tough to leave the comfort and security of the Cozy Rest, but if she wasn't wanted...

These were the things on her mind as Alec passed by the parlor doorway around three o'clock, soaked, flushed, and weary. Simmering with insecurity and distress, she called out to him. "Oh, Alec?"

Alec paused stiffly in the doorway, ruffling his damp hair. It stood up like a boy's. But the appealing image was spoiled by the rigid set of his jaw.

"What did Hal have to say about my car?"

"Hasn't gotten to it yet."

"But surely if you told him to step on it..."

Alec folded his arms across his expansive chest. "But I didn't. Told him you intended to stay, so there was definitely no rush on it."

Her eyes fell as she stroked Rosie's head. "Oh. I thought maybe you'd changed your mind, Alec."

"About what?"

"About wanting me to stay." She stared him down, hoping he'd reassure her with a repeat of last night's tenderness. To her dismay, his mouth split in a cold smile.

"Wouldn't dream of letting you out of my sight."

"So glad you care."

"Don't mention it."

All in all, she was so sorry that she had.

MRS. NESBITT WAS BAKING some sweet rolls that evening for Christmas dinner and suggested it would be the perfect time to bathe Rosie again, while the kitchen was warm.

The whole crew seemed to be on hand when Sara appeared with the baby and her gear. Everyone but Alec, that is.

Perhaps she was the biggest fool on earth, but she was having withdrawal symptoms. Hours had passed since their last terse exchange. He'd skipped supper, opting for a tray in his room. Timothy had been up to play cards with him for a while, but she'd checked minutes ago to find the bedroom empty. Tim was presently seated at the table munching on a bowl of Mrs. Nesbitt's home-cooked cranberry sauce.

The ladies quickly took charge of Rosie. Sara stood back and joined in the light conversation as they ran water in the sink and undressed the child. Finally she summoned the nerve to ask after Alec. Before she knew what was happening, Beatrice Nesbitt was bundling her into a green parka and sending her out to the barn with a lantern to light the way.

"FUNNY PLACE for a city boy."

Alec was standing over by the horse stalls when Sara revealed her presence. The barn was aglow with lanterns and moonlight, alive with animal sounds. She was half-sure she'd heard the echo of his voice, too, as though he'd been talking to Sugar and Spice.

He was saying nothing now as he leaned against a plank wall. She felt as welcome as a midwestern blizzard.

"I know you're the type to sulk on your own," she continued, swinging her lantern as she moved in closer. "But I'm not, Alec. I hate being alone."

"I'm not sulking."

"Oh, c'mon..." She paused, refocusing on more important things. "Look, there are some things I want to explain to you. Please."

"Oh?" His heart swelled with pleasure and relief. He charged over to her, took the lantern from her hands and set it on the ground. "Come over here, sit with me." He took hold of her arm.

"In a pile of hay," she said wryly.

"Sure. Great place for a roll."

She sagged in his grip. "Alec..."

"You're shaking," he said. "Come, sit down."

She collapsed beside him in the crunchy bed of dried grass and clover. They sat with shoulders touching. His feet were planted on the ground, hers didn't quite make it. "I've been turning things over in my mind and I think I know exactly why you're upset."

Alec studied his large, callused hands in the shadows. "Why?"

"Oh, I want to trust you with this, but..."

He snagged her chin in his hand, forcing eye-to-eye contact. "You can trust me, all the way."

"Okay. I've come to realize that I must've been a disappointment last night." Her throat tightened with dust, animal scents, and misery; she coughed to clear it. "As a lover."

"Oh, c'mon!" he thundered, dropping his hand from her face.

She gasped in surprise. "Don't be afraid to admit it."

He made a seething sound through his teeth. "I cannot believe this is your confidence."

"It's the only thing that's happened between us," she reasoned stubbornly. "There are no other changes to explain your brush-off. I thought if I cleared the air.... You see, I haven't made love with a man since before I gave birth to Rosie. That would make it close to nine months or so. And I'm a little padded in places, have a few stretch marks on my belly. The sentiment was there, in my heart, but I am out of shape, out of practice."

As if he'd ever want her to practice with anybody else. Alec's arms, resting on his knees, began to quake as her words sank in. She actually thought he was angry because she hadn't performed well in bed. He'd been so dazzled by her sensuality that he hadn't thought much of the small fan of creases below her navel, or the flare of her hips, or the ease with which he'd entered her.

All these things did verify motherhood, he realized. So she had given birth to Rosie. Thank goodness! One mystery solved. But was it Mel Slade's baby? How could she have been so foolish? How could she hope to shake him now, on this silly road trip?

His stoic front made her cry out in fury. "I should've known we were too far apart in experience to be good together. But you made some pretty bold moves to make it happen. Surely you must've known I might not be Venus?"

His eyes crinkled at the corners. "Quite honestly, honey, I was completely satisfied. Didn't I beg you to stay on at the inn when it was over?"

Relief softened her features. "Yes, I did wonder about that. A logical man being so fickle."

"Well, you've got it all wrong. Venus has nothin' on you." Alec laughed over the absurdity of it all.

She gasped, her expression changing shape in the shadows. There was a long pause before she spoke. "Oops, it seems I jumped to the wrong conclusion, then, doesn't it?"

"Absolutely." As angry as he was over her charade, he couldn't help softening his stand. She truly cared for him and wanted to please him.

Sara stared at him curiously as he caressed her temples, all the more mystified by his annoyance with her. "I must say I'm relieved and embarrassed all at once."

"Well, I for one, am just relieved," he confided.

"Why on earth..."

"There are so many questions I have concerning you, honey, but knowing that Rosie is really yours, is a great start."

She slapped his hand away, her eyes growing in amazement. "That she's *really* mine? What else did you think?"

He reared back a little. "I dunno. I thought maybe she was stolen, or purchased—"

Her gasp of sheer affront cut him short. "You're horrible!"

He was? He didn't feel that way. Hadn't expected this kind of response. "Think about it," he urged anxiously. "You don't handle her very well. Can you really blame me for wondering?"

"You had no right to wonder." She sputtered in rage. "Rosie is my flesh and blood—my baby!"

He took a nervous breath, completely unsettled by her vehemence. "I'm thrilled, of course. But you can understand my position, with all your secrets."

"Not so many secrets. And none of them concern you, Alec." Her mouth fell in disappointment. "I thought you accepted me as is. Trusted me on it."

"You did sound frightened on the telephone back at the café."

"Again, that's *my* private business! You just—" She burst into tears, keeping him at bay with a wave. "You shouldn't have doubted me about Rosie. Anything but that."

He felt like a grade-A heel, but wasn't accustomed to backing down. "You do handle her awkwardly," he insisted.

"You know, with that kind of tunnel reasoning, you are better off demoted."

"Not demoted, not demoted. Retired is the word. Just because you confuse names and things about yourself, *Kelly*, don't pull it on me."

"Kelly?" The name was dipped in acid on her tongue. "I'm suddenly Kelly now, for certain? I told you I'm Sara, trusted you believed at least that much."

"Don't know what to believe anymore," he admitted. "Not since Hal brought me the fax..."

"I thought he came to report on my car."

"No, I told him yesterday to stall the job. I'd contacted a friend at the Bureau and a reply had come in."

She sat up stiffly, her eyes shimmering with defiant tears. "Just what do you think you know, Alec?"

"More than I'd like." His profile was granite. "I half wish now that I'd left it all alone, but felt a moral obligation to check you out."

"That's a ridiculous excuse."

"Well, what if Rosie weren't yours? What if you were in some other big jam? It was tough, with my feelings for you growing so fast. But I was prepared to help, no matter what," he reminded her with a jabbing finger.

"How kind."

"It *was* kind, from my point of view. I was upset by the news I got, but I also kept the faith that you are a good-hearted woman. You could see how thrilled I was when you announced you wanted to talk. I want to help you through this. My faith in you stands firm."

"Gee, thanks. You run a check on me by day and seduce me by night. I'd say you had me under lock and key just in case it got ugly."

"Fill in the rest of the blanks for me," he pleaded suddenly. "Help me understand."

"Can't imagine why I should. Kelly's not wanted by the law, is she?"

"No."

Smugness flickered in her eyes. "I'd say you did only half

your job. Obviously you didn't bother to check up on Sara Jameson."

He prickled defensively. "How do you know I didn't?"

"Because you're behaving like a complete moron, that's why. Because you'd really have all the answers if you had. You're such an arrogant cuss, Alec. Isn't it true that you passed on the opportunity to check on Sara because you're so sure she doesn't exist?"

He couldn't deny it. "Once I found the credit card in Kelly's name, it didn't seem necessary. And the fax today confirmed your obvious trail. The Huttons are honoring your charges on that company card." He swung her back on the hay, crushing her with his weight. "Why would they do that for anyone but Kelly?"

"You wrote off Sara Jameson because her name wasn't on a stinking credit card. After I told you over and over that I am Sara."

They were so close their noses were touching, their hearts pounding in one furious crescendo.

"Even your suitcases bear the initials K.H."

"Oh, shut up, Alec. All the barking in the world isn't going to make you right. For the last time, I'm *not* Kelly Hutton." She sighed hard. "You blew this thing between us big-time. We would've been much better off if you'd taken my story at face value, believed in *me*."

"Guess you can't take the investigator out of the retiree."

"Aw, you've been hiding behind your old badge through this whole thing. Collecting facts on me, spying on me, judging me on the excuse that I'm a case needing attention. Don't you see if you'd just let go and loved me, we would've made it? Even your stupidity over Rosie's parentage wouldn't have gone unnoticed. If you'd just kept your mouth shut and waited, the truth would've fallen into place."

He leaned closer, pressing her back on the hay, hoping to intimidate her with his body weight. "Tell me what's going on. Right now. Everything!"

She pressed her nose petulantly up under his. "No. You don't deserve it and I've made a bargain to keep quiet." With a knee jab to his inner thigh she caught him off balance, and rolled out of reach. She was on her feet with lightning speed, picking up her lantern and stalked across the barn.

"This isn't over, Sara!"

She shook her fist, shouting into space. "Now he gets the name right! Ugh!"

12

ALEC WENT TO BED that night with Frosty's parting words ringing in his ears. Yes, he'd gotten the name right in the end. Sara. She'd given him no valid reasons for her situation, but there'd been no doubt that she was telling the truth.

In his own defense, he'd gotten it right earlier, too, when it really counted, at the height of orgasmic release. Surely she remembered that!

But in a way, Alec figured it only made his screwup all the worse. His gut instinct had steered him right from the very start, had told him Sara was a wonderful woman who adored Rosie as a mother should. He should have behaved just as she'd said, soft-pedaled his doubts, kept them to himself.

If only he could rewind the tape of the last few days and give her more faith, as the Nesbitt sisters had advised him to do.

That was another thing that pained him. Even Beatrice and Camille had been able to see and trust Sara's good qualities.

So why hadn't he gone with the flow and let things evolve?

Because old on-the-job habits were tough to break. He'd have been dead long ago if he'd fallen for pretty lies and acted upon wishful thinking.

Still, she should have been the exception.

If only he hadn't been so afraid of the feelings she stirred up in him, he wouldn't have used his profession as a smoke-screen for his interest. She'd had every right to chew him out. He had analyzed her mysteries for his own benefit. Made her his case, when in fact, he should just have let nature take its course. Surely everything would have come out in the end.

Then she would never have known of his doubts about Rosie. Unfortunately that had cut her deeper than he'd ever imagined it could. But he didn't know much about motherhood. And some mothers weren't so touchy about ownership. His own mother had abandoned him and his sisters whenever a half-eligible man picked her up in a bar.

Amazingly, Mrs. Nesbitt was the first real, live caregiver he'd ever felt close to. Beatrice Nesbitt, and Sara, under one roof—what a Christmas it could've been.

To think the confrontation in the barn had started out with her mistaking his ire for sexual disappointment. As lousy a detective as he was, she'd make a much worse one! He hadn't seduced her as she claimed, he'd surrendered to her magic, climbed into heaven for a hot, brief moment.

The woman was dynamite and didn't even know it.

How could he help but fall in love?

Ironically, accepting his certain love for Sara only heightened his sense of responsibility. He couldn't stop the facts from looping through his brain in search of a logical pattern. No matter that Sara was not Mel Slade's girl, Slade was still involved, and therefore a danger. The whole setup, Sara on the road with a bag of cash, charging things on a Hutton credit card, suggested that she was impersonating Kelly, leaving a false trail. For Slade's benefit?

Didn't Sara realize how dangerous a game she was playing?

Of course she didn't! For some reason she didn't.

The watch on the nightstand read 3:10. He considered waking her up, but that might waken the baby, probably the entire household. He'd set her straight first thing in the morning. That settled, he floated off to sleep.

"THERE HE IS, Miz Bea." Timothy's voice was a hiss of fear that echoed through the foyer as Alec stalked down the stairs

Christmas Eve morning.

Mrs. Nesbitt wiped her hands on her apron and gave the boy a gentle push. "Go have your breakfast, Tim."

Alec reached the foyer and stood buttoning the cuffs of his blue denim shirt by touch, his eyes never leaving the innkeeper. "What's up?"

Her ample bosom rose and fell beneath her paisley-print dress, her round face crinkled in unmistakable concern. "I have some news for you."

His large mouth curled sardonically. "Is it good news?"

"No," she said regretfully, biting her lip.

"C'mon, now, give."

"Very well. Sara left on the sleigh about thirty minutes ago."

"Huh!" His voice exploded like a crack of thunder. "Why didn't you wake me? You love doing that, for Pete's sake! You live for it!"

"I didn't know it was happening. I was upstairs in the sewing room wrapping a few presents." She set a plump hand on his arm. "Timothy helped her. He didn't know any better."

"Sara shouldn't be alone on the street. There are some real complications..." He trailed off waving a hand that ultimately landed on his brow. "Did she say what she was up to? Shopping?"

Mrs. Nesbitt hesitated. "It's a sure thing she's left for good. She had baggage and car seat in tow."

"She can't! It's not safe!" He whirled around thinking furiously. "Get me a parka and hat—and gloves."

Mrs. Nesbitt wrung her hands. "How will you get to town without the sleigh, Alec? Sugar's still here, I suppose, but she's so skittish in town—"

"Never mind. I'll walk, try to hitch a ride."

Alec did manage to catch a ride about a mile down the road, in a big, brown parcel-service truck on its way to Elm

City. As they rolled by the park again, he spotted the sleigh hitched up near the bronze statue of George Washington. At least Sara had made it this far. He took the truck as far as the Pump-U-Serve. Reliable Hal was big as life behind the counter, ringing up a purchase on the cash register for a teenager, the probable owner of a souped-up T-Bird parked out by the twin pumps.

Alec stalked round the station, anxiously waiting his turn. He peered back into the work area, grateful to see that the Lincoln was still there. He hustled back to the counter as the teen left.

"So, Hal." Alec rapped his knuckles on the worn Formica counter.

The blond man smiled, rubbing some grease off his chin with a handkerchief. "Just coming out to the inn for you, Alec."

His heart lurched. "What's happening? You seen Sara?"

"You mean Kelly?"

A trace of humor touched his mouth. "Well, Sara—Kelly to you, I guess."

"She's here in town, waiting for her car. Came in while I was delivering the sheriff his car. He's running late to his sister's and was in an awful rush."

"So who's in charge of law and order when the sheriff's away?"

Hal grinned. "Me. I'm a deputy. Naturally, this time of year, in rural country like this, the biggest hassle is the rash of Christmas Eve snowball fights."

Alec smiled tightly.

"Anyhow, about Sara-Kelly. Sorry she got to the bottom of our secret to hold the Lincoln hostage. If I'd been here I might have been able to stall her longer." He aimed a thumb back at the work area. "But Dad, who didn't know beans about it all, took a look at my work order for the car and promised he'd get her back on the road by noon. He was just writing up a credit-card slip when I walked in."

"Credit card?"

Faced with Alec's dark look he hastily added, "I sent Dad away, then, and explained to the lady that it was all taken care of by you."

Alec's exhaled in relief. "Where was she headed?"

"Leslie's. But before you hightail it outta here, I have to give you a fax."

Alec nearly jumped the chest-high counter. "Why didn't you say so right off?"

Hal moved toward his desk with aggravating deliberateness. "I was getting to it."

Alec settled back on his heels. "Sorry. It's not like me to lose my cool."

"The right girl can to do that to a man."

"Yeah." Alec took the sheet of paper Hal held out to him and scanned its contents. Jennifer had checked up on Mel Slade. He was on the rampage. He'd busted up the Super 8 Motel in Madison the other night, looking for Kelly Hutton.

That cinched things in Alec's mind. Sara had been set up as a decoy by the Huttons! And poor little Rosie was along for the ride. The rest of the message was rather cryptic for security reasons, but Alec understood that the Bureau was finally ready to move in on Slade if they could locate him.

Alec knew they'd love to use the Cozy Rest Inn as a trap for the hoodlum and Sara as the juicy bait. But he wasn't going to allow that to happen. He wouldn't mind donating his services to help nab the creep in the weeks to come, but Sara and Rosie had to be out of harm's way. Slade couldn't trace Sara here and he was determined to see that he didn't.

Alec thanked Hal and asked him to keep in touch.

"About the Lincoln, Alec—"

"With any luck it won't be leaving the garage just yet."

"So if I don't hear from you within the hour, you'll both be aboard the sleigh again?"

"Right." Alec smiled for the first time that day and saluted as he walked out the door. His grin was almost goofy with joy as he jogged the block to the main drag. It was going to be okay. As long as no credits went through on Kelly's account, Slade would never find them in this tiny town. Their Christmas was still on course, if Sara would let it happen.

HE FOUND SARA in the café. The place was nearly empty and she was seated in the back booth again with Rosie in her lap. She was facing the door and spotted him immediately.

He almost laughed out loud. With all her stuff piled high on the empty bench, she was actually looking around, as though searching for a means of escape! If he had his way, she'd never leave his sight again.

The only available seating space was right beside the girls, so Alec shoved in beside them, touching hips with Sara. She didn't acknowledge him, just kept her eyes aimed steadily ahead.

"You didn't even wait to say goodbye," he ventured.

"Goodbye, Alec."

"Look, Sara, I don't want to upset you."

"Then don't."

"We have to talk."

"I'm through talking to you."

"Okay, then listen. I've figured this thing out—most of it, anyway." He paused, giving her a chance to jump in. She took a sip of fruit juice instead, dribbling some into Rosie's mouth as well. "Kelly Hutton hired you to impersonate her on this road trip of yours, didn't she?"

"No law against that."

"No. I figure she paid you the twenty-five grand—"

"You searched my luggage!" She turned to him then, her eyes dark with anger.

"Yes. I hope you can just forgive and forget that," he said mildly. "The main issues are so very important." She made a snorting sound that made even Rosie start. "Why are you doing this gig, Sara?" He was again met by a stony silence. "Would it make any difference if I told you that Mel Slade is in the deepest trouble of his life? That the Bureau is ready to close in?"

"Makes no difference to me," she said coolly. "I've never heard of the man."

It was Alec's turn to snort. "Time's running out. You must tell me everything."

"I have a handle on things."

"Do you? What would possess you to drag Rosie around at this time of year in the first place? Put her in danger—"

"I didn't think there was any danger!" She paused, thinking back on her last call to Kelly. "And I'm still not sure there is."

"We're talking grave danger if you go on, especially if you're using Kelly's credit card."

She flinched under Alec's granite stare. "Okay. First of all, I'm doing this for *fifty* grand," she clarified in a defensive whisper. "Half in advance and half upon completion of the trip. I know it's dangerous to carry the money around, but there wasn't time to stow it anyplace back in Seattle, and Kelly didn't give it to me until the last minute."

"How did you ever hook up with a woman of her means in the first place?"

"Kelly and I met at a fitness center back home. She likes to keep toned, and I was...recuperating. Anyway, we struck up a conversation because we look quite alike. That's all we ever had in common, really. Her being a rich Hutton, and me being a poor widow."

"Recuperating? Widow?" Alec was shellshocked by the news.

"Yes." She took a deep breath, her expression reflecting her pain. "Anyway, within weeks she knew all about my circumstances— You see, I lost my husband Ethan shortly after Rosie's birth," she said in a small voice. "We were rock climbing in Mount Rainier National Park. Some stone gave way, we both slipped." She stopped and swallowed. "I was lucky—if you can call it that—to get caught up in some brush

on the way down. Ethan fell several hundred feet into a ra-
vine, broke his neck. Died instantly, they said."

"How horrible."

"Yes." She paused, her chin wobbling as painful memories assailed her. "Our marriage wasn't perfection, but we
were...fond of each other. Ethan was less adventurous than I,
more the studious type, a professor at a small college. It was
a nice life. Quiet and secure." She trembled and Alec put his
arm around her shoulders and pulled her closer. "Anyway, I
was hurt too. Busted collarbone, fractured hip, concussion. I
was laid up for a long time."

"Rosie..." Alec gave the child's fair hair a gentle ruffle.

"My sister looked after her while I was recovering. I had
contact with the baby, but was apart from her day-to-day
care. That's why I'm so clumsy at it, Alec. It'll take time to
build up my strength, get wise to Rosie's tricks and moods.
But she is mine—all mine!"

Alec blanched. "I wish I'd known."

"I made a bargain with Kelly not to tell anyone who I was,
or to travel with anyone."

"You cheated by bringing Rosie. So..." His eyes held a sad
plea.

"Why not cheat a little more and spill it to you?"

Alec nodded solemnly, thinking of the time he'd wasted
envisioning Slade with Sara, Sara in that peach negligée.

"Rosie was the only exception I thought it fair to make. I
couldn't bear to be apart from her any longer than I had
been. Otherwise, I followed instructions to the letter, making
the trip in her beautiful car, sticking to the itinerary she
mapped out, leaving the credit-card trail each stop. It was a
pretty sweet deal," she insisted, "all expenses paid on top of
the salary. And boy, do we need money for a fresh start,
Alec. Ethan's insurance covered my medical bills, but Rosie
and I have nothing more."

"The wisest thing to do is to call Kelly Hutton this instant
and tell her you're out."

"And give back the money?"

"If you must. Though she owes it to you already—for danger pay!"

"But I don't understand about this Slade. Who is he?"

Alec frowned. "First tell me what reason she gave you for this farce?"

"Reporters, she said. Kelly has a new love and wanted to spend the holidays with him, get the romantic fires going before the press invaded and spoiled things. Seemed straightforward and sincere. I figured any newshounds who got too close would see I was the wrong woman and back off. The idea was to keep one step ahead of them, keep them sniffing at the wrong trail."

Alec kissed her cheek and buried his face in her fragrant hair for a brief moment. "She lied. I'm sorry."

Sara wrenched free of him. "No way, I met her boyfriend. And I've been calling her at his Aspen home."

"She lied about the *press* being involved," he specified. "This Mel Slade is her real problem. She probably did want the heat off temporarily in order to ignite her new romance, but it's obvious that she wasn't thinking beyond Christmas, and cared nothing for your safety."

"She did seem more frightened during our last call."

"With good reason. You're a sitting duck, stalled in one spot."

"Who is this man?"

He hated to tell her, but making sure she finally understood the seriousness of the situation was paramount. "Slade's an old lover who's having trouble letting go. He's violent, into crime, and currently wanted by the Bureau. It's hard to say what Kelly thought Slade would do if he caught up to you, but it was a horrible risk to take, putting you in jeopardy the way she did."

"And I in turn brought Rosie into it!" She choked back a sob and hugged the baby so close Rosie squealed in protest.

With his point driven home, Alec sought to comfort her

and cuddled both of them as best he could in the cramped seat. "It's going to be fine. As long as you didn't use that credit card, Slade can't possibly track you here."

Sara sniffed, her moist eyes brighter. "I didn't. Except for a near charge at the garage. I didn't think it would matter to the false trail if I charged something on my way *out* of Elm City. But the owner, a Frank—"

"I was just there and Frank's son Hal explained how he intervened."

"Oh, yes," she said with a bit of her old spirit, "it was Hal who explained how my bill was your treat."

"Just want you here for Christmas, Sara."

"I intend to stay on now," she assured him. "But your way of ensuring it was a bit too heavy-handed to say the least."

He smiled guilelessly. "Guilty of loving you is all."

"Oh, Alec." She wrinkled her nose.

"What do you mean, 'Oh, Alec'?" He imitated her wrinkle in a mocking way, but was truly dying inside. For the first time in his whole life he was thinking about forever with a woman. He couldn't imagine going on without her!

She patted his hand on the table. "I don't wish to hurt you, but I intend to make sure my next long-term relationship is absolutely right. Sizzling chemistry isn't enough, just as the security Ethan offered wasn't enough. I want both in the deal! As well as a guarantee of one-hundred-percent trust."

"I stand for all that!" He winced at her curled lip. "Most it of it, anyway. I mean—in the future we could vow to always tell each other the whole truth."

"I just can't see you laying it all on the line for me," she said apologetically. As he inhaled to protest, she gestured to their public surroundings. "And this doesn't seem like the best place for further argument."

Alec balked. They were completely alone now save for Leslie who was at the other end of the café adjusting a wreath in the window. "It's a damn sight better than the crowded inn. Please, let's not tangle there."

She sighed with great reluctance. "Okay, here it is. I don't think you can lay it on the line for me, because you can't even sort things out inside yourself."

"What things?"

Again, she hesitated. "Take your retirement."

"I chose retirement—of my own free will!"

She shook her head slowly. "I think your injury slowed you down, and your superiors noticed, yanked you off the line."

He bobbed his head. "They might have acted for that reason, sure. But things have changed since. I'm as strong as an ox again."

She held up two fingers an inch apart. "Couldn't there still be just a teensy bit of difference in your before and after abilities?"

"No," he maintained staunchly. "I've worked my way back to peak condition and now all I have to do is prove it to the Bureau. Just like I'm trying to prove my love for you." He growled in frustration. "Why won't you see it my way? I've stumbled all over the place, but I'm finally back on track."

"I appreciate the fact that you've come to terms with your feelings for me. That's a wonderful start. But I don't think you've approached the career angle with the same kind of wisdom."

"I have!" He paused, held up a hand. "Okay, maybe my retirement was premature. I was angry that they didn't see my potential for recovery. But it was awful, doing all that sitting. Me, a man of action."

"From what Mrs. Nesbitt tells me, you were completely inactive before I came along—lost, out of sorts, hibernating."

He made a rumbling sound like a cranky bear. "I woke up!"

"Yes, only to concentrate on me and *my* troubles."

"I do admit to treating you like a mystery, at first anyway. It was the excuse of a confirmed bachelor who was afraid to admit he couldn't resist your charms. That was my biggest hurdle," he claimed. "I'm over it. I'm addicted to those charms."

The compliment didn't stir her as he'd hoped. "I won't allow you to lose yourself in me without clearing up your own denials," she insisted, growing impatient. "You can't go on avoiding your limitations, Alec."

"This is unfair and ungrounded speculation. The kind you didn't approve of in me."

"It's fair enough," she said softly. "As for proof, making love with your shirt on is a fine example of where you're at emotionally."

"But it all happened so fast between us—"

"No. I tried all the excuses and only one fits. It was your scar. It's not all that unsightly and still you tried to hide it. Deny its existence."

"You peeked under my shirt?" He was mortified.

"You peeked in my suitcases, and some other intimate places." She gave him a meaningful stare. "But that's really off track anyway. What's important is that you are haunted by the past, stuck in neutral over old disappointments. Me, I'm looking ahead. I've faced a couple of the brutal facts haunting me—one, that I couldn't have prevented Ethan's accident, and two, that I've missed some of Rosie's formative months and can't possibly recapture them. I figure you see your scar as a symbol of failure. You don't want to deal with it, so therefore you try to hide it."

"You're a master of concealment yourself, Sara. How can you be so tough on me?"

She lifted a finger in protest. "Ah, but my secrets with Kelly were temporary, all part of a job. You're in deeper trouble, Alec."

"So there's no hope for us?"

"I'm just saying we'll see."

He clenched his free fist on the lime-green table. "Is it so wrong for me to expect another chance from the Bureau?"

"But would it make a difference? I'm not the only one who

gets fatigued holding Sara for great lengths of time, for instance."

"That seems like a lame example."

"On its own, maybe. But there have been lots of other instances when your spirit seemed willing, but your muscles seemed weary."

Alec loosened his grip on her shoulders and rubbed his face with both hands. How humbling this was. Logical reasoning and educated guesses had been part of his job for years. Was it possible this little angel in tennis shoes could be right? Was he denying the truth about his physical condition?

He wasn't ready to concede that, though. But at the same time, more than ever, he wanted Sara and Rosie for his own.

How could he possibly turn around her thinking, or at the very least, convince her to give their relationship a real chance?

At least he'd stopped her flight. They would still have Christmas.

Sara squeezed his hand. "Please don't be too hard on me. Or on yourself."

He blinked, hating the burning damp behind his eyelids. "Just don't say we're absolutely finished."

"I didn't and I won't. That should settle things for now."

He managed a half smile. "Just answer me one more thing would you?"

She huffed in exasperation. "What stone's left unturned?"

He looked boyishly embarrassed. "About that negligée. Where did it come from? It's even more out of place on a road trip than your tennis shoes."

Sara's eyes twinkled with some of their old merriment. "My sister gave it to me after the accident. I know it's frivolous, but it was the perfect antidote to those drab hospital gowns I was stuck in for so long."

He brightened with relief. The gown was for herself. How simple. How utterly charming. But if he wasn't careful, he might not ever see it again. Pacing was everything now, taking things slowly, so as not to upset her further. He would swallow his hurt and disappointment and patiently take care of the next order of business.

Sara started when Alec started to rise from the booth. "Where are you going?"

He stepped behind the booth to the wall phone and dug into his jeans pocket for a quarter. "You're calling Kelly Hutton right now and cancelling your subscription," he directed gruffly. Meekly complying for a change, she scooted off the bench and handed him Rosie.

The conversation was short and to the point. Sara announced her bail-out in mid-route and Alec could tell Kelly wanted her money back. Upon his urging, she went on to say she knew about Mel Slade and was considering a lawsuit. Kelly suddenly insisted she keep the down payment, on condition that she return her credit card and Lincoln to Seattle. Sara agreed, saying she'd meet her back home after the holidays.

She hung up, a new person. "There, all squared. I'm cut loose, officially Sara Jameson again to the world at large." She slid back into the booth, raising no objection when he held on to the baby. "Now, what do you say we have lunch?"

NO ONE at the Cozy Rest expressed much surprise when the threesome barged into the service porch later that afternoon with all Sara's gear. The residents were in the midst of a taffy pull. Mrs. Nesbitt was standing at the cast-iron stove, stirring the contents of a huge kettle with a wooden spoon. Martha and Timothy were at one end of the long, stiff rope of satiny candy; Lyle and Camille were pulling at the other end.

"Just in time for the fun," Timothy rejoiced.

Sara shifted Rosie in her arms to give Timothy's cheek a pinch. It must have been tough on him, confessing to Alec that he'd helped her escape. She'd been so intent on escape, she hadn't thought how the boy would have to answer for what he'd done.

As angry as she'd been at the time, she'd also known full well that Alec would be devastated by her departure. And wasn't that kind of devotion something to take into serious consideration? Combined with her own loving feelings, it validated the wonderful sex they'd enjoyed, but she was unsure about a future together.

She couldn't get over that one last hurdle—Alec's denial. He was a strong man, no question. But he wasn't invincible, immortal, or twenty-two any more. Sara had learned much about limitations during her own convalescence—very much like his—and just as some things were lost, others were found. Accepting change was all part of the journey.

"Guess what, Sara?" Timothy said, bringing her back to reality. "Jim Nesbitt's coming home sometime tonight. Might be late. Miz Bea says if he is late, he hasta come down the chimney like good ole Santa Claus!"

Alec and Sara shared a puzzled look. "He sent a telegram?" Alec asked.

"Aw, no, Mr. Jim called on the telephone." Timothy, busy helping his mother swing their rope of taffy over the kitchen table, missed the significance of the news.

Mrs. Nesbitt bustled to the counter near the sink and picked up a pair of scissors. Moving to the table, she began to cut the length of candy into one-inch snippets. "Why don't you two get freshened up and come back and join us?" she suggested, not looking up from her task.

Alec opened the swinging door for Sara and Rosie to pass through.

When they reached the privacy of the foyer, Sara turned and gave him a raspberry. "And you thought my mysteries were strange," she whispered. Rosie imitated her mother, poking her little pink tongue out too, on a wave of drool.

"Double raspberries?" Alec clutched his heart in mock agony.

"Can you believe Jim Nesbitt got a call through?" Sara lamented.

"They all get calls through," Alec complained. "But you know what, I've given up caring. If Mrs. Nesbitt wants to slip through locked doors, flip me off my mattress, magically replenish the food in her cupboards, I say dandy. I'm all finished digging and probing into everything. Meet the new Alec Wagner. All snuggled and warm and dopey and looking forward to having the best Christmas ever."

Sara went on ahead up the stairs without another word. After giving him a raspberry again.

"Okay, okay," he mumbled to himself. "Keep a guy humble and proving himself." So what if he was an arrogant cuss accustomed to getting what he wanted? What he wanted right now was the jackpot of the average man, a pair of sweet raspberries for the rest of his life. He dared her to find fault with that!

13

SARA PUT ROSIE down for a nap and went to sleep herself, waking up sometime after sunset. In spite of all the drama surrounding the day, she found herself looking forward to the Christmas Eve festivities. She took the time to change into a blue silk pantsuit, and put Rosie in a red velvet jumper and white blouse.

She soon discovered that everyone had assembled in the parlor. Camille was busy pounding the keys of the piano, and Beatrice, Timothy and Martha were crowded around her bench in a semicircle, singing a carol. Alec and Lyle were kneeling before the tree in the midst of some operation. Alec was holding back some of the large pine tree's branches and Lyle was using a manual drill on its trunk, boring holes in it.

"What are you doing?" she asked in fascination, taking care not to step on the gifts as she came up behind the men.

Lyle greeted her with a cheerful nod. "Adding a few more boughs to the trunk."

"My Jim likes a full, rich tree," Mrs. Nesbitt explained over the chorus of voices.

Timothy was at Sara's side in a flash. "I'm getting more ornaments on the tree, after all. And we're having cold sandwiches for supper," he added, gesturing to the coffee table, which held a loaded platter, two salad bowls and a dish of shiny taffy, along with a silver coffeepot. "Need plenty of time to open presents and tell stories and play games." He exhaled, his small shoulders falling. "Whew!"

Sara joined the singers round the piano, coming elbow to elbow with Mrs. Nesbitt as Camille flipped through the pages of her songbook. "I wanted to apologize for the way I left today."

The innkeeper's round face softened in understanding. "You came back. That's all that matters."

"You're so kind. But what I mean is, we've never even discussed my bill. I left without asking for it." Sara grew sheepish. "My only excuse is that I was so very upset."

"Nothing to worry about," Mrs. Nesbitt crooned with a dismissive wave. "Alec's gift certificate covers a couple, so both of you are paid in full. All right?"

Sara stared at her in disbelief. "Did he know...that he could've brought someone else?"

Mrs. Nesbitt tittered. "I don't think he even noticed. He doesn't pay much attention to the small, but important personal things, does he? Needs a sweet woman and child to round off his sharp edges, put him straight when he's off balance."

Sara measured her with good-humored wariness. "You are a determined matchmaker, aren't you?"

Mrs. Nesbitt lifted a soft gray brow in speculation. "Happens to be part of my life's mission. Some unions are destined to be, but need a boost."

Sara was torn between blindly following fate, and holding out for the best of circumstances. Still, she couldn't help but be influenced by the innkeeper's support of her budding romance. Feeling a joy in the depths of her soul, Sara sang the loudest when Camille's fingers stole over the ivories once again. Even Rosie joined in, her toneless yammer adding an intriguing harmony.

Sara's eyes were continually drawn to Alec. She stole intermittent glances at him during the singalong. He looked ten years younger as he studiously kept the Christmas tree, loaded with shiny silver globes and golden strings of tinsel, steady while Lyle circled and drilled and jabbed extra lushly needled branches into bare spots. He appeared to be having the time of his life, enjoying the simple pleasures of the evening with a boyish wonder that rivaled Timothy's.

Alec caught Sara's eye as the music died away with a grand key-pounding crescendo from Camille. With deliberate care he curved his mouth into the sweetest, most kissable smile imaginable.

Mrs. Nesbitt came up beside him at the tree and gave his denim shirtsleeve a tug. "Did you notice, Alec? I hung mistletoe all over the place in here."

Deciding to give her a hard time, Alec looked overhead in confusion. "This room has no ceiling light fixture."

Mrs. Nesbitt huffed impatiently, grabbed a sprig off a nearby lampshade, took the necessary steps to Sara and jammed it in her tide of auburn hair above the ear. "There. Mistletoe. Everyplace." With a wink at the flustered Sara, the innkeeper took hold of Rosie and wandered over to the window seat.

"An offer I dare not refuse." Alec chuckled and closed the space between him and his love. Gathering Sara in his arms, he dipped his mouth to hers for a long, leisurely exploration. His pulse pounded in his temples as he slipped his tongue between her lips, tasting her thoroughly, as though for the last time.

It was no accident. He knew any time soon might very well be the last time.

Sara trembled as she was swept up into his desperate, urgent quest, acutely aware of his hands skimming the surface of her silky blouse as though looking for access to her bare skin. She'd never made a man feel crazed before. It was flattering and scary, an irresistible lure. But wanting her wasn't enough. He had to want better things for himself first.

It was Sara who finally broke free, feeling a little self-conscious over the intimacy they'd shared in front of everyone. But there didn't seem to be such a thing as moderation when they touched. Passion flared to life instantly, consuming them, isolating them.

Like a real family, no one seemed to be paying much attention. The couple proved no competition for cold roast-beef sandwiches, potato salad and fresh saltwater taffy. Everyone was seated in the cluster of comfortable chairs, holding plates and glasses in their laps, chatting merrily about the new fullness Lyle had given the tree. Mrs. Nesbitt had the baby well in hand for a feeding as the pair rocked gently in the innkeeper's favorite maple chair.

The sofa, however, had been left conspicuously empty. Sharing an amused look, Alec and Sara filled up plates and sank onto the sateen cushions.

"Did you know that I'm staying here on your tab?" Sara asked him, nibbling on a crust of homemade bread.

He stared at her in pleased confusion. "We going back to sharing a bed?"

She gasped self-consciously. "No, I mean that I spoke to Mrs. Nesbitt about my bill and she says I'm already covered because your gift certificate was for two."

Alec paused in thought. "Doesn't she think I would've noticed that perk?"

Sara grinned. "She's pretty sure you're a dolt, so I doubt it."

Alec knew full well that the certificate was for one. But he wasn't about to put the good-hearted old innkeeper on the spot. It was Mrs. Nesbitt's kind gesture and he had no right to spoil it. Even if he was left looking like a dumbbell. Wasn't that the overall theme of this trip?

They were halfway through their meal when Timothy suddenly remembered the outside lights. "Nobody turned 'em on!" With that, the energetic redhead scooted out to the foyer and flipped the wall switch. The panes in the bay window brightened with color as the bulbs trimming them sprang to life. Timothy darted back, half sliding, half diving to the tree.

He rubbed his hands with glee. "Let's open some presents!"

The adults chuckled. Martha reminded her son that they'd agreed to wait for Jim Nesbitt, but Beatrice intervened, suggesting that Timothy be allowed to open a couple of things. Alec donated his and Sara's box. Timothy quickly pulled off the green foil wrapping, whooping with joy when he discovered that the box held not shoes, but four Hardy Boys mysteries. "Jeepers, thanks." He rushed over to the sofa to hug the couple. "I'll read you every word," he vowed solemnly, as though promising to take a swing at world peace.

Alec chuckled, grazing his knuckles over the boy's crewcut head. "I think it's about time Rosie be exposed to the world of mystery, too. Right before her nap would be good, when she's fussy."

Martha sat down on the floor beside the boy and handed him the brightly wrapped box from Major Doanes, stripped of its twine and brown paper. Timothy peeled off the ribbon and paper to find wooden cars and a fox fur. "Look, Mom!" He held up the brown fur stole first. "A fox bitin' its own tail. Just what you wanted."

Martha gasped in delight, and taking up the stole, draped it across her shoulders over the fine knit of her white sweaterdress. "I'll be the fanciest lady in Elm City." She looked up to Sara for verification. "Don't see many furs this fine on the street these days, do you?"

Sara swallowed and answered with a frozen smile. "No. Can't say I've ever seen one."

"But it sure beats skunk," Alec whispered close to Sara's ear once Martha was busy with her son.

Sara nudged him, biting back a laugh. The Cozy Inn residents were certainly charmed by old-time customs. It was almost as if they lived in another world entirely.

Camille was passing out a china plate of cookies when a honk sounded outside. Speculation concerning the shoe salesman's return bubbled around the room and Mrs. Nesbitt leaned forward expectantly.

Timothy was up in a flash to climb into the window seat for a look down the driveway. "Nope, it's the tow truck."

"Hal?" Alec felt an adrenaline charge as he rose to his feet. "Excuse me for a minute." Not bothering with a jacket, he marched out onto the front porch. Hal hovered by his front fender, so Alec quickly took the path to the driveway, slipping a little in his moccasins. "Merry Christmas! Haven't you closed up shop yet?"

Hal took a deep breath, releasing it in a series of white puffs. "Got terrible news, Alec. That guy in the fax. That Mel Slade. He came into the station bold as you please, looking for your friend. Called her Kelly."

Alec rubbed his hands together for heat. "How could he have found us?"

"Dad's fault, I'm afraid. He got all mixed up and put the charge through on the credit card. If I'd have known, I could've closed up the station early. But he just showed up all of sudden, Alec. Announced his name all nasty, like it was supposed to mean something to everybody. Before I could deny anything, he found the Lincoln in back. Before I could stop him, he shoved Frank around a little bit."

Alec's hands paused in mid air. "Your dad okay?"

"Oh, yeah. Fine. But this guy's mean, Alec. Cut Dad's face with a sharp ring when he backhanded him. Dad was down when he admitted you were at the Cozy Rest. Gee, we're sorry."

Alec stared down the driveway, then beyond the split-rail fence to the road. "Wonder why he's not here yet."

Hal hesitated, but only for seconds. "Won't be long."

"Nice of you to stop out with the warning, Hal. Took guts."

Hal took a trifle offended. "I am the law right now. With the sheriff out of town."

Alec pressed his cold lips together, feeling an even deeper chill beneath his denim clothing. Damn, that was right. Hal from the service station was the Elm City law. Alec knew he had to take over. His brain raced as he formed the proper words that wouldn't insult this decent, but inexperienced man. Before the accident he would have just begun barking out orders. But things were different now. Slowing down had given him a new perspective on his actions.

Hal ended up helping him. "Of course I think we should work together on this, Alec."

Alec managed a smile. "I appreciate that. As you know, the phone service here stinks. What I need most from you now is to zip back to town and call in reinforcements. Who's nearest?"

Hal paused, his long face strained with thought. "Guess it's the highway patrol."

"Good. Summon them pronto. And call the number that appeared on the faxes. You got that one?"

"Sure thing. Copied it down just in case a transmission went wrong."

"Identify yourself and me. Ask for Jennifer. They'll connect you wherever she is. Tell her what's happening. She'll take it from there."

"What about you, Alec? Should I call in the neighbors to help?"

Alec shook his head forcefully. "No, it would be wrong to endanger anyone that way. Leave the inn to me." He clapped Hal on the arm and steered him back to the driver's seat. "Just get the highway patrol out here and fill them in on who we're dealing with."

Hal climbed back into the truck's cab and ignited the engine. "Don't worry, I'll tell 'em a real agent's in charge out here."

Alec only wished.

He returned to a parlor scene very different from the one he'd left only minutes before. The room was so silent you could've heard a pin drop, the tension as crisp as the crackling fire in the hearth. All eyes were on Sara, who was standing in the center of the festively decorated room, so very slender and small and obviously frightened out of her wits.

"I've told them about Slade," Sara said. "There is trouble, isn't there?"

"Yes." Alec quickly explained the crisis. Resentful murmurs arose in the room.

"I'm so sorry!" Sara cried. "This is all my fault."

Alec gave her a quick hug. "Don't be ridiculous, honey. We do foolish things for the people we care for. You only wanted a decent start for Rosie."

"I know what," Sara announced with a toss of her head, "I'll answer the door when he comes. He'll see I'm the wrong woman and he'll go."

"He won't be content with a look at you, Sara."

"I'll explain!"

"You can't prove Kelly's not here, that you're the one who's been traveling in her place. And even if you could," he added with great reluctance, "Slade doesn't operate on reason. He's a madman, especially where his women are concerned, and responds with violence always."

Sara sank against his length. "What have I done to us?"

Alec gave her a tight hug, then turned to the residents. "Does anyone have a gun? Of any kind?"

"Dearie me, no," Mrs. Nesbitt clucked. "Pitchfork out in the barn is the best we have." She rocked forward and stilled her chair. "I suggest you hide, Alec, with Sara and the baby. We can take care of this rube."

A hearty round of agreement rose in the room, startling the lovers.

"How could you possibly hope to defend yourselves?" Alec asked.

Camille sat up straighter on the bench, fingering the white collar of her black wool dress. "We've seen ourselves through plenty of trouble. This Slade wouldn't have a prayer against us!"

Alec threw his hands up despairingly in response to the hearty sounds of agreement. "If only you'd follow my lead!"

"We'll work together," Mrs. Nesbitt bargained.

"Indeed. We'll start by turning out all the lights," Lyle declared. He gave Camille's knee a pat and rose, giving his vest a sharp tug over his belt.

They waited silently in the darkness for a time, moving through the room as though on eggshells.

Their bravery was almost comical to Alec. "This would be an opportune time for the rest of you to hide," he suggested dryly.

Timothy had stationed himself in the window seat, so he was the first to spot their visitor. "Hey, there's a car out there on the road, by the Cozy Rest sign."

"Any headlights?" Alec demanded.

"No."

"He's our man."

Alec had been thinking hard during the wait and had come up with a game plan. He spoke loudly about caution as he stalked out to the foyer and over to the closet underneath the staircase. He needn't have worried about being heard, as they'd all followed him, eyes filled with excitement. How he wished for a little fear, just to keep them on their toes.

"I'm going to lure him out to the barn." Reaching inside the nook, he pulled a parka off a peg. Protests rang out as he slipped into the dark green jacket. He was amazed by the sentiment and baffled by their willingness to participate. No one had ever cared about him this way before. He cleared the lump from his throat. "Reinforcements should be here in short order."

He looked around, wishing he had something other than his house moccasins for his feet. But there wasn't time to hunt down his boots. "Bet you'd all be safe and sound if you crawled into this space under the stairs and closed the door after you," he announced. "The hinges are almost invisible to the naked eye. If Slade does dare to enter, he'll rip through this place like a tornado, too fast to ever find you in there."

"We'll put Rosie in there for sure," Mrs. Nesbitt decided. "Timothy, get her car seat. It's right behind you by the parson's bench." With Sara's help, the innkeeper ever-so-gently set the dozing baby in the seat and deposited her in the nook.

"She's really out," Sara noted, touching the baby's velvet cheek before they shut her in.

Lyle peered through the octagonal window beside the door. "He's halfway down the drive."

Alec was running as he moved down the hall, through the swinging door into the kitchen and on to the service porch. As quickly as he could, he lit one of the lanterns and burst outside to the path leading to the barn.

With the light of the moon behind him, the figure coming up the drive looked especially menacing and formidably tall. Alec made every move count, reeling in feigned surprise at the sight of the intruder, then breaking into a dash for the barn. If he could get Slade inside, Alec figured he could use his familiarity with the structure to get the drop on him.

But Alec never made it to the barn. Slade bore down on him with remarkable agility and speed. Youth and fitness were on his side, as well as custom boots just right for the weather.

The lantern fell against the snow fence lining the path as Alec slipped and fell on his back. He knew what Slade looked like and one glance told him there'd been no mistake about the identity of the intruder. The hood was a handsome man of twenty-five, with dark hair and eyes, who might have graced the cover of a business monthly or *GQ*. But there was a horrific rage distorting his features as he seized Alec by the throat.

"Where is she?"

"Who?"

"You know who! Kelly!" Digging his knee into Alec's chest, he slammed his head against the snow-packed pathway. "I've seen her car, the credit slip at that rinky-dink station. Where is she?"

Slade's tormented howl thundered in Alec's ears, the ground smacked against his skull. He mumbled incoherently, as though trying to find the right words. When Slade froze to listen, Alec snaked up and landed a hard right cross on his jaw. Knuckle hit bone with an echoing crack and Slade went tumbling off his prey.

Feeling a more worthy opponent now, Alec quickly rose to his feet and landed another punch to Slade's beautiful face. The man stumbled a little, but didn't lose his balance. Instead he charged at Alec again, hitting him at the knees, dropping him.

They wrestled in the snow with grunts and curses.

It was several minutes before Slade discovered Alec's weak left shoulder. He hammered his fist into the injured area like a club, over and over again, until Alec thought he'd faint from the excruciating pain.

Then a shot rang out. And Alec did pass out.

Sara came skittering to a stop several feet away, with the smoking gun still aimed in the air. Slade rolled off Alec as though he didn't exist, stood and ever so slowly started up the path. "Kelly?"

"No!" she shouted tersely. "She isn't here. Never was."

"Kelly..."

The gun shook a little as she brought it down and leveled it at him. It was a target pistol belonging to the major, remembered suddenly by Martha after Alec had charged outside. Although Sara had taken a firearms basic training course at a community center, she had accepted the weapon hesitantly. Now she gripped the walnut stock with care, remembering her gun instructor's advice to never aim unless you intended to shoot.

Could she shoot a human being?

It was during these precious seconds of indecision that Slade made his move. He lunged at her, grabbed her by the hair and wrenched the weapon away. He brought his head close to hers to study her face in the moonlight.

Sara stared up at him, frozen with fear. He surely was mad. His dark eyes held a glassy, inhuman quality that she instantly feared. His look of incomprehension told her that right now he was dealing with the fact that she wasn't the object of his obsession after all.

But what would he do if he caught on to *her* role? That she'd been the one luring him along for miles and miles through city after city?

"You know Kelly, don't you? Don't you!" He nodded, baring his teeth. "Oh, yes, I can see you do."

"Not w-well," Sara stammered. "She was here for a while, but she left. In a taxi. Her car is at the local garage—"

He stopped the flow of words with a hard backhand across her mouth, then shoved her to the ground. Sara, like Frank, was cut with his ring. A clean slice across the lower lip. But it was nothing compared to what he'd done to Alec, she realized angrily.

As Slade stormed toward the house, Sara scurried to Alec's side. She dropped to her knees, and cradling his head in her lap, rubbed his cheeks. "Oh, darling, wake up."

Alec's lids fluttered. "What's happening?"

"Slade is headed for the house."

"No!" Alec tried to sit up, but stiffened as pain shot through his left shoulder.

She eased him back into her lap. "It's all right. The others are ready for him."

"How?"

"I don't know," Sara admitted, caressing his temples. "But Mrs. Nesbitt assured me they were able, and we have to believe her, Alec. She's never been wrong yet."

"The gun..."

"Belongs to Martha's husband. Slade's got it now, I'm afraid."

Alec moaned again, his head lolling on her thighs.

"If they're all hiding inside—under the stairs for instance—there'll be no one to shoot."

"That's right, isn't it? Just...don't want to see anyone hurt."

"What else could those old folks possibly do but hide? Lyle's eighty!"

Alec relaxed a little. "Right, of course. Slade will tear through every room. By the time he's done, help will be here." Already there were sirens closing in. He shut his eyes with a faint smile. "Ah, what a woman."

"Me?"

"Mrs. Nesbitt."

"Thanks a lot!"

Alec managed a small chuckle, though it did send a jolt of pain through his ribs. "I was thinking for the hundredth time that Beatrice is the kind of mother every boy dreams of and deserves. Now, you don't want me to look on you as a mother, do you?"

Sara had to agree that she didn't.

From their position near the barn they could see down the drive and on to the road. Within seconds, Hal's tow truck and wailing patrol cars braked near the fence.

The sirens were quelled soon after, but were replaced by a high, reedy animal sound, a wail of terror. Suddenly Slade's dark figure could be seen scrambling up the winding drive and into the arms of the law. Two officers grabbed him and forced him to spread-eagle on one of the cars.

"Hot damn." Alec shifted and winced. "Help me up, Sara. Just a little boost."

"Help? You've used the word twice in past few minutes. How does it feel rolling off the sharp old tongue?"

His eyes narrowed and his voice dropped to a growl. "How would you like to roll off onto my lap for a paddling?"

She didn't crack a smile. "This is it, Alec. Your chance to face the whole truth about yourself."

He shuddered, more from his emotional torment than

pain, as he gazed up at her lovely face against the velvet-black sky. "You're cut." He gently touched her bloody lip.

She held fast to his hand. "Don't shift the attention to me and mine again. That trick's overdone."

He couldn't blame her for pressing the issue at a time when his diminished physical strength was obvious. Like it or not, his hard-slamming days were over. This grandstand attempt to single-handedly protect a house full of people confirmed it. He was damn lucky that the old birds of the inn were as tough as they were.

"Okay, honey. I admit it. I'm not quite up to spec, not quite my old self."

"Alec..."

He took a painful breath. "Okay! I may never be the same as I was. Close maybe, but never quite as sturdy, or a sure thing in the field as I'd hoped." He cupped her delicate chin in his hand with a sigh. "You were totally right about my denial. I'm a bullheaded front man who believed he could recapture that old infallible feeling."

"Anything else, as long as we're in the confessional?"

He bared his teeth in a self-conscious, half smile. "I did try to hide my scar from you when we made love. Out of sight, out of mind has been my motto." He sat up with a wince. "But tonight proves quite graphically that I can't deny my new limitations any longer."

"It's up to you, my darling. You can stand moping outside that closed door to the Bureau for the rest of your retired days, or you can walk through a whole new door with me."

Alec pulled her head down to his and gently kissed her unscathed upper lip. "Take me with you, Sara. Through the door—all the way back to Seattle."

"What will you do there?"

"Now who's spoiling the magical future? I'll have to think it over, look for an opportunity. I do have plenty of savings," he confided with pride. "Could retire permanently if I wanted to!"

She assessed him knowingly. "But you don't want to. Idle time makes you grumpy and bored and nosy."

"Sweet-talker. Now, help me up. Just a little boost that won't destroy the little ego I have left."

Alec and Sara walked arm on arm round the house to the front yard, parting company by the porch. He wanted to fill in the authorities and Sara wanted to check on Rosie and their brave cohorts.

Sara was amazed as she entered the parlor. It was almost as though nothing had happened. Everyone was relaxing, all no worse for wear. The lamps were back on, as well as the tree lights. Even Rosie was in the rocker again, snug in Mrs. Nesbitt's arms. True, Camille's cottony curls looked a little mussed as she leaned over the piano with Lyle, and Timothy had his nose glued to the bay window, watching the display on the road, but the battle waged outside had been the worst of it.

"Our girl slept through it all splendidly," Mrs. Nesbitt assured Sara, nodding down at the baby snuggled against her bosom.

Sara looked around the room. "Where's that brandy?"

Lyle gallantly played host, pouring them all full snifters. He held the decanter over the liquor trolley. "Do you think Alec..."

"I know so," Sara promptly replied. "Pour."

Alec appeared twenty minutes later, limping, with a bruised face, but satisfied just the same. He took an approving survey of the troops, then sank down in one of the deeper recliners and absently sipped the brandy Sara brought him. He patted her fanny with a comfortable familiarity as she perched on the arm of his chair.

"So, how did you handle things?" he asked, his eyes roaming over the tranquil, neat parlor. "Did you hide like I told you to?"

Mrs. Nesbitt smiled serenely. "Well, this Slade didn't see us, did he?"

Alec took another swallow of his drink. "No. Guess I must've hit him harder than I realized, though. He was nearly incoherent out on the road, came barrelling up to the patrolmen and begged for protection. Imagine, that dirtbag begging for a guard." Alec scowled, shaking his head. "Violent coward couldn't take half of what he dished out."

"What did he have to say, exactly?" Camille asked, patting her hairdo.

"Bunch of hooey about wraiths attacking him in this abandoned house." Alec rolled his eyes. "Can you believe it? Must be planning an insanity defense."

A round of cheers met the news. Alec handed Sara his drink, then leaned forward to peel off his parka, and gingerly removed the major's gun from his pocket. "Brought back the pistol. Slade dropped it along the drive."

"Thank you, Alec," Martha murmured.

"Thank you for thinking of it, Martha. Sara's firepower gave me just the distraction I needed. I took the precaution of unloading it out on the road. Though in its rusted state, I don't know how Sara managed to fire it in the first place."

"I'll take it off your hands."

Alec handed Martha the weapon, inhaling sharply as it passed beneath the glow of the table lamp. "You know, it looks brand-new back here in the light. But how—"

"You're upset, son," Lyle suggested, refilling his snifter. "Tough to unscramble it all."

"Maybe. Though I must say, I've managed to decode the most important mysteries in my way." To prove his point, Alec gave Sara an endearing squeeze.

The display delighted everyone.

"Hear hear!"

"Good show!"

"Another success!"

Another what? Sara met Alec's gaze, their confusion mutual.

Toasts in honor of the season followed. Buoyed by the

brandy and goodwill, Alec topped off the perilous night with one last risk, a marriage proposal.

Sara gasped, nearly toppling off his thighs. "Oh, Alec... Is this really the right time?"

"We don't mind!" the others chorused.

"I mean, don't you feel it might be premature?"

"Not at all," he said gently, grazing her cheek with his knuckle.

"I know I'm well suited for marriage," she said carefully, "having had the experience. But you've dodged commitment for a very long time."

"But I feel ready!"

"Making it legal is serious. What if the novelty wears off, once things simmer down?"

His denial was emphatic. "I can't imagine ever simmering down again with you and Rosie in my life."

"But it won't be like your field days, every case an adventure."

"There are different kinds of thrills, I've discovered. As for your unique powers, any woman who can charge a criminal with a target pistol, is a hundred percent pistol herself!"

She fluttered her lashes daintily. "Oh, that."

"You saved my life once tonight, honey," he said earnestly. "Save it for good, forever. I promise, I won't let you down. I'll work regular hours, be around for bedtime stories each and every night, loving every single minute of it."

"Sounds like the best kind of guarantee," Lyle interceded in fatherly judgement.

Mrs. Nesbitt clicked her tongue. "Indeed yes."

"But we'll be together—"

"Woman, I refuse to return to Seattle with you unless you're willing to make an honest man of me."

"Oh, Sara, please," Mrs. Nesbitt lamented, "if you don't bundle him off, I expect he'll try to hide out here through the spring thaw. And we're tuckered out as it is."

Sara sighed. "There's only the one way I can have you, then?"

"That's right. From here on in, I'm saving myself for the altar."

She leaned into his lap and hugged him fiercely. "All right, let's do it."

Whoops of joy filled the room, and hugs of congratulations exchanged.

"Hey, everybody, Jim's here!" Timothy raised the joyous alarm, then scrambled for the front door.

Mrs. Nesbitt nodded gently, her pleasant face joyful as she struggled to rise from her chair. Sara quickly crossed the room to scoop up Rosie just as a deep voice boomed in the foyer.

"Bea!" A blond and bearded man the size of a lumberjack, dressed in a gray car coat, burst into the room and lifted Mrs. Nesbitt off her feet. He twirled her around and around to the tune of her halfhearted protests. Out of breath as he set her down, she gasped, "Oh, Jimmy, this is bound to be my favorite Christmas of all!"

Alec embraced Sara and the baby, holding them close. "A favorite for all of us."

Epilogue

Six months later

"LOOK AT ALL the cars in Mrs. Nesbitt's driveway, Alec!"

Alec slowed their family van down on the two-lane road fronting the Cozy Rest Inn. The old gray lady looked much the same as it had during the holidays. What charm the Christmas lights had added then was compensated for by the lush green grass and blooming trees in the yard now.

"We may have to park out here by the fence."

Sara sighed in exasperation. "Alec, I'm not that fragile. Being pregnant is a cinch compared to my climbing accident. Exercise is good for me. Really!"

He smiled sheepishly. "Sure, sure. Sorry to be such a worrier."

"Worrisome is more like it. Relax. This baby will be every bit as heathy and wild as the one riding in back."

"Oh, no," Alec lamented teasingly. "A partner in crime for Rosie." He braked under a huge elm tree and killed the engine. He slipped off his sunglasses, set them on the dashboard and shifted around to unhook his rambunctious stepdaughter from her seat. "Boy, will your Aunt Bea be surprised to see you tearing around with twice as much hair and triple the wiles."

Alec ushered Sara and Rosie inside the house, the coolness of the foyer a welcome relief from the blazing sunshine. Alec nudged his wife when he spotted some dirt on the innkeeper's spotless black-and-white-tiled floor. "Wait till she sees this mess!"

Sara chuckled as she looked around, absorbing the details

to get a sense of the place again. She peered into the parlor, remarking to Alec that it looked much larger without the grand Christmas tree. Still every bit as inviting, though, from the billowy lace curtains to the fluffed-up furniture cushions.

Alec had a tight hold on Rosie's hand as she tap-tap-tapped on the foyer tiles in her white walking shoes. People were passing through the hallway and the rooms, carrying purses and cameras, paying no attention to one another, something Cozy Rest residents would never do.

Something was off here. The prickly hairs on his neck told him so.

Sara returned to his side and adjusted the plastic barrett in Rosie's thick, golden curls. "Any familiar faces?"

"Not yet. Though—" Alec stooped a little to peer up the staircase "—I think I see a paisley hem on the descent."

To the couple's mutual surprise, it was Leslie Anderson from the town's café who was wearing Mrs. Nesbitt's house-dress.

She greeted them with equal surprise. "You're back!"

"Yes," Sara said, extending her hand. "Back and married and pregnant."

Alec's large mouth quirked playfully. "Care to top all that?"

Her forehead puckered. "You might be surprised."

Sara took Leslie's arm. "So where's Mrs. Nesbitt? And all the others?"

Leslie shushed her and looked round self-consciously. "Let's go in the kitchen." She led the way, greeting people along the hall. Once in the kitchen, she picked up the tele-phone.

"That thing finally working?" Alec asked teasingly.

Leslie smiled and dialed. It turned out that she was phon-ing Hal at the Pump-U-Serve, summoning him to the house for a reunion.

In the meantime, she invited the Wagner family to make themselves comfortable. Rosie certainly did, tottering around on the linoleum babbling, her yellow sundress floating around her chunky legs. She opened a cupboard door, exposing her ruffled panties as she bent over to peek inside. Sara, who was watching her daughter, could not help noticing that the cupboard shelves were empty. Alec took in the scene too, his raven brows joining in suspicion.

"I have lots to tell you," Leslie assured them. "But I thought Hal could help tremendously."

Sara sank into a bow-backed chair, smoothed her white-eyelet sundress over her legs and wrestled Rosie into her lap. "Leslie, where is Beatrice? Why are you wearing her out-dated clothing, three sizes too large for you?"

Leslie opened her mouth to speak, then clamped it shut again as a young couple came through the swinging door. "Know it's near closing time. Just wanted to say goodbye," the man said. "Fascinating place. Hope to see you at your café."

"Fascinating place?" Sara repeated. "Why is the inn full of browsers, Leslie?"

"Because it's a farm museum in the summertime," Leslie explained haltingly. "I run it."

"When did all this happen?" Alec demanded.

"About fifteen years ago," Leslie admitted.

"What!" Sara's tone was steeped in disbelief.

"An inn in the winter, full of food and people and life?" Alec queried doubtfully. "Transformed to a neat, empty museum in the summer? Doesn't seem logical."

Leslie backed off as the pair prepared to pounce on her. "I'm afraid you're going to find all of this nearly impossible to swallow."

"Try us," Alec urged impatiently.

"Right." Leslie took a breath. "Where to begin?"

"Anyplace," Alec urged, with traces of a scowl.

Leslie nodded. "This place is open to the public from June to September, tours available."

"Serving as an inn during the winter," Sara sought to verify.

Leslie looked more and more uncomfortable. "Not really, not officially. That's where it all gets a bit tricky."

More people entered the kitchen. As they peered into every nook and cranny, it became evident that there was not a crumb of food in the house. Even the old refrigerator was dark and empty.

Sara and Alec exchanged a troubled look. This was nothing like the joyous homecoming they'd anticipated.

Hal showed up shortly thereafter and greeted the Wagners like long-lost relatives. Alec felt a bit better, a touch of the old comfort. But the innkeeper herself had been the highlight of their stay, the subject of many a conversation over the months. With a sigh of relief Leslie noted that it was indeed time to lock up and excused herself to do that.

Hal sat down at the table, stretched his legs and asked the Wagners for details about their new life together.

"We're getting along great," Alec reported. "Sara's three months pregnant, I've been doing some freelance security work. We're still in our settling stage."

Leslie reappeared, looking a little more relaxed. "We won't be disturbed anymore."

Hal nodded. "So what have you told them so far, Les?"

"Not much. Guess I felt I needed some collaboration on the more ticklish details. Some of your plain talk, Hal."

Hal drummed his blunt, greasy fingernails on the table. "Okay, folks, here's the skinny."

"All we want is to see Mrs. Nesbitt," Sara persisted. "Is that so hard?"

"Well, yes," Hal said mildly. "It's impossible, as a matter of fact. For you see, your lovely hostess Beatrice Nesbitt has long since passed over."

"What!" the couple chorused again.

"She died nearly two decades ago," Hal affirmed.

"But how, h-how..." Sara stuttered, completely baffled.

"The lady you met, the lady you fell in love with, was a ghost."

"But she was so real to me," Alec protested. "My ideal, my savior."

"Just as she undoubtedly set out to be," Leslie said soothingly. "I know what I'm saying because Beatrice was precious to me too, my grandmother in fact."

"You never said so."

"I couldn't, Alec, for reasons I'll explain. But remember how interested I was in the happenings at the house? That's because all of this is mine. Bea and I were very close, so she chose me to handle her estate, carry out her wishes."

"Exactly what were her wishes?" Sara asked.

"More than anything she wanted this place preserved and a functioning relic of the thirties. That was her favorite time of life, you see, and she felt that future generations could, through her farm, have a taste of living history, see how life used to be. Grandma believed strongly in education. She was especially content back then, and wanted to share the feeling." Leslie sighed hard. "Little did I realize that I was preserving her nest for her spiritual visits as well."

"You expect us to believe that she was a ghost?" Alec asked angrily. "That she took this living-history thing so seriously that she stayed on herself?"

"Guess I'm doing this rather clumsily. We've never had a couple return this way, catch things as they truly are."

"What about everyone else?" Alec demanded. "Timothy? Martha? Camille? Lyle?"

"All ghosts," Hal maintained. "When you stepped into the house last Christmas, you were moving into another dimension, joining the gang in 1938. That's why I refused to come in back then. I wasn't part of your world and the house would've been cold and empty to me." Hal shivered a little. "And may I say spooky."

Alec thought things over. It seemed too incredible, downright impossible. But if it was true, it would explain Mel Slade's horror when he shot out of the house. It was a sure bet those old spirits gave him a spin through the darkness he'd never forget! And the major's old gun being rusty out on the road. That was probably how it would have looked if left sitting untended for sixty years.

Alec didn't believe in ghosts, but so many facts backed up their claims.

"What did you mean about couples, Leslie?" Sara thought to ask.

"The high jinks center around romance, uniting soul mates who have lost their way," Leslie explained. "It all started shortly after I restored everything to its former glory and opened the museum. I have never seen Beatrice here myself the way you did. Rather, she comes to me in dreams. And the strangest dream of my life was one shortly after her death, when she floated by to tell me she intended to occupy the inn every winter to play matchmaker to a couple who were meant to be together but were missing out on their destiny because of earthly circumstances."

Humor touched Leslie's round face, so like Beatrice's. "I thought I'd eaten something funny for dinner that night, let me tell you. But darned if a couple didn't pop into the café one night a week before that particular Christmas, announcing that they were lodgers at the Cozy Rest Inn."

"Most people are staying at the modern Cozy Rest on the other side of town," Hal put in. "It's run by Mrs. Nesbitt's son Gerald, Leslie's father."

"Ah, the source of my brochure boasting modern conveniences," Alec said.

"Yes, and the origin of your gift certificate, Alec," Leslie added. "Your taxi driver got lost by Beatrice's design I'm certain and you ended up on the wrong side of town. Same with you, Sara, skidding round on your own."

"But how did you know that first couple was from the old Cozy Rest in particular?" Sara challenged.

"They caught the whole town's attention by coming in on Grandma Bea's old sleigh."

"What did that prove?"

"There was no horse pulling it!" Hal said.

"But Sugar and Spice—"

Leslie raised a palm to Sara's objections. "Spice was pulling the sleigh, I'm sure, just as he did for you. But don't you see? Both the farm's Belgians went to their reward decades ago, back in the forties."

"Even the horses were ghosts?" Alec thundered.

"Yes, invisible to all of us. The first sign that we've got action at the museum is usually the sight of the old black sleigh zipping along the streets on its own!"

"It would explain why people were staring," Sara reluctantly admitted.

"And smiling," Hal presumed. "This is a nice little town that's proud of its ghostly secret."

Sara frowned, tucking her auburn tresses behind her ears. "So your life in town is completely separate from what happens here in the off-season."

"Exactly," Hal confirmed. "It's why you had trouble with the telephone. You were in 1938, trying to dial out to 1997! Whenever one of the residents called out, they were speaking to someone in their time zone. You, on the other hand, were trying to reach people in modern times and short-circuited the wires, so to speak."

Alec stroked his chin. "So when Timothy made that call for me and got old Ben at the station, who was he speaking to?"

"*My* grandfather," Hal replied. "Little Timothy probably knew him, didn't he, Alec?"

"Yes. No wonder you were so interested in everything Ben said."

Hal sniffed a little. "It was like spinning back in a time machine for Frank and me. Not everyone stranded at the inn comes to the garage. And no one's ever gotten Ben on the line before. You were clever to think of Timothy as a source for the telephone."

"Well, logic suggested he could get it to work, but that's as far as my brainpower took me."

"So what happened to Timothy?" Sara asked anxiously. "He so wanted to be a healer."

Leslie smiled. "He followed through. Became a doctor, settled here permanently. Why, you met his son in the café, remember? Spoke to him in the bookstore too."

"That was Tim's son?" Alec marveled. "Damn weird, but really moving."

"He knew who you were, of course," Leslie confided, "but like the rest of us, didn't want to give things away, spoil it for his father, or any of you back at the inn."

"The photo in the garage that you were asking about, Alec, that was Ben, of course," Hal admitted. "There you were, convinced he was alive and well, and there he was, big as life in the ancient photograph, his name embroidered on his uniform. That was a close one. Would've hated being the one to spill the beans. I imagine Beatrice would've gotten in touch with me somehow."

Alec shook his head slowly. "Two dimensions, in motion at the same time. Amazing. Beatrice goaded me into having faith, but never in my wildest dreams did I imagine how much I'd need."

Sara, who had been quietly trying to put together the pieces of the tale, spoke haltingly. "So if what you're saying is true, we were the special love match of the season, meant to connect, but not quite making it ourselves."

Leslie pursed her lips. "Yes. Considered an emergency in progress by Beatrice—lost soul mates lured to the inn for a dose of her special nurturing."

"Can't say I like your description much," Alec said sulkily. "Emergency, indeed."

Sara laughed. "Indeed. Why, Alec, you might have lasted another whole week on your own!"

"Please tell us you're joking," Alec urged in a last-ditch effort to deny the story. "Tell Beatrice to show herself, and we'll all have one last laugh on needy old Alec."

"Wish I could," Leslie murmured. "It would mean the world to me just to see that grand old operator for even a moment."

"I'm fascinated, but I'm also terribly disappointed," Sara confided. "I so wanted Rosie to see Mrs. Nesbitt again. They got along so famously."

At the sound of her name, Rosie came alive in Sara's lap, squirmed free and scooted for the swinging door with amazing agility that made her parents proud. The adults all trailed after her like sheep.

Rosie headed for the parlor where she patted tables and chairs, chirping all the while. Sara summoned Alec to a bookcase. There were the Hardy Boys books they'd presented to Timothy, side-by-side with his old ones in their paper jackets.

The liquor trolley was there as well, the bottles and cut-glass decanter empty. Thoughts of the brandy got Alec to thinking about the third-floor sewing room. "Anything up there?" he asked Leslie.

"Certainly. Shall we take a look?"

Sara poked her tongue out at Alec when he asked her if she was up to the climb. "I'm fit as can be—father hen!"

He kissed her nose. "There's a name I can live with."

Alec led the way into the cheery attic room. The sun was beginning to set, sending bright golden rays through the long narrow windows of the pentagonal tower. The room was as he remembered it, the brown velvet recliners flanking the huge walnut cabinet, with the pole lamp in the background. The pedal-operated sewing machine and the ice-cream churn were still on display in a far corner as well.

Alec was mildly embarrassed, thinking how amused the sisters must have been over his references to their *antiques*.

Sara folded her arms across her chest. "Why are we here, Alec?"

Alec crossed the hardwood floor and opened the cabinet doors. "There, you see," he said triumphantly. "An old radio! I couldn't believe the inn folks were cut off from the world. It also explains the rumble of voices I heard—that they tried to brush off."

"Just didn't want you to catch one of their old-time broadcasts," Sara surmised. Seeing something new and tender in her husband's eyes, she stared up him, waiting for a further explanation.

"This room means a lot to me," he admitted huskily. "It was up here that the sisters basically kicked my mule's butt into gear and ordered me to have faith in you!"

She gasped in mock horror. "Oh, really."

"Showed me more love and support than I'd ever known." He turned back to the cabinet with a wistful sigh. "I'm sure it's a lost cause, but I have to test this thing out." Alec knelt before the rectangular radio with its huge mesh grille, glass-covered channel indicator and two large brown dials for volume and tuning. He turned the knobs and listened for any signs of life.

"Mrs. Nesbitt! Where are you, my darlin'?" he shouted in exasperation.

Rosie came ambling up beside him as he fiddled with the machine. He gave his baby stepdaughter an affectionate squeeze. "What do you think of all this, Jingle?"

Rosie reached over and patted the right-hand chair. "Bea-Bea."

Suddenly the radio came to life, and Jack Benny's voice filled the room. The group gasped as a human form began to take shape in the chair.

Sure enough, it was Beatrice Nesbitt, wearing the same dress Leslie wore, though she filled it out much better. She was exactly as Alec remembered, her hair wrapped in the braided coronet, her fingers busy with a needlework project, her voice rich and loving and playful.

"My dears! How fine you all look."

Soft joyous sounds of wonder filled the room as everyone greeted the old woman in their own special way.

Alec was last to speak, his voice husky, warm, and grateful. "You are a rascal."

Beatrice beamed dreamily. "A compliment, to be sure. Remember me always, Alec. You might even wish to name that precious child you're having after me." Blowing them all kisses, she vanished along with the radio frequency.

A hush fell on the room, broken by Rosie as she tried to climb up in the vacated chair. Alec stood up on shaky legs.

"Oh, Alec." Sara put her arms around him. "She cared for you so very much."

He swallowed hard, finding his throat nearly swollen shut. "She cared for all of us. It's so hard to accept that she's really gone."

"But is she?" Leslie protested lightly. "I myself believe she can pop in anyplace, anytime, that she *prefers* this house at Christmas."

Sara stood on tiptoe to kiss her husband's cheek. "And she'll always be in our hearts, Alec. The best place for anyone."

The ladies were right, he knew. This was a happy closure, the best under the circumstances. Alec cringed playfully. "Gee, I guess the pressure's on about the namesake. Hope our baby is a girl."

Sara laughed and looped her arms around his neck. "I think we can pretty much count on it. Mrs. Nesbitt was right about everything else, wasn't she?"

Filled with an exquisite sense of contentment, Alec pressed his lips to Sara's temple. "Absolutely, my love. Absolutely."

Take 4 bestselling love stories FREE

Plus get a FREE surprise gift!

It's hot...
and it's out of control!

This January, Temptation turns up the heat. Look for these bold, provocative, _ultra_-sexy books!

NIGHT HEAT
by Lyn Ellis

Tripp Anderson had been hired to protect beautiful, sexy, _rich_ Abby Duncan. Keeping his gorgeous client safe wasn't hard—keeping his hands off her _was_. But when Abby was threatened, Tripp vowed to look after her, even if it meant keeping watch day and night. Little did he expect his night _watch_ to become night _heat_....

BLAZE! Red-hot reads from Temptation!

THE MEN OF BACHELOR CREEK

Alaska. A place where men could be men—and women were scarce!

To Tanner, Joe and Hawk, Alaska was the final frontier. They'd gone to the ends of the earth to flee the one thing they all feared—MATRIMONY. Little did they know that three intrepid heroines would brave the wilds to "save" them from their lonely bachelor existences.

Enjoy

#662 CAUGHT UNDER THE MISTLETOE!
December 1997

#670 DODGING CUPID'S ARROW!
February 1998

#678 STRUCK BY SPRING FEVER!
April 1998

by Kate Hoffmann

Available wherever Harlequin books are sold.

A showgirl, a minister—
and an unsolved murder.

EASY VIRTUE

Eight years ago Mary Margaret's father was
convicted of a violent murder she knew he
didn't commit—and she vowed to clear his
name. With her father serving a life sentence,
Mary Margaret is working as a showgirl in Reno
when Reverend Dane Barrett shows up with
information about her father's case. Working to
expose the real killer, the unlikely pair also
proceed to expose themselves to an unknown
enemy who is intent on keeping the past buried.

**From the bestselling author of
LAST NIGHT IN RIO**

JANICE
KAISER

Available in December 1997
at your favorite retail outlet.

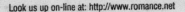

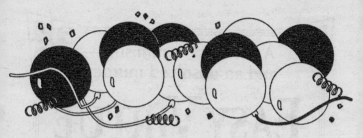

Ring in the New Year with

New Year's Resolution:

FAMILY

**This heartwarming collection of three
contemporary stories rings in the
New Year with babies, families and
the best of holiday romance.**

Add a dash of romance to your holiday celebrations
with this exciting new collection, featuring bestselling
authors **Barbara Bretton, Anne McAllister** and
Leandra Logan.

Available in December,
wherever Harlequin books are sold.

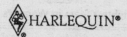

Free Gift Offer

With a Free Gift proof-of-purchase
from any Harlequin® book, you can receive
a beautiful cubic zirconia pendant.

This stunning marquise-shaped stone is a genuine cubic
zirconia—accented by an 18" gold tone necklace.
(Approximate retail value $19.95)

Send for yours today...
compliments of ◆HARLEQUIN®

To receive your free gift, a cubic zirconia pendant, send us one original proof-of-purchase, photocopies not accepted, from the back of any Harlequin Romance®, Harlequin Presents®, Harlequin Temptation®, Harlequin Superromance®, Harlequin Intrigue®, Harlequin American Romance®, or Harlequin Historicals® title available at your favorite retail outlet, together with the Free Gift Certificate, plus a check or money order for $1.65 U.S./$2.15 CAN. (do not send cash) to cover postage and handling, payable to Harlequin Free Gift Offer. We will send you the specified gift. Allow 6 to 8 weeks for delivery. Offer good until December 31, 1997, or while quantities last. Offer valid in the U.S. and Canada only.

Free Gift Certificate

Name: _____

Address: _____

City: _____ State/Province: _____ Zip/Postal Code: _____

Mail this certificate, one proof-of-purchase and a check or money order for postage and handling to: HARLEQUIN FREE GIFT OFFER 1997. In the U.S.: 3010 Walden Avenue, P.O. Box 9071, Buffalo NY 14269-9057. In Canada: P.O. Box 604, Fort Erie, Ontario L2Z 5X3.

FREE GIFT OFFER   084-KEZ
ONE PROOF-OF-PURCHASE
To collect your fabulous FREE GIFT, a cubic zirconia pendant, you must include this original proof-of-purchase for each gift with the properly completed Free Gift Certificate.

084-KEZR